ST. PETER'S BONES

For Frank Gingrich
Let this book be a blessing
for you.

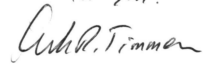

KENNETH R. TIMMERMAN

D0062150

Cassiopeia Press

ISBN 978-0-9797229-1-2

Order online at www.kentimmerman.com

Cover photos: U.S. Air Force photo, Owja, Iraq, July 22, 2009, by Staff Sgt. Luke P. Thelen. Released by MNC-1 PAO/114th PAD, Department of Defense; St. Joseph's cathedral, Ankawa, Iraq (author's collection). Back cover: author photo by Gunnar Wiebalck.

Disclaimer:
The scenes recorded in *St. Peter's Bone's* are fictional and a work of the imagination. Any resemblance between the characters in this book and real persons would be, to quote a famous passage from the 9/11 Commission report, "a remarkable coincidence."

Published by Cassiopeia Press, Rockville, Maryland 20814
1.0

Timmerman.road@verizon.net

Author bio available at:
www.kentimmerman.com

ADVANCE PRAISE FOR
ST. PETER'S BONES

"Kenneth Timmerman has wrought a wildly inventive and highly gripping thriller that encompasses the secret and long-hidden origins of Islam, the tomb of St. Peter in Rome (or is it in Rome?), the embattled Iraqi Christian community, and the scope and magnitude of today's jihad against the West... That makes *St. Peter's Bones* more than just a great novel, although it is assuredly that as well: it is also an enlightening insight into today's increasingly conflict-ridden relationship between Islam and the Judeo-Christian/post-Christian West."

—**Robert Spencer,** director of JihadWatch and author of the New York Times bestsellers *The Politically Incorrect Guide to Islam (and the Crusades)* and *The Truth About Muhammad.*

"This is a book no major New York publisher had the courage to print. You owe it to yourself to read it and to defend your freedom by doing so."

—**David Horowitz,** best-selling author and founder, David Horowitz Freedom Center

"Timmerman's taboo-breaking thriller portrays authentically the politics and passions fueling the deadly persecution of Iraq's ancient Christian community: an unintended but ruinous by-product of Operation Iraqi Freedom. It's a powerful book America's political leadership on both the left and the right would prefer you not to read."

—**Dr. John Eibner,** CEO, Christian Solidarity International (CSI-USA)

"This novel sheds light on one of the most overlooked foreign policy catastrophes of our times—the flight of Iraq's ancient Christian community under siege from al Qaeda and other extremists...Kenneth Timmerman's riveting tale is a story in urgent need of telling."

—**Nina Shea,** Commissioner, US Commission on International Religious Freedom

"In *St. Peter's Bones*, Kenneth Timmerman does more than share with us an intriguing mystery rooted deep in the lore of Assyrian history. It provides insight into how Christians wrestle with their place in Iraq. One of his characters, Burhan Salahuddin, an Islamist but a potential ally of Christians, observes that, *"There are no secrets in Iraq......There are only stories that don't get told."* One of the stories not told is of the burden that Christians in Iraq bear."

—**The Rev. Keith Roderick, D.D.,** Secretary General, Coalition for the Defense of Human Rights

"The persecution of Christians throughout the Middle East and Muslim world is one of the most important stories that have been ignored throughout the conflict in the region, and it's embarrassing that we're not talking more about it. *St. Peter's Bones* provides a compelling insight into their current and historical struggles and ordeals. We need to get Americans and the U.S. government actively focusing on how we can help endangered Christians to survive."

—**U.S. Representative Pete Hoekstra**

ST. PETER'S BONES

For the brave Iraqi Christian interpreters who risked their lives to help their American liberators, and for the families of the martyrs.

Dear friends, do not be surprised at the painful trial you are suffering, as though something strange were happening to you. But rejoice that you participate in the sufferings of Christ, so that you may be overjoyed when his glory is revealed.

I Peter 4:12

Prologue

Anno Domini 582, somewhere near Damascus, Syria

Surely you were guiding my steps when you brought me to the tent of Abu Talib, that rascal, and compelled me beyond my better judgment to book passage with that filthy Bedouin and his caravan of sixty lame camels for the treacherous desert journey to Mecca. For it was here, at night, during our first halt, that you brought the boy to me.

The young fellow could not have been much older than 12. And yet, despite his very young age, his frail features, his coat of many colors that seemed to be made of so many discarded rags, he attracted quite a crowd around the fire that night when we made our first halt. With eyes like a falcon, and long slender hands that clearly had never known a day's labor, he seemed to combine the harshness of the desert with the soft luxuries of a courtesan. He entranced us with his tales of Hubul, the moon goddess of the Black Stone, who speaks to him in his dreams, whispering of the three daughters she begat in secret congress with the Sun. He entranced us with his tales of imaginary battles with vast armies upon a rocky plain, of a bearded Knight worshipped by all as he wielded a great Sword of Justice, killing the treacherous Jews.

Abu Talib smiled as his young nephew spoke of these things. But as I listened to him recount his fantasies and dreams, the most extraordinary thought occurred to me: what if one could channel these pagan beliefs, bend them, so to speak, to your will, O Lord? What if one could use this illiterate boy from the caravans as a messenger of your Holy Spirit, to bring your Word to the desert tribes of Araby who until now have resisted all efforts to bring them to the true faith?

But I am plagued with doubts. Is it you guiding me, Lord, to this boy? Or is it another, one who would lead me from the path of righteousness into Pride, Arrogance, and Self-Aggrandizement?

—from The Secret Book of the Order of St. Hormizd

1

Al Qaim, Iraq

There was just a sliver of moon as we moved through the date palm grove on the outskirts of al Qaim. Up ahead of us, the window of the crumbling mud-brick house glowed faintly through the blanket someone had hung over it from the inside. We had left our HUMVEEs back on the main road, more than a kilometer away. My heart was pounding as much from fear as from exertion. I felt sure its loud thumping would give us away.

Sgt. Manny Diaz, of City of Commerce, California, led our small team of Special Forces operators as we ran quickly but quietly from tree to tree. Deron was on point. Willy, Frank and Mojo covered our flanks and our rear with me in tow. When we went out on operations like this, they always allowed me to carry weapons for my personal protection, even though I was a civilian. Anybody looking at us would have thought I was just another member of the team, until I opened my mouth. Catching my breath, hidden by the still-warm tree trunk, I gripped my Glock 19 in both hands, aiming vaguely at the ground. But truth be told, my hands were trembling.

It was early March. By this time in the war, five years after the U.S. deposed Saddam Hussein, the Americans had finally begun to take Iraq's borders seriously. Al Qaim shared a rocky desert with Syria, and was the preferred insertion point for al Qaeda and their Baathist allies to bring foreign jihadis, money, and material into my country. It was also the site of one of Saddam's nuclear weapons plants. When the UN arms inspectors finally discovered it, they were embarrassed and said nothing, since they had believed it was just a fertilizer plant as Saddam had always claimed. In the distance we could see the ruined tower of the uranium distillery framed against the evening sky. Somebody with a sense of humor had strung white Christmas lights from it in the form of a heart. That was one of the many things that had changed since the fall of Saddam. People actually laughed and made jokes, without always looking over their shoulder.

I am not a violent man by nature. Many of my countrymen, who can take the life of a man as easily as others brush their teeth, would undoubtedly call me a coward. I remember how I dreaded my eighteenth birthday, because I was sure to be called up for military service. With Saddam, the next war was always just around the corner. We used to say that the lucky ones were sent out on construction details, building gigantic palaces for the megalomaniac who ran our country. But some of them weren't so lucky; whatever they saw, Saddam didn't want them to tell anyone. We said they were "growing old in secret," to disguise what we all knew had happened. Saddam had them taken out into the desert and shot.

Until recently, we wore balaclavas on operations like this. The American press referred to them as ski masks, but that is not accurate. The face gear the SpecOps guys gave us was thin and made out of a nylon-based fiber so we could operate in the heat. It was nothing like a ski mask, except that it covered the face.

But now, as the United States was seeking a graceful exit from Iraq, we "terps" had been ordered to participate in the interrogations without our balaclavas. This was intended to show that the dangers we faced had somehow decreased, and that the war was winding down. My elder cousin Gewargis resigned when that order was given, even though he'd been working with the Americans from the beginning. Gewargis, who grew up in my uncle's tiny electronics shop with a soldering iron and a tiny screwdriver in his hands, taught me how to repair broken radios and TVs almost before I could walk. I can still remember the first time he revealed to me the mystery of the crystal, bending over a mess of circuit boards with his green eyeshade and suddenly making wild music erupt from the pile of scrap. "I love the Americans," he said. "I'd do just about anything to help them, because they are helping us to recapture our country, to give birth to something like normal human decency after thirty-five years of a nightmare. But the nightmare lives on in these Baathist criminals. Don't the Americans understand that we lived in fear for thirty-five years, and that these Baathists own our fear? There's no way I'm going to let them see my face."

Maybe it was because I was that much younger, and had only lived for a handful of years as a teenager and young adult under Saddam that I didn't take Gewargis seriously. We were living in Karada by then, a mixed Baghdad neighborhood where we had moved once the church bombings began, and opportunities were limited. What was he going to do as a Christian in Baghdad if he didn't work for the Americans? Salvage old TVs?

"Get out, Yohannes. Don't press your luck," he said. "Soon the Americans will be gone. Who's going to protect you then?"

An aching hollowness gripped my stomach as I thought over what I knew about the man we were hoping to arrest tonight. For a moment, as my chest heaved in the gathering darkness, I wondered whether I had made a mistake. Perhaps I should have played it safe and heeded Gewargis' prudent advice. Perhaps I should have left my job and gone back to take care of my family. It was as if my gut was warning me that something was dreadfully wrong. Could I have escaped all the deaths and the sorrow and the agony by that one small sacrifice?

But it was already too late. We were about to move.

"Go-go-go!!" Sgt. Diaz mouthed to us, pumping his fist as he and Deron ran the last few meters across the open mud to the farmhouse. The instant that we joined them, chests heaving, hugging the dirty plaster that still clung to the crumbling brick walls of the farmhouse, Sgt. Diaz and Deron kicked open the door and I saw the muzzle flash and heard the rounds from his M-4 carbine slam into the far wall.

"Everyone down! Get down now! Down on the floor!" he shouted. No one expected me to translate, since the violence of his gesture was easy to comprehend.

We heard another quick burst of gunfire, and then shouts from the men inside. Sgt. Diaz kicked the legs out of the cheap wooden chair on which our target had been sitting, sending him crashing to the cement floor. Two younger men, completely bewildered by the intrusion, tried to stand up from the table, their hands in the air, but Deron motioned to them with his assault rifle to hit the ground as well. A Soviet-era pistol clattered off the table to the ground, and Deron kicked it away toward the door. All of this happened in about two seconds. We knew our target only as Abu Hassan. We believed he was the leader of a stay-behind network operating in this sector of the border region. Even with the thick beard, I recognized him from the grainy photographs we had been shown in preparation for tonight's mission. Something about his eyes disquieted me. They were cold, fearless, hard, and narrowing, like the eyes of a snake. I kneeled down to him and hissed into his ear in Arabic: "How many more of you are there?"

He just grunted, and turned his head painfully against the cold cement so he could look at me with one eye. Deron had pinioned his arms behind his back with a foot and was getting out plastic cuffs to secure him.

"We know there are five other men in your cell," I said. "Where are they?"

He tried to spit at me, but he couldn't get his head high enough into the air and just got himself wet. "They're with your mother. And when they're through with her they're going after your sister, you son of a whore."

Willy and Frank ran out through the kitchen to the muddy courtyard behind the house to look for the other cell members, while Mojo searched the small house. In a few minutes, they gave the all clear.

By this time, Sgt. Diaz had Abu Hassan back in the chair, his hands cuffed behind his back. He was dressed like a peasant in a dirty grey dishdash that swept the floor, a black and white-checked keffiyeh wrapped around his head and a web belt and a holster at his waist. When we burst in, he and the two young Syrians had been looking at a schematic diagram of our firebase, twenty klicks to the southeast. He had circled the point of entry, and made crude marks where crash barriers and sentries were posted. In a suitcase along the wall we found five million Iraqi dinars—the equivalent of around $5,000—and two suicide vests.

That was how the Baathists operated. They gathered the intelligence, the explosives, and provided the cash. Then they recruited young Arabs from outside Iraq to come blow up Americans and called the whole show, "al Qaeda."

I pulled Sgt. Diaz aside and asked him quietly to let me have at the two young men alone. "They don't have a clue what's going on," I said. "They can tell us if there's anyone else here that we've missed."

"Negative, Johnny," Sgt. Diaz said. "We're going for the big fish first. We want the network, not the bit players."

He must have read the panic in my eyes. Even though I had covered my cheeks and forehead with lampblack, Abu Hassan had seen my real face. And while "Johnny" wasn't my real name—at least, not my Christian name—he'd be able to find out soon enough the identity of the Iraqi terp who had collaborated in his arrest from other detainees, once we took him into custody.

"I will make your sister wish she had not been born," he hissed again. "And then I will come for you. With a pitchfork."

He coughed as he said this, making his chair clatter against the floor, until I realized that he was not coughing but laughing. It was the type of joke the Baathists found funny. "I'm coming for you, Johnny. You will never be safe. Every night you are going to be thinking of me, wondering if it's me you hear or just the wind. Johnnee... Johnnee."

He whispered my Americanized name with utter contempt, taunting, making sure that I understood he knew it was a nickname and that he would find out my true name soon enough. Even though the early spring night was still cool, I felt the sweat begin to pool at the back of my neck.

"Hey-hey-hey!" Sgt. Diaz said, whirling around, picking up on his trick. He slapped Abu Hassan so hard that he fell over onto the cement floor, chair and all.

"Go out and wait in the HUMVEE," Sgt. Diaz told me. "We'll take Abu Hassan and his friends back home and see how he likes to talk to serious people. Tell him that, Johnny."

We knew from detainee interrogations that Abu Hassan was in charge of bringing suicide bomber recruits into Iraq from across the border in Syria, and that he commanded a whole series of safe houses near Al Qaim and in Syria itself. But at this point, we didn't yet know who he was, even though we had finally arrested him.

As Sgt. Diaz tightened the cuffs around Abu Hassan's wrists I told him that because he had refused to cooperate with us, we were going to take him to an interrogation center where professionals were waiting to ask him questions. I must not have conveyed Sgt. Diaz's threat convincingly enough, because he just stared at me with dark unblinking reptilian eyes, as if he would murder me on the spot. For a moment, I felt that I couldn't move, mesmerized, frozen. And then he spat again, this time barely missing my boots.

We are Assyrians, among the first Christians evangelized in what the West used to call the pagan world, sons and daughters of giants both living and dead. How many young Assyrian men bear the name

Sargon, in honor of our greatest Emperor? His palace now lies in ruins, scattered piles of stones and mounds of dung surrounded by the dirty back alleys of Karamlesh. And yet, here was Nineveh, fabled capital of the eastern world, navel of the universe, birthplace of civilization. Our ancestor Hammurabi penned the first universal code of human rights, granting each individual protection from arbitrary injustice, even by the state. How far we have come since then! How many leagues have we traveled backward toward savagery?

My Assyrian nation, I am only beginning to understand how rich your blood flows in my veins. We are not conquerors any longer, or oppressors of captive peoples. Ever since St. Thomas made his first trip to our homeland, nearly two millennia ago, we have been washed in the Blood of the Lamb, our sins redeemed. Here in this land where the Sword rules supreme, Christ's blood made it easier for us to stretch our necks toward victimhood. Hopeful, trusting, believing in the better nature of our adversaries, we were betrayed again and again. Today we are learning to beware our friends.

The night my father lost his leg, the few Americans soldiers remaining in Baghdad all seemed to be staying on base. I do not hold it against them; such were their orders. As they saw it, their mission was not to occupy Iraq, but to liberate it. And they did. But when they freed us from the iron fist of Saddam, they set loose the hordes of minor demons he had held in check for thirty-five years. Free of their chains, like Prometheus after the eagle has plucked out his liver, they thirsted for blood. As always, it was Christian blood they sought and tasted first.

In our adopted neighborhood of Dora, car bombs started to go off within months of the liberation. I was just 23 years old at the time. We lived just six miles south of Saddam's former palace, now called the Green Zone, across a few bends of the Tigris. My father, Toma Boutros Yohanna, had been a minor functionary in the Ministry of Agriculture, but because he had been forced to join the Baath Party to keep his job under Saddam, the Americans tossed him out after the Liberation. His moustaches were still black then, and he used to stroke them in the evenings, sitting in front of the blackened TV after another day of futile wandering in search of work, slowly sipping the sweetened black coffee my mother would bring him. In a way, the six months or so that he remained unemployed saved our family from the wrath of the Baathists once the insurgency began. Even the jihadis, the *taqfeer*, accepted the fact that the Americans eventually hired him back. If the Christians didn't work, they couldn't pay the jizya, the protection tax decreed by the Muslim prophet. It was only later that they came for Baba and killed him. Like so many others.

It began slowly at first. Myrna and Emad, my aunt and uncle, lived six blocks away from us. Emad was my mother's older brother, the one who owned the TV repair shop and who, like Gewargis, could make broken circuit boards and twisted wires sing. One night in March, intruders broke into the house next door to them and murdered the elderly Christian couple who lived there. The man's throat was slit. The woman was found naked and violated. The murderers left a crudely worded letter behind them, vowing to kill all the Christians in Dora if they did not leave. Myrna was trembling when she carried the letter over to our house. Mother just held her, trying to calm her sobbing, patting her back as she gasped for air.

11

Two months later Miryam Yonan, a young woman I had known in high school, was riddled with bullets by gunmen in a drive-by shooting. Miryam always wore a white scarf around her hair when I passed her on the way to the Protestant girl's school she attended. Later, in high school, she would take off the scarf once she was in class, and we all wondered at her smooth skin, the perfect ears, her green eyes. We said she was like a butterfly that had just emerged from its cocoon. She had been so proud to get a job as a secretary in the Green Zone, working for an American company. When she opened her remaining eye in the ambulance after the shooting we all said she was lucky to survive, but I'm not so sure. After the way they tore up her face, no man would think of marrying her.

Then in July, the jihadis entered the home of one of our neighbors on a Saturday evening and murdered their 16-year old son and an eight-year old daughter. The parents had been attending mass at Mar Gewargis and had left them behind, thinking the teenage boy could take care of his younger sister, just as he always did. They cut the genitals off the boy and stuffed them in the girl's mouth, after they violated her. Suffering and loss were not enough, in the eyes of the jihadis. They did such things to create shame, to push us beyond our limits so we would leave.

My parents worked in Mar Gewargis—St. George's—in their spare time. My mother, an elementary school teacher, taught catechism. My father worked as a guard during Saturday evening and Sunday morning services. By that time, two years or so after the liberation, the jihadis had learned they could kill more people by staggering the explosions. First, they set off a small bomb in a doorway or underneath a car. Once the police and the medics and a good crowd had gathered, they set off a second, bigger bomb. That's how they achieved such high kill rates. It worked almost every time.

That's what they were hoping to do when they set off the first bomb at Mar Gewargis church that August. The blast ripped into the alleyway along the side of the church, just as people were entering for Sunday morning mass. There was blood everywhere and screaming as people tried to rush outside to make sure no one they knew had been injured. Baba stood there, desperate, like some kind of Ottoman sentinel, his black moustaches streaked with grey, the dusty cartouche belt slung across a shoulder, trying to hold them back. "Get back in the church! Back in the church!" he shouted as they bumped up against him. He took out the old Iraqi-made pistol they had given him and fired into the air once or twice to get people's attention. He was glancing behind him, toward the street, where he knew death was lurking, frantically trying to herd people out of the way.

He was pushing the last family and their baby through the door into the side chapel off the nave when a black and orange taxi with the second bomb came rushing toward him, filling the narrow alleyway. He dove onto the backs of the couple with their baby, and that is certainly what saved all of their lives. The white hot wind from the explosion tore the heavy wooden doors from their hinges, and one of them smashed into Baba, nearly crushing him. He woke up in the hospital a few hours later with broken ribs, badly bruised, missing his left leg from the knee down. My mother was holding his hand when he opened his eyes.

"Hannah," he said, giving her hand a squeeze. Then he winced with pain and closed his eyes again momentarily. "Is the baby alright?" he said finally.

"The baby is fine," my mother said. "Everyone is fine. And you are alive."

"God is merciful," he whispered.

That was Baba. A much braver man than I am. And one who eventually paid the ultimate price.

Living as Christians in Baghdad has never been easy, but since the liberation of our country by the Americans it has become a daily race with death. Don't get me wrong: I welcomed the liberation, and so did most Iraqis. But as Christians, we were afraid that the relative peace Saddam had granted us over the years would disappear once the brutal order he had imposed on the country was shattered. "When they want to make an omelet in the East, they use Christians as eggs," Nana Soraya used to say. Under Saddam, we had controlled mayhem, organized murder. If you were lucky and kept quiet, you would be allowed to live; some even prospered, counting their blessings, holding their breath. Once Saddam was gone, we just had mayhem.

Over the centuries, we Christians of the East have survived the collapse of empires. We have survived wars and pogroms, even attempted genocide. We were taught to rejoice that our suffering allowed us participate in the sufferings of Christ, "so that you may be overjoyed when his glory is revealed."[1] We were taught to submit to the earthly Prince, whoever he might be, because only Christ is King. And so we remained unorganized and unarmed as Sunnis and Shias and Kurds formed militias, relying on the new order imposed by the Americans and watching the chaos that ensued like helpless members of a Greek chorus as the tragedy reaches the crescendo of its utterly predictable conclusion. Only rarely in the

---

[1] I Peter 4:13.

14

history of our Assyrian nation have we defended ourselves. Some say that because of this, we have survived. I am no longer sure.

Mojo was working on Abu Hassan's beard when Lieutenant Colonel Danny Wilkens, the S-2 from the Big Snake—Camp Anaconda—came into the small cell. We had worked together before on detainee interrogations, and he was smart, tough, but fair. He was not a large man so he used his brain to break the taqfeer, although once, I saw him hurl a man twice his size against a cinderblock wall, knocking his breath away and his self-confidence with it. They brought Colonel Wilkens in for the hard cases.

"I want all of it off," he said.

Mojo gave a big grin, waving the shears in front of Abu Hassan's eyes carelessly, snipping the air. He wore blue latex gloves, and had spread a plastic sheet on the cement floor of the cell. His own reddish-blond beard and disheveled hair were ragged from a lack of trimming. The special operators were allowed a license in their personal grooming not granted to regular soldiers, and Mojo was no exception. He wore a red kerchief around his head, making him look like a cross between a woodsman and a hippie.

"Even the moustache?" he asked, pointing the scissors toward Abu Hassan's upper lip.

"What do you think, Johnny?" Col. Wilkens asked me. "All the Saddamists wear moustaches. It might give us an advantage."

I turned to the filthy Baathist whose wiry black facial hair had fallen in clumps to the floor. I wanted to retch from the smell. "They want to shave your moustache, too," I said. "I can ask them to stop." "They can do what they like. For now," he said. "It might be easier to identify him if you leave it on," I said. "Don't worry. We'll be able to identify him without that. Tell him that we know where the money he brought in from Syria came from. I want to see his reaction," Wilkens said.

So I translated that information. Abu Hassan sneered. "You know nothing," he said.

"We know the name of your contact on the other side of the border," Wilkens said. "And we know the bank accounts he is using in Qatar. You were planning murder. You know, if I hand you over to the Iraqi authorities, premeditated murder carries the death penalty."

As I was translating his words, Col. Wilkens kept staring into his eyes, not aggressively or smugly, but with a hard, even gaze, trying to gauge the man's fear. That was his method. "Fear is your friend," he said once, "in the bedroom and in the battlefield." But I could tell that Abu Hassan was not afraid. "Let's leave him here to think about his options," Wilkens said.

His interrogation technique was a far cry from the imaginings of the Western journalists, who screamed about the Americans "torturing" prisoners in Iraq. And while I'm not convinced that using intelligence and cunning was more effective than brute force, I had seen Col. Danny Wilkens get results before, without ever laying a finger on a prisoner. It was almost funny in a way. The Baathists were expecting to be beaten. They were expecting to be striped naked and thrown into a wet cell, and get their genitals wired to an electric generator. After all, that's what they had always done with their victims. When the Americans didn't use such techniques, it threw them off. And that's when they started to talk.

But Abu Hassan was different. For three days, Wilkens would go into his cell with me in tow, and during each interrogation session Wilkens would throw out additional details he had learned about his network, his plans, his accomplices, then dangle in front of him the endless torment he would face at the hands of his fellow Iraqis if Wilkens turned him over to the judicial authorities. Abu Hassan didn't seem to care. It was almost as if he knew that the Americans couldn't touch him, that whatever they discovered about him, he knew just that little bit more about them. As long as he was able to keep his secrets, he was dangerous, and both he and Wilkens seemed to know it.

"Why are you called Abu Hassan?" Wilkens asked him one day.

By this point, the dishdash was gone and he was dressed in clean, orange overalls. His hair had been washed, and his swarthy beard was starting to grow dark on his face.

"Surely you've learned enough by now about Arabic culture, Colonel, to know how we chose our nicknames?"

"So how old is your son? How old is Hassan?"

For the first time in the week he had been in custody, a trace of emotion seemed to trouble the prisoner's reptilian eyes, giving them just a vague hint of moisture. He quickly fought it back, and looked away with self-disgust.

"He is dead. You Americans killed him. One of your F-16s and your 500 pound bombs."

"I keep my son away from the battlefield," Wilkens said evenly.

"You brought the battlefield to us," he replied, the contempt returning to his voice.

I didn't understand what Col. Wilkens was doing, and I must have let my misgivings show.

"No, you brought the battlefield upon yourselves. Just translate, Johnny. No one forced you to start this war. You could have taken your place in the new Iraq and you would be rich by now. Instead, you chose the coward's way. You chose to fight like women, clawing in the dark."

When he heard these words, I saw a fire light up in Abu Hassan's eyes, and he struggled against the chair. If his wrists hadn't been bound together, he would have tried to strike Col. Wilkens. The American smiled.

"You and your kind are writing a new chapter in the history of Baathism," he went on. "You're not nationalists. That's just the lie you tell yourselves. This chapter is called the Mother of All Cowards."

"We are defending our homeland!"

"No, you're not. You're murdering your fellow citizens."

"They are citizens of nothing." He spat in my direction. "These are the cowards, with their suffering savior who carries his own cross and climbs up onto it without a fight. We will drive them all from Iraq."

Wilkens got up, and signaled for me to join him at the door. "We'll soon see where the glory lies, *Saddoun*."

He didn't even bother to look behind him as he walked out to take notice of the utter shock that came across Abu Hassan's face at hearing his real name for the first time. But I saw it. No, I relished it. Abu Hassan was stunned. He had completely underestimated the intelligence and cunning of his

American adversary. He had been unmasked. Stripped of his anonymity, he was more vulnerable than the poor wretch he had thrown naked into the damp cell. Once we knew his name there was nothing more he could hide. Or so I thought.

Later, Col. Wilkens told me how he knew.

"Every human being has a genetic fingerprint," he explained. "We got Saddoun's DNA from his facial hair. "

"But who did you match him against?" I asked. "How did you know where to look?"

"We *are* the United States of America, don't forget," Wilkens laughed. He was not a large man, but he had a way of uncoiling his shoulders in a stretching motion that made him appear much more powerful and larger than he was. "We have big fast computers, with huge amounts of data. And DNA is one of the things that we run on all detainees. We also had to do some detective work. That's why I asked him about his son. There are several members of his family who have children named Hassan. But only one whose son was killed in a bombing raid."

Saddam Hussein had three half-brothers, he explained: Barzan, Sabbowi, and Adnan. All three were the sons of Saddam's stepfather, an illiterate shepherd named Ibrahim Hassan. Saddam's real father deserted the family when Saddam was a young child, and it didn't take long for him to develop a deep hatred for his stepfather. The shepherd beat him, and once his three sons were born, he treated the young Saddam like an interloper. By the time he was twelve, Saddam took refuge in the home of a maternal uncle, a cashiered officer named Khairallah Tulfah. He learned to read by the light of an oil lamp and fed his spirit on his uncle's tales of exploits with pro-German officers in the Iraqi army during World War II. Uncle Khairallah had a dream that Arabs would one day be free of foreign occupation and foreign rule. The Germans were the only ones who respected the Arabs as equals, he told the young Saddam. The British were just after their oil. "That's the back story of Baath party ideology," Wilkens said. "Basically, you've got Nazis with hummus."

For the rest of his life, Saddam had a troubled relationship with his three half-brothers. At times, he held them closer than any political ally, putting Sabbowi in charge of the party intelligence apparatus, and giving Barzan control over the family fortune, which he invested in secret accounts in a dozen countries from his headquarters in Switzerland. At other times, they grew apart. At one point in the 1990s, it was rumored that Barzan was flirting with a Western intelligence agency.

Both Sabbowi and Barzan were eventually captured by coalition forces, put on trial, condemned to death, and executed.

"We knew less about Adnan, the youngest of the three," Wilkens said. "We think he was killed during the air raid on the restaurant in al-Mansur on the first day of the war, the raid where we had hoped to get Saddam."

Adnan's son Saddoun had a boy named Hassan, but so did two other of Saddam's immediate family members. One was attending an exclusive boarding school in Switzerland, while the other lived in Qatar with his grandmother, Saddam's widow.

"When I asked him about his son, I didn't know about the bombing raid. But I did know where the other two Hassans were," Wilkens said. "That's the beauty and the limitation of DNA. You can tell paternity 99.99 percent of the time. But when you're dealing with a large family such as Saddam's, you need more to go on."

So Abu Hassan was Saddam Hussein's nephew, and his real name was Saddoun Adnan al-Ibrahim al-Takriti. As I repeated it out loud, I felt an uncomfortable shiver run down my spine. Before, I had felt the presence of evil. Now I knew I was facing the Devil himself. And he knew my face, my voice, even my name.

Soraya, my great-grandmother, was born in Tabriz at the turn of the century, when that country was still called Persia. She was widowed at the age of 22, not long after she bore a single son to her husband, Boutros. "I asked God to take me instead, but He had other plans for me and that Issa," she told me when I was just old enough to remember. We called her Nana Soraya, the grandmother we never had. She lived with our family in Baghdad until she died in 1987.

Issa, her son, was my mother's father. His name meant "Jesus" in Aramaic, the language of Christ, the language we still use in church and among family. But from listening to Nana Soraya, he bore little resemblance to his namesake.

Tabriz in 1922, when Nana's husband Boutros was martyred, was in the final throes of the genocide. A Kurdish warlord, in league with the Persians, had recently murdered the young Patriarch of our church, who had brought 150 of his best soldiers to the Kurd's palace unarmed as a token of peace.

21

The Kurdish prince put on a banquet in their honor, and asked for one of the Patriarch's daughters in marriage to seal their agreement. That's the way things were still done in those days. The young Patriarch acquiesced for the sake of his people, who had suffered mightily from the hatchets and the Remingtons and the scimitars and the butcher knives of the Kurds, Turks, Arabs, and Persians who were bent on eradicating all trace of them from our historic Assyrian land. As the Patriarch and his warriors were getting back into their carriages, heavy but joyous from the meal, the Kurd summoned the thousand warriors he had dissimulated behind the rocks and in the hollows around his palace, and gave the order to open fire. After the massacre, he personally went to the Patriarch's carriage and cut off the finger bearing the signet ring he had so recently kissed as a token of peace.

"Here is my token of peace," he said, holding aloft the slain Patriarch's finger and the large ruby ring.

Such were the stories Nana Soraya nourished me with throughout my childhood, cradling me in the ancient walnut rocker she managed to save from their stately house in Tabriz after the mob set it on fire and murdered her husband.

My Assyrian nation, murdered and martyred. And yet rising, generation after generation, like a Phoenix from the assassin's flames.

LTC Wilkens was flipping through a stack of documents the next morning when he called out for me to enter the small office he kept at battalion headquarters. Behind him, thumb-tacked to a portable corkboard, were photographs of Saddoun, the two Syrian suiciders we had arrested along with him, and another half dozen heads, some of them burned or disfigured beyond recognition—the remains of "successful" suiciders. Looking at the pictures, something in me snapped.

"I can't go back in there, sir. I just can't. For so many years these monsters were killing my people. You heard him in there."

"Yes, I did," Wilkens said.

This wasn't just any Baathist, but Saddam Hussein's own nephew! I was still trembling at the thought that I had been in the same room with him, close enough to touch him, and that I was still alive.

"Look, Johnny. You're one of the best terps I've ever worked with," Wilkens said.. "I don't want to push you too hard. You have family, don't you?"

I nodded. "Just on the other side of Mosul. My mom and my kid brother and my two sisters went back up there after my Dad was murdered in Dora."

"You never told me. I'm sorry to hear that," he said.

He was young to be a Colonel, barely 40. But there was a depth to him you didn't always sense in the American officers. His soul had been moved by this war. It was almost as if it was personal for him, just as it was for me.

"Why don't you take some time off and go see your family? It's not an easy time to be a Christian here. Just this morning, the police found the body of Archbishop Rahho, the one who disappeared after saying mass last week in Mosul. He was a personal friend. I could do nothing to find him," Wilkens said.

"Maybe Saddoun wasn't involved in that," I offered. "There are plenty of jihadis to go around."

"Maybe. But maybe he did know, and I was too slow in breaking him."

He came around to sit on front of the desk, and motioned for me to take the plastic armchair in the corner. I picked up the stack of paper that was piled on it and handed it to him. He looked at the top document, thought for a moment, then carefully folded back the red cover sheet.

"Any idea what this is? We found it when we went back through the safe house where you captured Saddoun."

I glanced down at the handwritten script on the top sheet, and did a double take.

"It's not Arabic or Persian, as far as I can tell," Wilkens said.

"That's correct, sir. It's Aramaic," I stammered. "The script is similar to what we use in the church. It looks very old."

"Can you read it? Give me an idea of what it says? I've sent it down to Baghdad for a full translation, but they haven't sent anything back up to me yet."

There were perhaps a dozen pages, faint photocopies of what appeared to be a handwritten letter or series of documents, written in beautiful calligraphy with some kind of quill pen.

"We think it might be some kind of code," he said.

I found it hard to believe that Saddoun and his murderous cronies could be using my language to devise some kind of secret operational handbook. For the text that Col. Wilkens had handed me read like excerpts from a diary, written as a coherent narrative of a most peculiar sort. As I leafed through the pages something gnawed at me, a glimmer of recognition, like a memory on the verge of consciousness, slipping in and out of the light. There was something achingly familiar about these words, but I wasn't quite sure what it was.

"I don't think it's recent," I said. "Here, listen to this."

The first two pages appeared to be a fragment. Without the beginning or the end, it was hard to know precisely what they were about. But on the third page there was a date and a place name to mark the beginning of a new entry.

Anno Domini 595, Damascus, Syria

Ubul Kassim turned 25 this year, and while in many ways he remains a slow student, with a constitutional aversion to the written word, he has compensated for this illiteracy with a prodigious ability to memorize large strings of numbers and blocks of text, as if he were reading them directly from printed ledgers. This genius of his has already begun to pay off, for the wealthiest trader in Mecca, a woman named Khadija bint Khuwaylid, recently hired him as her principle camel-driver and put him in charge of a caravan of 120 animals and forty armed men! Alas, he knows little of commerce, and would have traded away the entire cargo of hides, raisins, frankincense, myrrh, dried dates, and silver he was carrying for a pittance if I hadn't interceded on his behalf. As it was, I arranged for a local merchant to pay twice the going rate for his goods, allowing him to take back to his mistress a full complement of rich Damascene fabric and other luxuries as she required. "This

25

should help you to win the good graces of your mistress, Mustafa," I told him.'

"But she is old, Master. She has already worn through two husbands."

"What do you care about this?" I said. "The sooner she completes her days here on God's earth, the sooner her empire will be fully in your hands. You must demonstrate your worthiness to her at every occasion. Soon, because she is an older woman who has no offspring of her loins, she will come to depend on you entirely."

I had to pay that trader off with a large purse of good Roman gold from the treasury of our Order. We shall have to consider it an investment in the future of the church.

Col. Wilkens just shook his head, quietly chuckling, when I had finished my rough translation of this passage. "Now I see why no one has gotten back to me on this. Do you have a clue what this is all about?"

I must have turned white. My fingers were trembling. I was leafing through the rest of the pages, careful not to meet his eyes, and I was troubled by what I saw. For anyone brought up in my part of the world, the first wife of the Prophet Mohammad, the wealthy trader widow Khadija, was as familiar as their own grandmother. It was something Muslims were taught from the earliest age, and that we as Christians assimilated through an unwanted osmosis. The Prophet of Islam married the richest woman in Mecca, and her money helped him to establish himself and his new religion. But these pages hinted at a much darker secret than the purely mercantile history the Muslims themselves found comforting. There have long been rumors, propagated by Muslim scholars of old, that the Prophet Mohammed received his education, and indeed, a good deal of his theology from a wayward Nestorian monk named Bahira. Could he possibly have kept a diary? And if so, what use could it possibly be to Saddoun?

"Sir, would you mind if I took a copy of these pages? Perhaps while I am on leave I can translate them for you. Maybe there will be something in them of interest."

"Be my guest," he said.

He made a photocopy of the document minus the Top Secret cover page and gave it to me. Then he reached into his drawer and took out a small box and a pen.

"I'm going down to Camp Cropper in Baghdad with Saddoun. Maybe our civilian friends can get more out of him than I could. But before I go, I wanted you to have this."

He gave me the box, which contained a commander's coin from General Petraeus himself, and two of his business card. On the back of one of the cards he had printed an email address.

"If anything happens, contact me using this private email address. You have done invaluable service to your country and to mine. I will make sure that my country honors its debt to you. It's a dirty world out there, Johnny. Bad things always happen to good people."

Wilkens didn't tell me that his tour of duty was up, but there was something fatalistic about his words and his demeanor, as if he knew that this meeting would be our last. Perhaps it was just the warrior in him, who refused to fully believe the plans he made for the future, driving him to live so intensely in the present.

Little did I know it as I took my leave of Lieutenant Colonel Wilkens that afternoon, but a new chapter in my life was about to begin—a terrifying chapter, filled with live ghosts and the living dead.

2

Northern Iraq

I caught a U.S. Marine helicopter from Forward Operating Base Tiger, where we had been based for the past two weeks, up to Camp Marez at the Mosul military airport. My few belongings fit into a small sports bag I carried over one shoulder. It was almost dark by the time we landed. At Camp Marez, I took the white and orange minibus that carried the Iraqi employees home from work to the central bus station, where they could take another minibus or the service—collective taxis—to their final destination.

I didn't know any of my fellow passengers. There were three young women around my age, two older men, and myself, in addition to the driver and an armed guard. The women sat in the middle row of seats, and talked quietly amongst themselves for most of the short drive. Up ahead, as we approached the center of the city, we could hear a riot of beeping cars and the bright three-note trumpet blasts of trucks, honking at each other in wild rapture even though they knew there was no place to go. And then the horns went silent as the eerie tones of the call to evening prayer erupted, first from one hidden mosque, then another, and another, until it drowned out everything else. The man next to me leaned forward and addressed the young women. "Cover yourselves, my daughters. We're almost there," he said. They had been lost in conversation and hadn't seen that we had nearly arrived at the outdoor bus station. Quickly, they pulled scarves out of the pockets of their coats and wrapped them around their heads. Their giggling stopped, their smiles replaced with urgent sideward glances, the telltale furtiveness of fear.

I felt naked and under a microscope arriving like this in downtown Mosul, surrounded by mosques, on a minibus that everyone knew was bringing Iraqi employees back home from work on the American base. As we got out, I surveyed the crowd, their faces flicking in and out of the shadows as they moved. I had no doubt that Saddoun would try to make good on his promise, and my stomach was knotted with fear. Was it the man at the kiosk selling newspapers? How about the soft-drink vendor? Or was it the two young men with the Baathi moustaches and black vinyl jackets who had nothing else to do but scrutinize the passengers as they disembarked? They were leaning against the glass window of a kebab shop, picking their teeth, as the purple neon sign blinked overhead. Which ones were reporting to Saddoun?

For a moment, I contemplated walking straight out of the crowded square to the mosque up the street by the Nineveh Bridge to make them think I was a Muslim. But then I remembered that I also was carrying the two black Armalite cases containing the pair of compact Glock 19 automatic pistols that LTC Wilkens had given me.

I might be naked and under a microscope, but I wasn't defenseless. I met the gaze of the two Baathis with the moustaches and let them know it.

When I finally got home to the refugee housing complex where my family lived in Karamlesh, just east of Mosul in the Nineveh Plain, my mother and youngest sister were already in bed. Everyone else was out. I went quietly into the tiny bedroom I shared with Marcos when I was home and dumped my gear in a corner. Marcos's bed, as usual, was unmade, covered with clothes and a still-damp towel. On the tiny desk in the corner was a small computer screen—something he had "salvaged" from a government office during the liberation. It didn't look like it was hooked up to anything.

I lifted the mattress off my bed, sheets and all, and slid it halfway onto the floor. Then as quietly as I could, I took the slim Armalite cases with the 9 mm pistols and, kneeling on the concrete floor, I attached them to the underside of the bed frame with black bungee straps. Just as I was pulling the mattress back onto the bed, I felt a presence behind me and whirled around.

"I keep the bed made for you," my mother said, "just in case you come home like this some evening and no one is around."

"*Yimaa*, you scared me!"

She gave a quick grunt, pecked at her straggling hair, and pulled the nightdress around her. "I should think you've seen plenty of things more scary than me."

I laughed, and then she reached for me and folded me into her arms silently, just as she always did, reading my state of mind through our embrace.

No questions. No deceptions. No expectations. That was Mama. She had lived so long with absences she dared not tempt fate.

31

Kyrieh… Kyrieh Elayasson.

Kyrieh… Kyrieh Elayasson

In the distance, down the freshly-washed street, we could see the beginning of the funeral procession led by a single priest dressed in long white robes, the color of redemption and eternal life. The wide main street of Karamlesh formed the outer limit of the old town, but the crowds had turned it into a narrow pathway. On the town side, men and women emerged from their cramped, low houses and stood together in neat rows facing forward, somber and orderly, as if attending church; on the far side, a more helter-skelter group of onlookers had gathered to watch the townspeople and the procession as the priests and the mourners slowly made their way to the church. A group of men carried bouquets of red tulips and a large portrait of Archbishop Paulos Faraj Rahho, whose mutilated body had been found just the day before. Then came the pallbearers with the casket, a phalanx of priests in simple black suits and white collars, the church dignitaries with their purple and red sashes and black hats, and then the women of his extended family, all dressed in black but wearing headscarves of different colors, white and royal blue and deep crimson. There was no wailing, no ululating such as one hears at Muslim funerals. There was no shouting, no public anger, no political slogans. Just the quiet chant of the Kyrie, and a single bell tolling from St. Paul's church at our back. That was how we Christians mourned our dead. If you listened carefully, the shuffling of feet in the dust beat the air like the wings of an escaping bird.

Yousrah, my youngest sister, had lined up with the virgins along the outer wall of the church. There were about twenty of them, all dressed in black trousers, white blouses, and long black leather jackets, with white damascene scarves draped over their heads whose tasseled ends they gathered in front of them. Each of the girls held a small white basket. When the casket arrived, they silently moved toward it and showered it with rose petals, as the pallbearers walked up the few steps into the nave. Following alongside the pallbearers was my uncle Boutros, my mother's oldest brother. Although he was not a priest, he had worked with the church all of his life in Mosul, and was the last person who had seen Archbishop Rahho alive. He carried the Archbishop's pastoral staff, St. Peter's staff. It would be laid to rest along with his body in the crypt behind the altar.

"Boutros will now have to get a job," Mother said, once her brother had followed the casket into the church. I thought I detected the hint of a smile, but she carefully suppressed it. That was so like her: irreverent, practical, always leaning forward. But she also was my conduit to the past, the voice of our ghosts.

"He's not the only one," said Rita. "But there aren't any jobs here. The Kurds won't allow it."

Rita was 26, two years my junior. We all thought she should have gotten married years ago, but none of the men her age lived up to her standard—or so she said. She had mother's sharp tongue and tough intellect, but none of her subtlety or her humor. She had completed her law degree in Baghdad after the liberation and worked as a women's activist with the Assyrian Democratic Movement, now legal after years of opposition to Saddam.

She was less tough than she let on to be. After Baba was killed, when they firebombed Mar Gewargis, I would surprise her sometimes in the mornings, sobbing quietly as she combed out her long auburn hair. These were emotions that were forbidden to us. With all the suffering of our Assyrian nation, our martyrs whose blood was always fresh, to give in to sadness meant giving up. Still, I was less worried about Rita than I was about Yousrah and Marcos—not because of any particular emotional fragility, but because of the jihadis.

Yousrah had just started classes the previous autumn at the University of Mosul. Although it was just a twenty-minute bus ride from Karamlesh, the university was a world away, outside the fragile security zone where we now lived. Karamlesh was still the Nineveh Plain, our ancient Assyrian homeland, now protected—or occupied, as Rita would argue—by the Kurds. But for all the problems we had with the Kurds, Mosul was worse. Mosul was jihadi land, and Christians were considered fair game by predators of all sorts. To make sure she was safe, Marcos rode with her every day on the bus, and I know that they held hands as they crossed the bridge into the badlands and prayed. Marcos stayed in Mosul driving a taxi while Yousrah attended classes. It gave him something to do and brought in some extra money, he said. But I knew he also did it for the thrills. Outside of working for the American military, it was the most dangerous thing an Iraqi could do, especially an Assyrian Christian. I suppose it was a kid brother thing, his way of saying, 'don't you see? I'm as tough as you.' But I wasn't tough, no matter what he thought. Our world was too bleak and too dangerous to be tough.

For as long as I was away, working with the Americans, I was powerless to alter these arrangements. But now that I was home, I was determined to put a stop to the daily bus rides. Surely the murder of Archbishop Rahho should have made it clear that the jihadis could strike anyone, no matter how powerful, who dared to step onto their turf. We were all just living on borrowed time.

I needed to tell Marcos that I prayed, too, and that praying wasn't weakness, but faith in a God who surely must be somewhere, weeping as our small lives were extinguished like the last embers of the evening fire by the breath of dawn.

After the service, Mother took Marcos and Yousrah back the refugee-housing complex. I went with Rita to drink tea at the local ADM headquarters, which was just down the street from the church.

The main street was gradually emptying out as the out-of-town dignitaries and on-lookers made their way to the parking lot at the edge of town, where dozens of tour buses were parked. A handful of young men with short-barreled Kalashnikovs strapped across their shoulders stood outside the Party building, talking with people as they went inside. The low, blue building had an open forecourt directly off the street, and was impossible to defend even with professional soldiers. But these guards carried their weapons as if they were fashion appendages. At least they kept the barrels pointed to the ground, I thought. I just shook my head when I noticed that their fingers were curled around the trigger, not flat out against it as the Americans taught. That was the way Palestinian guerillas carried their weapons in the Arab movies. It was stupid, dangerous, and inefficient.

The forecourt was full of Party dignitaries sipping tea, most of them standing. A few older men sat around a low plastic table, smoking, enjoying a brief burst of springtime sunshine, after all the rain of the past few days. One of the guards started to frisk me until he saw Rita.

"*Shlama, rabia!*" he said, welcoming her. "Who is your friend?"

Rita gave the young man a little shake of the head and one of those smiles she reserved for hopeless suitors. "My long lost brother, Yohannes."

"Ah, the one who works with the Americans?" the guard said.

I nodded warily, not too happy that he knew this.

"Don't worry, we're among friends," Rita said, catching my arm.

"So was Bishop Rahho," I said, "when he was murdered."

She gave me a dirty look and dragged me inside by the arm. The main room of the Party headquarters was almost smaller than the courtyard. As was the style with all public buildings in my country, the room was walled with cheap sofas and a series of small tables, each bearing a metal tray with a half dozen glasses of sweet tea. The old male servant who served the tea inevitably overfilled the glasses, so you couldn't touch the tray without getting your fingers sticky. The older men poured hot tea into the saucers then soaked it up with a sugar cube. The air was so thick with cigarette smoke it was hard to breathe.

"Welcome home," Rita said, with a chuck of her head at our surroundings. Was this home? After the years I had been working for the Americans, bunking in sandbagged trailers with young men from places called City of Industry, California, and Oshkosh, Michigan, who rarely smoked, never drank tea, and chatted with their families over the Internet when they weren't playing video games, I wasn't quite sure. The Americans seemed to create the world

anew wherever they went, whereas we seemed mired
in our old ways, ways of violence and betrayal, dark
secrets and forbidden places, unable to grasp the
changes taking placed around us. Rita grabbed a glass
of hot tea from a fresh tray the old servant had
brought out from the kitchen alcove and handed it to
me, then took another glass for herself. "At least, let
me introduce you to some of my comrades."

Politics has always bored me, and Rita knew
this. Politicians could sit around for days discussing
how to divvy up other people's money, and when
they were finished they still would stuff half of it into
their own pockets. Rita thrived on the talk because
she felt they could remake the world. It was an
aspiration if not a reality she shared with the
Americans.

"So when are your military friends coming
here to help us?" the party secretary asked me. I think
she introduced him as Jamal something.

"They aren't," I said bluntly.

"Why not? They've helped the Shias.
They've helped the Kurds. Now they're even helping
the Sunnis. Why won't the Americans help us?"

"Because we've never planted car bombs and
blown ourselves up in crowded markets," I said.

He gave Rita a look that questioned why she
had brought me here in the first place.

"I'm not suggesting that Assyrians should do
such things. I'm just telling you the facts of life.
We're going to have to rely on ourselves."

"I agree," he said. And then an aide came up
from behind him, and pulled him off by an elbow to
greet someone important.

Rita caught my eye and nodded over to one of
the sofas on the far side of the room, where a thin
woman in blue jeans and a black t-shirt sat with a
small child on her lap and two others alongside her.

She couldn't have been more than thirty or thirty-five; but she looked at least fifty. Her eyes seemed to have receded deep into her face, and the skin of her neck sagged. The four of them sat forward in a kind of dull expectation, eternally waiting for something to lift them out of their misery. The children just stared at the floor, listless, not fidgeting or anything, but this wasn't a sign of obedience or parental training. There was death in their eyes, silence in their souls. It was a look I had come to know well.

"They're hungry," she said, in answer to my unspoken question. "They come here once every fortnight to receive aid, when we have anything to distribute. This woman's husband was abducted in Mosul last year, along with another one of their children. The jihadis wanted $40,000 in ransom. She sold everything they had, and so did the man's brothers, but they couldn't come up with more than one and a half copybooks—$15,000. The kidnappers were neighbors. They went to the local mosque. They called the brother and put her husband on the phone. He pleaded with them to come up with more money. In the end, they gave the kidnappers the $15,000 they had gathered and got the boy released, but not the husband. The kidnappers dumped his body along the side of the road a few days later, minus the head. That they delivered in a plastic bag to her house."

Every family who lived here in Karamlesh and throughout the Nineveh Plain had a similar story. Most were refugees, just like us, who had fled from tragedy, only to be greeted by more violence in what they had hoped was a safe haven. Why can't we live as ordinary folk, as people in America or in Europe? But that doesn't appear to be God's plan for us in this place, in this time. If God does indeed have a plan.

Rita was very popular, and soon she got sucked into some political discussion. I wandered off after a bit and decided to head home. I turned the corner onto a side street not far from the ADM building, when a man I didn't recognize stepped toward me from a doorway. He wasn't armed, and he wasn't threatening. But something about him put me on edge. He wore a dirty white shirt and his face glistened with old sweat. The skin of one cheek bore the deep pockmarks that plagued so many Iraqis, reminders of an age before vaccines. And he wore the Baathi moustache.

"Yohannes Yohanna?" he said. "*Johnny?*"

"Do I know you?" I asked.

"I have been sent by Abu Hassan," he said, without answering. "He asked me to give you a message."

"Who is Abu Hassan?" I said.

I never thought they could find me so quickly, here, in the heart of the Nineveh Plain. It was a bad sign, and a familiar one. This is what the Baathists did in their endless sadism. They wanted you to know that they were tracking you. They wanted the thrill of feeling your fear before they slowly extinguished your life. I was determined not to give him that pleasure and worked hard to keep my voice level.

I turned to leave, but before I could spin around a second man emerged from the alleyway from behind me and punched me hard on the ear. The pain was startling, sharp, stinging. As my hands went up involuntarily to protect my head, the first man punched me in the stomach, driving me into the crumbling plaster wall, and then they grabbed one of my arms and whipsawed me onto the ground and began kicking me. I must have cried out as I bucked and rolled, because suddenly I heard a woman calling out from a window up above. *"Mann le l'tekh?* Who's down there? Is that you, Boutros?"

The first man grabbed my hair and yanked back my head and bore down on me, just inches away from my face, and covered my mouth with his hand. He was sweating now, and as I struggled to break free, he drove his knee into my stomach until I couldn't breath. Seeing my fear, a sick grin twisted his face. I was ashamed.

"Greetings from Abu Hassan," he hissed. He held up a finger for me to be quiet, and I could see now that he was wearing brass knuckles. I nodded, and then he let go and the two of them got up.

Just before they ran off into the alleyway, he turned to me. "Stay away from St. Hormizd. That's his message." And then they were gone.

I picked myself up and brushed the dust from my clothes. My jaw was numb, but it was not broken. In an instant, my fear became anger—anger with myself for being so stupid to believe I could be safe. Saddoun was right: he could find me anywhere, even here in Karamlesh. As I walked quickly back home, the wadded copy of Saddoun's ancient document I had stuffed into my back pocket burned like a branding iron into my flesh. Whatever secret it contained he clearly wanted to keep, and he was prepared to kill for it.

A large yellow banner with the words, "Hope in Our Savior," in Aramaic script, hung over the main entrance of the refugee-housing complex where Mother and the family had found shelter after the fire-bombing of Mar Gewargis in Baghdad the year before. When I first came to visit, shortly after they moved in, I remember commenting on those words to Shimun Goreal, the block leader, when I saw him outside. I asked him if this was the name of the neighborhood church. He laughed.

"No, that's the answer of Mr. Elias every time someone has a complaint," he said. "The plumbing doesn't work? The windows leak? The electricity went out? 'Hope in our Savior,' that's the answer we get. But don't get me wrong," he added quickly, seeing an armed guard approach. "Mr. Elias is our benefactor. Without him, we wouldn't even have a roof over our heads, never mind the leaks. See? He even provides us with guards to protect us."

The pre-fab housing units looked like they had been built fifty years ago and been badly maintained since then, but Mr. Elias had them hastily erected just a few years ago as Christians started fleeing Baghdad and other cities around Iraq. He always seemed to choose the worst piece of property for the refugee centers, on the outskirts of our towns. They had sprung up all across the Nineveh Plain and in parts of Iraqi Kurdistan where Assyrian towns and villages and farm settlements had once thrived. Rita claims it was part of some deal he had struck with the local Bishop, where he would rent worthless property, generating fresh revenue for the church, in exchange for his political support. While Mr. Elias claimed he was motivated out of the kindness of his Christian heart, in fact his real goal was to win the acquiescence of the beleaguered Assyrians in northern Iraq to annexation by the Kurds, his political allies. Mr. Elias became the godfather of the church, and the arch-nemesis of Rita and her secular political friends. They said he spent all his money building empty churches and cemeteries, whereas if he really wanted to help the people he would be building schools and investing in local businesses that could create jobs.

Our unit was identical to the eighty-six others in the low-slung ochre complex: two tiny bedrooms, a small common room, a kitchen, and a "wet room." (You could hardly call it a bathroom, since the shower and the toilet were holes in the cement floor). The complex gave onto a vacant field at the edge of town, where chickens and sheep grazed through garbage and plastic bags. A few motorbikes were parked around a pool of sewage between two of the buildings, where despite the cold weather a few children were running barefoot.

I asked Mama what she knew about Mar Hormizd.

She was the keeper of our histories, guardian of our family memories, repository of our Assyrian soul. Some people might wonder why you were asking such a question out of the blue. But not *Yimaa.* She took each question like each new tragedy that befell our people as an opportunity, 'a teachable moment,' she called them.

As always, the first thing she did was brew coffee. This was a relatively elaborate process, involving a small brass pot with a narrow neck into which she measured water, finely ground coffee, sugar, and a pinch of cardamom. The trick was to make it boil just slightly, so the coffee foamed up to the rim without spilling over, then put it back on the heat just an instant to reach the boiling point a second time. Stirring. Thinking. Contemplating where to begin.

"When your Nana Soraya was a young widow freshly arrived from Tabriz after the massacres, she was taken in by a family who worked as gardeners at the old Nestorian monastery in Al Qosh, where the Nineveh Plain dead ends into the wild mountains that form the border with Turkey. Remember: she had an infant child with her—that would be Issa, your grandfather—so their generosity was very real. She stayed with them for many years, until Issa went down to the University of Mosul and made a name for himself as a young firebrand poet and Arab nationalist. People came to her to hear her stories of the genocide, the kindness of the American missionaries in Tabriz, the treachery of the Kurds, the utter duplicity of the Persians."

"I remember," I said, passing the cup with the hot fragrant coffee before my nose. The long afternoons in winter sitting on Nana Soraya's lap in the big house in Dora were like a faraway dream of goodness before the world began to collapse into fear and suspicion and I grew up.

"In those days, the monastery of Mar Hormizd was world famous," Hannah went on. "The Papal nuncio used to come to al Qosh, as did Bishops from all over Europe and the Middle East. No one ever saw them outside the monastery, but they always would come to the gardener's house to listen to Nana Soraya. That's how she found out the real purpose of their visits. They came to devote a secret cult to St. Peter's bones.

"Legend has it that St. Peter was executed in Babylon after bringing the Gospel to the remnants of our Assyrian kings. Believers rescued his body, just as they did the broken body of our Lord, and brought it up to Al Qosh where they buried him in a cave hollowed out of the flank of the mountains. Centuries later, a church was built to conceal the spot. Later still, a hermit priest named Hormizd expanded it to become a monastery."

St. Peter's bones? How could that be? Weren't they supposed to be in the Vatican? He was the Vicar of Christ, the founder of the Church of Rome. What would Saddoun care about some Christian relic, should it exist? And what did that have to do with the manuscript we had found in Saddoun's safe house? My mind was spinning.

"Is that true?" I asked. "Is St. Peter really buried in the monastery of St. Hormizd?" But Hannah just laughed.

"That's my Yohannes," she said, stroking my hair. "Still asking that question, ever since you were a child."

"Well, is it?" I persisted.

She pursed her lips and gave a little shrug, turning her head aside from the hand with which she had offered the story, as if to disown it. "It is what it is," she said finally, just as she always did.

Here she was, two generations later, a refugee just like her grandmother. Her beautiful black hair was now streaked with grey, but her eyes were still alight, and I could see in them burning the embers of memory just as I remembered how they had burned with Nana Soraya. Like mother, like daughter, down through the generations. Were we equally doomed to repeat the past as we were to resemble our forebears?

I dared not contemplate fully and consciously what I feared the jihadis might be plotting. But in the back of my mind I knew: if they knew about St. Peter's bones, they would do everything in their power to destroy them, just as they had destroyed our villages and our churches for generations whenever they had the upper hand. They would destroy anything that contributed to our Christian culture, our Assyrian heritage, given an opportunity.

There was only one hope, really: the Americans. I resolved to tell the whole story—or at least, the important parts—to my supervisor. Surely he would know what to do.

And then I resolved to read the manuscript fully. Perhaps it would provide some clue as to Saddoun's intentions.

A few days later, I took a minibus to Erbil, the capital of the Kurdish region, to report back to work at Triple Shield. For most Christians living in the north as "internally displaced persons," it was difficult to travel from the Nineveh Plain into Kurdistan. Although the Kurds had seized control of our area and were providing nominal security, legally we were still attached to the Nineveh governorate—which meant Baghdad, Sunni suiciders and al Qaeda. As the Kurds had done elsewhere to limit the encroachment of al Qaeda into their region, they had set up border checkpoints on the edges of the Nineveh Plain, in this case, just on the other side of the narrow bridge that crossed the Greater Zab river. I could flash my contractor's ID card, and enter without question. But most Christians who had come to the north after their homes had been bombed in Baghdad or Basra or even Mosul couldn't get Kurdish residence permits. This made the ninety-minute ride to Erbil like a journey to a foreign land, but without a passport. Instead of Arabic, everyone spoke Kurdish, which is closer to Persian than to Arabic. And if you chanced to speak Arabic, the Kurds looked at you with suspicion, as if you were a Baathist, an enemy. Sometimes they took people out of cars or the minibuses and turned them back if they didn't like their names or their ID cards or just their accents. Sometimes they just beat them and let them go.

Erbil was a boomtown, growing in every direction across the flat, rocky desert, without style or grace. Gigantic billboards in the northern suburb of Ainkawa, where Christians had lived for 2,000 years, advertised a new "American village," a gated community built to resemble something in southern California, right down to the twin garages, grass lawns, and SUVs parked out front. I got out of the minibus at St. Joseph's cathedral, and walked the short distance to the U.S. Consulate, a city unto itself hidden behind high walls, next to the Ainkawa police station.

At first glance, from the street, you would never suspect there was anything behind those grey walls. The distant buildings were low enough to be invisible to the street, and there was no obvious vehicle entrance or traffic. I presented my contractor's ID to the guard outside the gatehouse, and even though we recognized each other, he scanned it and indicated that I should pass through the metal detectors. I placed my mobile phone and the Glock 19 I carried in the small of my back in a wooden box, after I popped out the magazine and showed the guard the empty chamber. He nodded, and gave me a stiff cardboard chit with a number on it, so I could reclaim them when I left. Anyone who had a shred of sanity carried a personal weapon these days, and the guards were used to it.

Once you push through the bulletproof glass door into the American compound, the smell of diesel fuel and the din of the gigantic generators assail you. The generators were as big as container trucks, and fed power to invisible offices deep inside the warren of cramped, narrow streets set behind their high walls. The first time I came here I felt like a rat entering a maze.

Cory Reed, my boss, worked out of a large but disheveled villa within the walled American compound. On the walls were detailed maps of Erbil, Kirkuk, Suleymaniyeh and Mosul—the major cities in the north—that came under his supervision. Red explosion points marked the location of recent clashes, and smaller red pins marked this month's IEDs. When a road got too red, he gave the order to his drivers to avoid it.

A large white board behind him had the names of his team leaders and their assignments for the week. Triple Shield did executive protection, escorting U.S. diplomats and visiting journalists. They also provided locally hired interpreters to the military and to their civilian clients. I had been with the company for four years, first in Baghdad then up in Erbil. The retired British, Australian, and U.S. military men they hired as bodyguards got upwards of $1000 a day for their services. Because I was a local hire, I was paid one tenth of that amount. Still, I earned in one day as much as my kid brother Marcos earned in a month driving a taxi, so I couldn't complain.

"Where you been, Johnny?" Mr. Reed asked me.

"Col. Wilkens gave me some time off to be with my family."

"Is that right?" he said. "Well, he didn't tell me jack all."

Cory Reed had been a CIA station chief somewhere in the Arab world. After 9/11, he retired with the equivalent of a two-star general's pay, and let everyone he met know it. During a clandestine trip to Afghanistan during the late 1990s, a Tajik warlord had given him a pair of brass balls the size of large grapes, attached to the ends of a smoky leather thong. He worked the balls like Muslims handled their worry beads, flipping them around his right hand until they clicked into each other and bounced back from the contact with a sharp metallic sound. He was clicking them now. *This is not how I had imagined our meeting. I desperately wanted to tell him about St. Peter's bones and Saddoun's threats.* But he had something else in mind.

"You know something, Johnny?" he said. The balls went *click*. He wasn't waiting for an answer, just punctuating his thoughts. "You lied to me."

"Lied to you? " I asked.

"About your family. You *[click]* lied to us on your employment interview."

"I don't understand. What are you talking about, Mr. Reed?"

"You are *family* with Tariq Aziz. You know who Tariq Aziz is, don't you"

Click! went the brass balls.

"Yes, of course. He was the deputy prime minister under Saddam. But you say I am family with him? What do you mean?"

"You have the same last names. Yohanna. He's Mikhail Yohanna. You never reported that. You are *family* with Saddam Hussein's big honky sidekick *[click]*, and you never reported that."

I didn't like where this was going. It sounded like Mr. Reed had put two and two together and made twenty-seven.

"It's true," I said. "We have the same last name. So do thousands of other Iraqis."

"But you're his relative. And you never told us that. Even that *[click]* raghead Saddoun knew that."

The sound of Saddoun's name had an unpleasant effect on me. I could feel the cold stare of his reptilian eyes bearing into the back of my neck just before he sank his fangs into my flesh. I felt weak, my stomach suddenly empty. What did Mr. Reed know about Saddoun? And why would Saddoun have been talking to him, anyway?

"My father's grandfather and his grandfather were brothers," I said. "What does that make us?"

"Too close for comfort, as far as I'm concerned," Mr. Reed said. "You're fired. And not only are you fired: you will never work for an American contractor or the US government again."

I couldn't believe what I was hearing. I had worked for Triple Shield for four years, gone all over Iraq, and taken part in dozens of takedowns of jihadi cells. Col. Wilkens had even given me a commander's coin from Gen. Petraeus himself in recognition of my service. The truth was, I had never met Tariq Aziz, nor would anyone in my family admit to the distant tie after what he did to my grandfather, Issa. That's why it had never occurred to me to report it. As far as I was concerned or my family was concerned, Tariq Aziz was the enemy.

"That's just so wrong, sir. Do you want to know the real story? It's not at all—"

"—Look," he said, holding the leather thong in the middle and letting one of the brass balls drop until it hit the other, sending it upwards like the arc of a pendulum. "I don't care what the real story is, or even if there is a real story. You lied on your employment application and that's a firing offense. Period. End of story. End of the *[click]* mother of all stories. Now please hand over your contractor ID."

He tapped the metal desk impatiently until I placed before him the stiff, photographic identity card and the bead chain, my ticket to freedom within my own country. Setting them on the desk was like taking off my clothes and my boots. I felt naked and at least six inches shorter.

In a daze, I cleared out the few things I kept in a locker in the employees' trailer –a handful of spent AK-47 shells that one of our targets had fired at me before Sgt. Diaz took him out, my balaclava, a change of clothes, a few books. Then I swung by the quartermaster's trailer to pick up the last of the money that was owed me for my work with Col. Wilkens. I couldn't believe that this was it, that I wouldn't be coming back. It had all happened so quickly. Whatever Saddoun's emissary had meant about staying away from St. Hormizd meant nothing now, I thought. Without my contractor's ID and my job with the Americans, I was nobody. I had no power. I didn't know their secret. Surely I couldn't present any danger to them now.

But I was wrong.

I was still in a state of shock from my encounter with Cory Reed when Marcos and Yousrah returned home from Mosul one evening much earlier than normal. It was several days after I was discharged from Triple Shield; perhaps even a week afterwards, I can't recall. But after I learned what had happened to them I knew I had to take my family away from Karamlesh, out of Iraq, if we were going to have any chance of surviving at all.

Yousrah was still trembling when she and Marcos opened the door to our tiny housing unit at Hope in Our Savior. Marcos's shirt was streaked with blood and ashes. He was doing his best to be angry, shouting as he slammed the paper-thin door behind them, but I could tell he was more afraid than angry.

"*Brata... brata,*" Mama murmured as Yousrah flung herself into her arms. She stroked Yousrah's dark hair and held her as my younger sister sobbed her heart out. Mama didn't need to ask questions to understand what had just happened. She whispered words of comfort dredged up from generations of tragedy, always on the ready, never stale, and never wrong.

Marcos stamped around the room, until finally he exploded.

"*Yimaa*, stop! We need guns, not tears. Not compassion. We need guns, Mama."

She ignored him for as long as she could, until he interrupted her ministering again. He wanted to know where he could find Rita and her friends so they could take action.

"You, Marcos. *shtuk*—hush!" she hissed at him. "You will get us all killed."

When finally he calmed down, I learned what happened.

They had been running late in the minibus on their way to Yousrah's classes at the University. For some reason, the Kurdish militia held them up at the last roadblock before the bridge into the badlands of the city, making everyone get out so they could check their identity papers and thoroughly search the bus. When they finally got on their way again, they saw Marcos's taxi overtake them, the driver from the night shift waving as he spied Marcos with my sister inside the minibus. Apparently, the Muslim driver, Mahmoud, had also been running late. Normally, he would be waiting at the taxi company office when Marcos arrived after dropping off Yousrah at her class. But today, he must have had a last minute fare. Fare-paying customers were so unpredictable in Mosul that he couldn't afford to pass up any opportunity. He was rushing back to sign off his shift and return to his family so Marcos could take over.

Not two minutes later, a muffled explosion made the closed windows of the minibus suck in and out like a death rattle, and then they screeched to a halt, the road blocked by the burning hulk of the taxi.

Mahmoud's black bubbling head lay slumped over the steering wheel, while the engine and the vinyl and the seat cushions inside were all in flames. Marcos cut himself on the twisted metal trying to wrench Mahmoud's body out of the wreck, smearing blood and ashes all over his clothes.

"They were coming for me, don't you see?" Marcos said angrily to me. "They were coming for me because I am a Christian. It was just an accident that Mahmoud was late, that we were late. It was me they wanted, don't you see?"

I nodded sympathetically. He was probably right. The attack was probably just a random act of violence against a Christian whose comings and goings had attracted attention because of their regularity. There was nothing personal about it, nothing focused. The target was our Assyrian community, not Marcos, not Yousrah, not Mama, not me. In truth, it happened all the time.

But I couldn't get Saddoun's evil reptilian face out of my mind. What if the attack on Marcos's taxi was the work of Saddoun and his thugs? *We're here and we're serious*, they were saying. *See? We can get you and anyone in your family at any time we wish!*

That was when I began to make plans to get my family out of Karamlesh, out of Iraq. Thus began our descent into nightmare.

There were several more intact passages among the pages of the ancient manuscript we had taken from Saddoun. The language in which they were written, while literary, was not ambiguous. As I read through them, I hoped and prayed that the reason he had them with him when we arrested him was because he was seeking to get them translated into Arabic. For the story that was beginning to emerge from them was deeply troubling. Perhaps Saddoun suspected that I had been given a copy of this document. Perhaps that was the real reason why he was pursuing me? If so, I realized, there could be no turning back; I could no longer pretend innocence or ignorance. Like a young woman who wakes up after her wedding night a transformed person, I could not unlearn the startling teaching of these pages now that I had read them. If, of course, they were authentic and true.

Anno Domini 613, Yathrib

Things have not been going as planned.

Yesterday, Mustafa came up from Mecca and complained to me that no one is taking him seriously. Except for his wife, who is so enamored of him she would believe any inanity coming off his lips, no one believes the legend that Bahira and the Brothers crafted so carefully for him about finding revelation in a cave. In his city, the other tradesmen he has approached claim he is just a sick man having seizures or fits. Worst of all is his wife's cousin, Waraqa, considered a wise man by everyone in Mecca, who has translated the words of our Savior into the local dialect. I tried to reason with him, as one man of God to another. But Waraqa just laughed and recalled the time when Mustafa had his first seizure at the age of four, nearly forty years ago. "Lo, and he fell down in a field and shouted out loud that demons were splitting his stomach in two, as if searching for something inside," he said, slapping his thigh between bouts of hilarity as he mimicked Mustafa's propensity for rotund oratory. I did not share in his levity.

"Surely," I said, "is it not in the best interest of the faith, here in this pagan land where men and women dance naked around that abominable stone and fall down in worship before a whole pantheon of false deities, to help one arise up who can turn the people toward repentance and prayer to the One God Almighty?"

"Aye, so it would," rejoined Waraqa, "if you found such a one who was truly willing to repent. This man knows no humility. Nay, even worse: should he succeed, I dare say he would want to be Pope. Woe unto you should you continue to promote his cause."

I was shaken by these words, and delivered Waraqa's blunt warning to the other Brothers of the Order. We agreed to send an emissary to Babai in Nisibis to seek his counsel. After such great hopes of expanding the faith, Mustafa's own failings, his tendency to pick fights, his greed, and the rumors of wanton and even lewd behavior that dogged him, may prove the stronger party of all.

Yathrib, of course, was the common name for the city of Medina, which was not far from Mecca, where Mohammad and his followers fled after losing their battle with the Quraysh in 622 AD. Apparently, it also was home of the Nestorian monastery to which the monk Bahira belonged.

Anno Domini 619, Yathrib

It is not surprising that my efforts to teach Mustafa about the three-fold nature of God have foundered, when even in our own church opinions diverge. I fear the fine distinctions between the human and divine nature of the Son, as they were so delicately elucidated by the founder of our Order, are simply lost on this simple soul, who worships so deeply at the alter of the material world and covets earthly power, earthly treasure.

One day, after a lesson devoted to the breath of God as Holy Spirit, ever present throughout the ages, inspiration of the Prophets, Mustafa turned to me in derision. "What, you would have me tell my followers to worship the Wind?" Another time, after I attempted to explain that Jesus was born of Mary, just like any other man, but was also and at the same time the only son of God, sent by God the Father into the world for our salvation, he came back and said, "O Esteemed Hormizd bint Bahira, as surely as the Prophet was born of woman's womb I tell you: Allah had no son."

As he grows increasingly frustrated with the refusal of his own tribe, the Quraysh, to accept his teaching, I find that his mind wanders whenever I attempt to teach him right doctrine. His sole interest is power, not truth; domination of men, not submission to God's will; and I find increasingly that he subtly alters the texts that we have crafted for him to memorize in order to enhance his standing with the Quraysh or to justify this or that personal weakness, such as his lust.

So it was that he came up with the notion, after a day spent observing the Quraysh in their worship of Hubul al-Ilah at the horrible shrine of the black stone, of a pagan trinity whose Godhead he announced. It was meet and right for his followers to bow down before al-Lat, al-Uzza, and Manat—the three daughters of al-Ilah–if the Quraysh would bow down alongside his followers in worship of the One God he now called Allah. The brothers were terrified when I reported this back to them; they tore the cloth from their backs and beat the bare skin with knotted cords until it was bleeding and raw, begging the Lord to forgive them for having helped birth such blasphemy.

I reproved Mustafa when I saw him next, but the success of these verses had gone to his head. "What would you have me become?" he said. "A voice who cries out in the wilderness, and who gets his head lopped off on the orders of a woman whose attentions he spurned? Or one whose words can make his enemies kneel to worship the One True God?"

I fear, if he is successful and wins over the Quraysh with this blasphemy, that he will abjure our counsel and rely increasingly on his own inventions and political skills. The brothers agree that we must use all of our powers to get him to recant this blasphemy and return to the narrow path, even if it means interceding with the father of that poor six-year girl with whom he is smitten, to give his blessing to Mustafa's lust.

Every Christian brought up in this part of the world knows that our lives hang on the slenderest of threads. We like to call it the grace of God, and surely that is the truth. But on a more mundane and practical level, we live because the Muslims allow us to live. We die when they grow weary of tolerance, or when we refuse to pay the tribute, the *jizya*. Only the strongest of warrior kings has succeeded in rolling back the advancing waves of Islam, men like Charles Martel, who stopped the Saracen hordes from sweeping into northern Europe in 732 AD, or like Godefroi de Bouillon, who led the first Crusade to retake the Holy Land. As I read this passage, I knew without the slightest doubt that Saddoun and his thugs would not hesitate for a second to kill anyone who came into possession of these pages, for they had the power of calling into question the very origins of their faith. I could burn the actual pages, but not the knowledge that they contained. Surely that was the meaning of the words Saddoun's thug had hissed at me. *Stay away from St. Hormizd.* They would stop at nothing to keep these pages and the original book of which they were a copy from ever seeing the light of day.

But what could I do, a lone person, without power or influence? Surely, my first responsibility was to my immediate family, not to history or truth or any of those grand notions the politicians like others to die for. I put those thoughts away along with the incendiary manuscript pages, which I stuffed behind the black Armalite cases containing my Glock 19s.

3

Amman, Jordan

As head of the household, I traveled to Amman ahead of the others to start our application for refugee status. With letters of commendation from my unit commanders, and several citations for meritorious service, I expected to be welcomed with open arms at the U.S. embassy. When I finally did get an appointment with a consular officer, after being rebuffed several times by the Bedouins at the embassy gates, I had everything ready in a dark blue binder, with all of my documents in glassine inserts. I had a photograph of me with Sgt. Diaz, Willy, Frank, Deron and Mojo, and another one with Col. Wilkens. I even had photocopies of several of the identification passes I had been issued over the past four years.

"That's very nice," said Thomas McGuinty, the blond-haired consular officer, as he leafed through the binder. "So what do you want me to do with this? Start a fan club?"

"No, sir," I said. "I need your help to get me and my family relocated to the United States."

He burst out laughing when I said that, then caught himself and covered his mouth.

"And why do you think I would do that?" he asked finally. "There are only about one and a half million Iraqis who want to move to the United States. What's the matter, isn't freedom good enough for you people?"

McGuinty was maybe 30 or 32 years old, just a few years more than me. He told me right off the bat that he had never served in Iraq and had no desire to ever see the place. But I was directed to him as the embassy's liaison person to the hundreds of thousands of Iraqis now living in Jordan. Many of them, like me, were Assyrian Christians, and couldn't return home because of the jihadis and the Kurds.

"My father lost his leg trying to protect the congregation at his church from a car-bomber. Last year he was killed when they firebombed the church again. I worked for the coalition for four years as a translator. The jihadis put me on a list of collaborators they posted in the mosque near our home in Karada last year. If I stay any longer, I will be killed," I said.

McGuinty got up from behind his desk and pulled up a metal armchair, so his knees almost touched mine. He gave me a look up and down that for an instant reminded me of Saddoun: probing, acute, like a bird of prey. I met his eyes and they were ironic, almost sassy, inviting.

"You're a big, strong man," he said finally, more friendly now. "Got a wife? Children?"

"No," I said. "A younger brother and two sisters."

"Are they here with you in Amman?"

"Not yet. I need to get them an appointment with you or with the United Nations so they can get visas to leave Iraq. I was told you have a program to help former translators and their families."

He laughed again, a stiff little contemptuous hiccup, then covered his mouth. "Well, now. That might actually make this insane administration look good. But never mind."

He reached over to his desk to a pile of forms, then asked me for the names of my brother and sisters and wrote them down.

"What about your mother?"

"Yes, my mother, too," I said, and spelled out her name.

He looked at the form, sighed deeply, then reluctantly handed it to me.

"Alright. They can use this with the airline in Erbil. I'm assuming that you *are* going to fly them down here, right?"

"Yes, the road is too dangerous."

"So I hear. Well, this gives you two months to get them down here."

The form certified that the persons listed below had an appointment with a consular officer at the U.S. Embassy in Amman to begin processing their application for refugee status. Then he gave me his card and got up.

"It's Johnny, is it?" he said, as I prepared to leave.

"That's what people call me, yes."

"I put my cell phone on the card. Call me over the weekend if you like and you can tell me all about Iraq. I'm sure I will enjoy it, coming from you."

I managed to get Marcos and Yousrah to Amman on a flight in early July, but my mother and Rita refused to leave Karamlesh. Hannah was fatalistic: this was her homeland, and the jihadis could kill her just as they killed her father and grandfather, but she wasn't going to give up her identity in exchange for her life. Rita was more prosaic: the political fight they were waging with the ADM was gaining traction, so now was not the time to leave. I tried everything to change their minds. I reminded them of the car-bombing that just barely missed Marcos and Yousrah, that I had no job, that we had an opportunity of starting a new life as a family in America. But nothing worked.

When I took Marcos and Yousrah for the promised appointment at the embassy, McGuinty's former friendliness had vanished. He told us coldly that we would have to go to the United Nations High Commission for Refugees, the UNHCR.

"We used to have a program to help translators and people who worked for the so-called Coalition, but not their family members," he said. "And at any rate, that program has been scaled back and moved to Baghdad now that Iraq has become a sovereign country again."

I couldn't believe it. He had said nothing about this when we first met. Indeed, he had encouraged me to bring my family to Amman! Then I realized that I had never called him since our first meeting, as he had suggested. Apparently this was his revenge.

Marcos sensed my silent outrage, and hissed urgent questions at Yousrah and me in Syriac. I had already explained to him that relocation was going to take time, but he wanted everything to happen immediately. He was incapable of believing that a U.S. diplomat couldn't simply snap his fingers and stamp visas into our passports and whisk us into a nice house with three bedrooms and two baths in Southfield, Michigan, where many of his friends had gone. When Yousrah and I got up to leave, he took McGuinty's two hands and shook them earnestly.

"You can help us, right?" he asked, his English spotty and to the point.

"No, I can't," McGuinty replied. "Now, good-bye."

Back outside in the dry dusty heat of early afternoon, Marcos was furious with me. "You didn't tell him what happened to us?" he shouted. "You didn't tell him how Papa was murdered? You didn't show him all your letters from the U.S. Army?"

"Of course I did, Marco," I said gently, trying to calm him down. But he brushed off my arm as I attempted to steer him down the hill, away from the embassy compound, the surveillance cameras and the Bedouin guards. I didn't want for them to hear us speaking in Syriac, just in case they could make out a few words. That would immediately identify us as Christians, in case they hadn't figured it out already. At times, Christians simply disappeared in Amman, but there was no point in explaining that now. There would be plenty of time to explain to Marcos the threats we faced, and the compromises we had to accept if we wanted to stay alive, even if I myself sometimes rejected them.

The form McGuinty gave me said that Iraqis seeking relocation as refugees had to first register with the UNHCR. Their professional staff would examine our documents and work with us to find an appropriate country for resettlement. Iraqis who had worked for the Coalition would receive priority treatment along with their immediate family, and would be put on a preferred list for entry into the United States. As I read the paper over carefully, I convinced myself that McGuinty had just been giving me a hard time, wanting to embarrass me in front of my family. My case was a perfect match for the U.S.

resettlement program. The stop at the UN was just a formality. Nevertheless, when I went to the UN office a few days later, I decided it was better if I went alone. I didn't need Marco blowing his stack at some UN functionary. Amman is a large city, built on steep hills, and there is very little public transport. I was in a hurry the day I finally went to the UNHCR, eager to get back before either Yousrah or Marcos returned. Our cramped basement apartment in the crumbling Christian slum of Jebel Ashrafieyeh was on the opposite side of the city from the US embassy and the UN compound, so I figured I needed a good half hour by taxi each way.

I went up to the small square near the Armenian Church on the street above us, and jumped into the first taxi that stopped. I told the driver where I wanted to go and he set the car in gear immediately, before we had even agreed on the fare. At first, in my eagerness to get to the UN office, I took his haste as a mirror of my own. Besides, the car was air-conditioned and the windows were tinted, making it a refreshing respite from the dusty summer heat.

Before long, I sensed that something was wrong. The driver was in his early twenties, dressed in fashionable jeans and a clean t-shirt, with a trim beard. But when he looked at me in the rear-view mirror as we raced down the hill I noticed that his eyes were red. He was driving erratically, sitting way back in his seat, swerving to avoid people and parked cars as if they were distant objects in some video game. The Mercedes sedan was too new to belong to him, I thought. Then I noticed that the picture on the cab license, taped to the passenger side sun visor, was not him.

He asked me if I wanted him to wait while I went to the UNHCR.

"I don't think that will be necessary," I said. "I've got some other people to see, too."

He thought for a minute as we swerved down the curving street until we reached an interchange where I knew he had to turn left to head back up toward the Fifth Circle and the UN complex. Instead, he turned in the opposite direction.

"I think you've made a wrong turn," I said casually, not wanting to show concern.

"Just give me a minute," he said. "I promised a friend I would pick him up."

"I'll pay you the full fare," I said. "Not the *service* fare."

"*Mafi moushkeda*—no problem. We're almost there."

I didn't like the idea that we had strayed from the main road, and that we were heading in exactly the wrong direction, through a semi-deserted area of auto repair shops and empty lots, but I couldn't exactly jump out of the taxi at the speed we were driving.

"You know, last week I brought a man like yourself over to the UN, and he didn't want me to wait," the driver said, as he raced up a hill I didn't recognize. "He was a Christian, just like you. Next thing I heard, they found him in the desert on the other side of the border a few days later. Plainclothes police got him."

I hadn't told him I was a Christian, but Muslims seemed to know instantly, no matter what you said.

"It's likely to take quite a while," I said. "And if you don't mind, I'm going to be late for my appointment if we don't get back to the main road."

"*Mafi moushkeda.* Just another minute. We're almost there."

We were halfway up the hill to the Rabah Ammon, across the valley from where we lived in the opposite direction from the UN complex, when he stopped the car on a curve, pocketed the keys, and got out. A blast of dry summer heat hit me from the open door. "I'll be right back," he called over his shoulder. I watched him disappear into a small shop on the far side of the deserted street.

I was tempted to get out of the car right then and there, but I was halfway on the other side of Amman from where I had to go and there were no taxis anywhere nearby. I resolved that if he didn't immediately head back down to the main highway, I would force him to stop the car and I would get out.

He came back carrying a pack of cigarettes he apparently had just bought. He started the car and turned to me.

"Can I borrow your phone?" he said.

"Excuse me?"

He held up his own cellphone, and showed me the blank face. "The battery went dead. My friend wasn't there where he was supposed to be," he said.

"Look, if you're too busy to take me to the UN compound, I'll find another taxi," I said.

"*Mafi moushkeda*—don't worry, we're going right now."

I had heard the phone trick before and it made me doubly suspicious. Gangs of jihadis liked to track their victims through their cell phones, and make threatening calls at all hours of the day or night. It was a form of harassment, but at times it got deadly.

We went up another hill, still heading in the wrong direction, then went up a broad, steep side street. At the top, a white Nissan was parked with the hood up. Two men our age were loitering around the front of the car, but no one seemed particularly worried about the engine. "Here are my friends," he said.

Opening the window, he called to them. "*Yallah* Mahmoud. Let's go!"

The other two men slammed down the hood, jumped into the car, and started it right up. My driver did a U-turn and started racing back down the hill to the main road, the other car close behind us.

"We need to head back to the Fifth Circle," I said to him.

"*Fi dagheghah*—Just a minute. We have one more stop to make," he said.

By now, I was sweating. All my nerves were alive. I was looking at every car we passed, every street corner, every shop, for some opportunity to jump out of the car and make a run for it. But he was going too fast. And then I noticed with some relief, we began heading back in the right direction, so I settled back to wait.

We reached the main road in the downtown area, but instead of taking it toward the Fifth Circle, we went back up the hill toward the Jebel Ashrafiyeh, where we had started out more than twenty minutes earlier. But this time, he was going along Quraysh Boulevard, a rim road that leads to the outskirts of the city. Looking back, I saw the white car still right behind us. Suddenly, the driver stopped, and I saw a wild look in his red eyes as he lowered his window and waved for the other car to pass him and pull up in front of us. There was bloodlust in his eyes, a look of predatory hunger, and in that instant I saw the gleam of a knife. Before he could turn around, I jumped out of the car and started running down the hill while he was shouting and calling to his friend to chase after me. Twenty meters behind us was a narrow alleyway that gave onto a steep set of stairs leading down to the next curving road that circled our hill. I ran down the staircase three steps at a time until I reached the next road, then followed it a short distance until I came to another alleyway and another set of stairs. My heart was pumping so fast I couldn't hear anything behind me, but I didn't dare to turn around to find out if they were there.

On the street below, I found a taxi parked in front of a shwarma shop and jumped in and locked the door. The driver must have thought I was crazy, dressed in a suit and sweating like I had just come off a football field, but I noticed with relief that a tiny virgin Mary was dangling from his rear view mirror.

"I cannot tell you how happy I am to see you, my brother," I said. "Please, just drive—quickly now!" I said.

The driver was an old dried out man, and his battered orange Nissan seemed even older than he was. The clutch was worn out, but once we got going down the hill, it seemed to work okay. Later, he told me his story. His name was Ibrahim, and he was a Palestinian Christian from a village near Beit Jallah. But for now, all I cared about was the distance we were putting between us and the men who had just tried to kidnap me. Ibrahim and his battered Nissan were my angel's wings.

Ibrahim let me off at the top of the hill, and I walked down toward the blue UN flag that hung atop the guardhouse outside a large, three-storey villa. The sidewalk was packed with people: young couples with small children, single men, old people. Almost all of them had a single sheet of paper in their hands. The young man ahead of me had green eyes and an Assyrian face, but when I tried to catch his eye to ask him a question, he dropped his gaze to the ground. We shuffled forward in the dull summer heat, leaning into the hill, a silent procession of the damned.

Once the guards let me inside the cool marble villa, I was sent to be interviewed by a woman wearing a white Islamic headscarf and a thick choker to cover her neck. Luckily for her, the office was air-conditioned, because she was wearing a dark-green *abaya* all the way to her shoes, with a white damascene pattern to offset her arms. You couldn't see her wrists or her ankles beneath the covering. She introduced herself as Huda.

I told her that I had been a translator for the Coalition in Baghdad and in Mosul, and was hoping to be resettled in the United States. She pulled out a form and prepared to write. When she heard my name she looked up from the paper sharply.

"You are a Christian."

She spat out the words, her lip visibly curling up in contempt.

"Yes, we are Assyrian."

She wrote our names on the paper, then stapled the ID photos I had given her of the three of us and slid it toward me across the counter. "This is your refugee document. Come back in six months to renew it."

"I hope to be resettled by then. The Americans have a special program for people who worked for the Coalition. See? Here are the letters of commendation I received from my American commanders," I said proudly, opening my book to the glassine page where the letter from LTC Wilkens was displayed. "You should have a copy of these for the file," I added.

"That won't be necessary," she said. She didn't even glance at the letter, or the binder. She pushed the form with our photos more insistently until it tapped my hand. "Come back in six months." And with that, she waved me away and signaled for the next person to come up to her desk. There was nothing more I could say.

I climbed back up to the top of the hill where Ibrahim was waiting. He shrugged when I showed him the refugee document.

"I've taken people here dozens of times," he said. "Make sure you make copies of it while it's still fresh. After a couple of years, no one can read the originals any more."

"A couple of years?" I said in disbelief. But Ibrahim just shrugged again, his head tilted to one side as he listened to the engine and played the clutch, coaxing the ancient car into gear.

"God is merciful. At least you have some money and a roof over your head," he said, after we had crested another hill and the car picked up speed and began to descend into a smoke-filled tunnel. "Just don't let the police pick you up. They're sending Iraqis back across the border. Especially if they catch you working."

I was just settling into the life of a refugee, but I was beginning to think we were no safer here in Amman than we had been in Karamlesh. Later, I would learn the odd contradictions of this place. Although the royal family and government ministers sent their children to Christian schools, you had to be careful about what you said and how you appeared before Muslims. Every week, one or two Christians would get kidnapped or murdered, or a church would be set on fire mysteriously. The newspapers always painted such incidents as criminal attacks, but everyone knew what was really going on, The jihadis controlled the mosques, the schools, and much of the police. As Iraqi Christians we lived outside the law, outside of society, like ghosts hovering at the edges of a world to which we once belonged. And so we huddled in our basements and whispered to each other at church, afraid to go out, afraid to work, afraid to be seen together.

In the evenings, the three of us went out into the tiny backyard of our apartment to drink coffee, watching the hills of Amman emerge from the dusty brown haze and begin to blink as people returned home from work. The hills were so steep that our backyard sat on the roof of the building on the street below us. In the distance, we could see Rabah Ammon, where once an ancient city stood. This is where King David, driven by guilt over his own adultery, sent Uriah the Hittite to his death in a hopeless battle. Today, it looked like any other part of Amman, scarcely a bump in the starry fabric of the city. We had a few plastic chairs we had picked up from the Chaldean patriarchy down the hill, and a cardboard box we used as a table. Once the rains returned in October, the box collapsed. But soon it was too cold anyway to sit outside and take coffee in the evenings. Sometimes, late at night, Marcos took pebbles from the rooftop and hurled them into the distance, his form of defiance, I suppose.

Exile forced Yousrah to abandon her studies. To beguile the time, she volunteered at the church school with Father Shemoun two days a week, teaching English to refugee children. Marcos worked there as a guard; although to his chagrin, this being

Jordan, he was unarmed. The school itself was illegal but tolerated by the authorities, just so long as it operated on a part-time basis, as a supplement to the government schools which Iraqi children could now attend if they dared. For years, they were banned even from government schools, so the older children had fallen way behind in their studies.

As the months went by without further incident, I lulled myself into believing that if we were careful and stayed underground we would be safe in Amman until the Americans approved us for resettlement. But I should have known that this was just an illusion, and that no amount of discretion would save us from the long arm of Saddoun and his thugs.

One evening toward the end of winter, my mother phoned from Karamlesh. We normally spoke to her on Sundays, but this was just an ordinary day. Her voice was rushed, and I could tell that she was worried, even though the line was bad.

"Are you alone?" was the first thing she asked me.

As it happened, I was. Both Yousrah and Marcos were at the church that evening at a planning session with parents.

"You must be careful, Yohannes. Those people have come looking for you."

"What people, *Yimaa*? What do you mean?"

But even as I put the question into words, I knew the answer and dreaded it.

"When you were working," she said. She paused, trying to find innocent words, as if she was afraid that someone could hear her. "A man you spoke to. He has friends. They wanted to talk to you. Yohannes..."

A scratching sound came over the line, so I couldn't hear what she said next. This often happened with the local phones in Iraq. Normally, I didn't think anything of it. But today, I wasn't sure.

"...know where you are," she was saying.

My mind was racing. Clearly, she was talking about Saddoun, although I had never mentioned him to her and she wouldn't recognize his name. What could he and his friends possibly want with me now? I had stopped working with the Americans months ago, and knew nothing more about him than I had learned during the few interrogation sessions where I had translated for Col. Wilkens in Mosul. I had spoken about the secret document we found on him to no one, and only Col. Wilkens even knew that I had seen it. Why would he send someone to visit my mother? Surely they must know that I had left Iraq. What danger could I possibly be to him or his friends? Besides, he had been arrested by the Americans and was probably rotting away in a cell somewhere at Camp Cropper by the Baghdad airport.

"*Yimaa*, are you okay?" I asked her. I had to repeat it several times through the static.

"Yes, yes, *bruna*," she said. "What do you want them to do with an old woman? But you must be careful. They said you would know what it was about."

I hadn't told her about the man who had approached me in the alleyway after Bishop Rahho's funeral, warning me to stay away from St. Hormizd. In the months since leaving Karamlesh, I had tried to put the encounter and the secret document out of my mind. I was about to tell her not to worry, that I was just working for Father Shemoun, the 45-year old priest who ran the Chaldean Patriarchy in Amman, when I realized that the pastoral care he provided to the thousands of Assyrian Christians who had fled certain death in Iraq must have angered Saddoun and his friends almost as much as my working for the Americans had done.

"*Yimaa*," I said. "*Yimaa?*"

The phone had gone dead.

Spring came to Amman early that year. You could tell because the streets leading down through the souk to the central mosque were all packed with young Arab men, walking hand in hand, smoking, laughing. The hills opposite us lost some of the chalky whiteness of winter, and from place to place you could see dark patches where tiny garden plots were coming back to life between the distant houses.

Father Shemoun was animated as he spoke to the Americans who had come on a fact-finding mission. He had asked me to translate, because his English was spotty. There was a former Governor from a southern state, who exuded geniality: a bronze-headed giant with chiseled features who headed a group called Christians United; a swarthy Catholic priest from Philadelphia whose ample stomach burst out between the buttons of his clerical shirt; and Dona. She stood nearly shoulder to shoulder with Father Shemoun and wore fashionable jeans, a long black tunic that came down to her thighs, and a yellow and green silk scarf decorated with a mosaic of finely designed branches, their tips alive with springtime vigor. Her large deep-blue eyes seemed to hold everything in a firm grasp, like a horse-trainer who walks into a new stable and with a single word instantly commands even the most difficult animal.

"*Shlama, Rabi Yohannes,*" she said as she shook my hand.

"*Enee ashooreetah?*" I said, surprised. "Dona Hollinger?"

She gave a good-natured laugh. "*Eh! Pa ana ashooretewan.* I am Assyrian, too. It's actually short for Damreena. I was born in California. My father's American. Are you surprised?"

She wore simple silver loops on her ears and a silver cross around her neck that seemed to reflect the playful light of her eyes.

"Abouna asked me to translate for him and the others," I stammered in Syriac. "I can see that won't be necessary."

Suddenly I felt an arm around my shoulder. Father Shemoun had snuck up behind me and was smiling broadly.

"Yohannes joined us last summer, and already I don't know what I would do without him," he said proudly. "Of course you must stay," he said, turning to me. "I want you to tell your story, too."

Father Shemoun had asked four men from the congregation to remain after the morning mass so they could tell their stories to the Americans. I knew one of them vaguely from Baghdad, and recalled that his son, who was my age, had been murdered by the jihadis. I had crossed him several times in the Green Zone, where he worked as an electrician. Muslim gunmen had ambushed the mini-van bringing him and a few others to work one morning, spraying it with automatic weapons fire. I remember the incident because the jihadis kept on firing for nearly a minute after the mini-van crashed, slicing the bodies into pieces.

The father's name was Behnam Toma. He sat along the wall with the other three witnesses in a simple, straight-backed chair, clutching a plastic bag with bread he was taking home to his family. Above him was a portrait of the Virgin Mary, the mother of

75

our Savior, gazing down in compassion. His voice cracked with emotion when he got to the part about searching for his son's body in the morgue.

"It took me three days to find him," he said. "It was so hot. And they had fired so many bullets at him that—that—"

He started to sob. Father Shemoun bowed his head and said a brief prayer in Aramaic, making the sign of the Cross in the air. I turned to the former Governor, an athletic man in his early 50s, dressed in khaki trousers, an open shirt, and a blue blazer. He was leaning forward intently, kneading his hands together so you could see the white of his knuckles.

"I knew this man's son in Baghdad," I said. "He was decapitated by the weapons fire. That's why the family couldn't find him in the morgue. This was the summer after the bombing of the golden mosque in Samarra. There were so many bodies they had to stack them out in the courtyard in the heat."

The former Governor shook his head, then looked at Behnam Toma with deep, soulful eyes, and placed his hands on his heart. "I am so sorry," he said. "There is no consolation I or anyone can offer you, except to know that now he is with the Lord."

I translated what he said for Mr. Toma, and that seemed to relieve him.

"Thank-you, sir. Thank-you. Please help us, sir."

I didn't translate that, but Dona turned to the former Governor and whispered something to him. He reached out his hands, taking hers and the hand of the Catholic priest, and bowed his head to offer a prayer. I felt Dona's hand reach toward mine and saw that everyone else was holding hands, so I took it and closed my eyes and prayed fervently that the Lord would forgive me for my sinful thoughts. Her hand was warm and strong and her skin was smooth, like the breast of a dove. I mustn't have heard a word of the former Governor's prayer, because the next thing I knew Dona was pressing my hand insistently. I opened my eyes and saw her indicating Mr. Toma and the others. I felt myself reddening, so I looked down at the floor and smiled inwardly when I heard Dona translating the former Governor's prayer.

"*Melkoota d'Shmaya,*" I whispered, correcting her grammar. In our language, unlike English, we conjugate both the gender and the person of our verbs, even when referring to the Kingdom of Heaven.She nodded slightly, correcting herself. I think only Abouna Shemoun noticed, and he smiled.

"I only learned Aramaic as a teenager," she whispered, after she had finished. "But don't tell them that!"

"Of course not."

"You should come with us to the Embassy. I will ask the Governor to put you on the list."

And that was when I saw Saddoun.

We arrived at the Embassy the next morning in two separate taxis. I had ridden over with Father Francis Pacelli, the Catholic priest from Philadelphia. By the time we got there Dona, the former Governor, Frank Aiken, and Gary Utz, who headed Christians United, were waiting for us on the sidewalk just down the hill from the Bedouins who were patrolling the perimeter wall. Saddoun was on his way inside when he saw me and froze me on the spot with his reptilian eyes.

"What's the matter?" Dona said. She followed my gaze and saw Saddoun, just as he was closing his mobile phone. "Do you know that man?"

"He—he's Iraqi," I said finally, when I could find my voice again. By that time, Saddoun had disappeared inside the embassy. "He's a former Baathist, a relative of Saddam."

"What's he doing here?" Dona asked.

"The last time I saw him, he was headed down to Camp Cropper in plastic cuffs for extended interrogation. It just doesn't make any sense."

I was stunned and was staring at the place where Saddoun had just disappeared when I felt a heavy arm come down on my shoulder. Father Francis must have heard us conversing in Swadaya, and came up behind us, unaware of what had just taken place. "Ah, to be young and without the vows," he said, giving us a huge complicit grin. "Of all the seven deadly sins, the worst is not the one you think."

He gazed down wistfully at his stomach, which he hefted like a bowl full of jelly with both hands. Tiny drops of sweat had formed like oil on his sun-darkened neck, and his tousle of black-grey hair was streaked as if from exertion. He wasn't really as fat as he tried to make himself appear. His arms and shoulders were thick with muscle. Damreena laughed and I tried to smile, but my mind was on the evil one who had just returned to my life. What was Saddoun doing here? How could he possible be a free man? And entering the U.S. embassy willingly, without a hitch, like an expected guest? As we approached the Bedouins, a young dark-haired man emerged from inside the embassy, carrying a piece of paper.

"Good morning, Governor Aiken," he said. "I have five persons in your delegation. Is that correct?"

"That's right. There's me and Father Francis here...."

The young Jordanian examined the names on his list earnestly and checked off the names. "And you, sir, would be Mr. Utz," he said, turning to Gary Utz, who towered over him by at least a full head. He ushered us past the guards and through the vehicle entrance, without us having to show any identification.

"When most Iraqis come here," I whispered to Dona, "the Bedouins just insult us and won't let us through the gates."

"It helps to have a Governor along," she whispered back.

"Or apparently, to be a relative of Saddam."

Instead of taking us into the main embassy complex, our escort led us through a small garden to a modest-sized pavilion built of polished Jordanian sandstone. It had floor to ceiling windows, sculpted columns, and an elegant marble portico where limousines could pull up to discharge guests. Could this be where Saddoun had gone? Surely I must have been mistaken. How could he possibly be free and here inside the U.S. embassy?

Another man, an American, greeted us just in front of the double glass doors. He was wearing a suit despite the heat, and sheltered his eyes from the direct glare as we arrived.

"I'm Harvey Windred, the DCM," he said. "Ambassador Hough is looking forward to meeting you, Governor. We have coffee and refreshments waiting for you."

The reception area looked like something out of a French palace, with huge windows, a pair of gigantic crystal chandeliers, and a long dining table laid out with coffee pots, a brass samovar, and ornate silver platters of *mamoul* cookies, various sorts of *baklawa*, and small poppy seed cakes. Father Francis gave a little gasp as a white-gloved steward handed him a porcelain coffee cup and pointed him toward the food.

"You young folks had better get something," he said. "You never know when you're going to eat next."

Dona took a small plate and handed it to me, then hesitated before taking one herself. "What do you think looks best?" she asked. There was a girlish innocence to her that made my fear of Saddoun appear unwarranted, an intrusion from another more dangerous world where sweet cookies contained poison and cars blew up on the streets. I tried to relax and let myself slip into the comforting order of Dona's universe. But even as I bit down into the light pastry, I half expected my mouth to explode with a bitter almond taste and to start gagging in agony. I couldn't stop thinking about Saddoun.

The DCM reappeared and announced that the ambassador was ready to receive us. He ushered us down a corridor into a large comfortable living room. Ambassador Forest L. Hough was standing just inside the doorway, his hand outstretched, a pinched, almost painful smile on his face. He was a slight, small man in his early forties, and for an instant I thought Gov. Aiken would crush the frail bones of his hand in his bear paw grip. But he didn't wince, and pointed us to white damascene sofas and plush easy chairs, each with its own end table so we could put down the coffee cups we had carried in with us.

"We thought we would share some of our findings and maybe offer a few constructive ideas on how this embassy could better serve the refugee community and the goals announced by the president when he was still a candidate last year," Gov. Aiken began. "And then, Father Francis has a particular subject relating to the church he would like to raise."

"Of course," the ambassador said, setting back in his sofa, bringing his long thin fingers together in a tent beneath his chin. "Since you've just arrived in Amman, let me bring you up to speed on what we are doing at this embassy."

The ambassador launched into a bureaucratic speech, to which I only half listened. He talked about "processing" refugees, especially interpreters who had worked for the coalition, and about specific numbers and targets set by Congress. As he was saying these things, I watched Gary Utz shake his head in disbelief. He exchanged a glance with me, but I just shrugged, wondering behind which door Saddoun was listening to us.

"With all due respect, Mr. Ambassador," he cut in. "Sitting with us right here is one of those interpreters, and he can't get the time of day out of this embassy."

I looked down at my hands and said nothing, but out of the corner of my eyes I saw Thomas McGuinty, the consular officer I had met many months ago, turn toward the ambassador and shake his head. The ambassador nodded for him to speak.

"That's just not true. I met with Mr. Yohanna on two separate occasions and gave him instructions on how he should pursue his application," McGuinty said.

"You just told him to go to the UNHCR," Gary Utz said in exasperation. He was close to shouting by now, and the ambassador visibly recoiled, taken aback by his sudden emotion. "That's not an answer. Or perhaps you're not aware how Christians are being treated by the UN intake officers?"

"They are very professional, Mr. Utz. I can assure you that," McGuinty said.

"Have you gone to the churches to talk to these people?" he asked.

"It's not my job to go to church, Mr. Utz."

The two of them glared at each other for an instant, and if they hadn't been separated by the large sandstone and glass coffee table, I am sure that Utz would have taken him down. He was a former Marine, and despite having reached middle age, he still ran marathons and looked almost out of place in the dark suit he had worn for this meeting.

Dona jumped in then. "I work with newly arrived refugees in California, Mr. Ambassador. I've seen lots of cases where the UNHCR has turned down Iraqi refugees with legitimate claims, and recommended others for resettlement whose claims were patently false. The only difference we've been able to find is that the ones who get turned down are Christian, and the ones who get approved are Muslims."

Gov. Aiken raised his eyebrows, and offered a smile of sympathy to Ambassador Hough.

"Mr. Ambassador," he said with a chuckle. "We didn't come all the way to Amman to have an argument with you, but to share with you some of our findings. After all, this is our war and these are our refugees, no matter who happens to be in the White House."

The Ambassador turned to Jasper C. Ganz, the man he had introduced as his public information officer, and asked him to call the Consul General to come down. He reached into an inside pocket for a cellphone, revealing a stiffly starched white shirt and a pair of burgundy suspenders.

Gary Utz was still seething, and turned his head away pointedly from McGuinty, who had a self-satisfied smug on his face. Father Francis waded in.

"Perhaps while we are waiting, Mr. Ambassador," he said with his thick Philadelphia accent, "I can raise with you an issue of particular importance to the church."

"By all means, Father."

Father Francis clasped his hands beneath his chin as if he was about to pray, and thrust his jaw forward. He was going to impart some great truth, and wanted the ambassador to understand the import of his words.

"As you may be aware, the Christians of Iraq are the descendants of one of the oldest Christian communities in the world. They were proselytized by St. Thomas; and some say, by St. Peter himself. For centuries, Iraq has been a backwater of the church. Until just recently, the Chaldean patriarch was just a bishop. Because Saddam Hussein tolerated the Christian presence in Iraq, no one wanted to draw attention to it by elevating him to Cardinal."

As he was speaking, Jasper Ganz shot me a dark look that penetrated to my very soul. I was starting to wish I hadn't taken up Dona's suggestion to come to the embassy.

"I can reveal you today that Saddam Hussein made a secret pact with the Catholic Church in Rome," Father Francis went on. "Yes, this is true. He agreed not to persecute Christians for their faith—although he certainly persecuted them for disobedience, as he did everyone else–if the Church would not elevate opposition to his regime into a sacred cause. This deal, if you wish, was negotiated during a discrete visit to the Vatican made by Tariq Aziz at the start of the Iran-Iraq war in 1980. Tariq Aziz was a Christian, as you probably know. His real name was Mikhail Yohanna—like our friend Yohannes, here."

He nodded toward me, and I gave the ambassador a timid smile, acutely aware that Ganz was still glaring at me. Dona was clearly surprised to hear this. I resolved to tell her about my family later on.

"In addition to ignoring calls from the Islamists to kick the Christians out of Iraq, Saddam agreed to protect certain sites of exceptional importance to the church. The most prized of these is the former Nestorian monastery at al Qosh. While probably you have never heard of it, the Vatican Curia for generations has sent bishops to al Qosh to study the ancient manuscripts preserved there. We believe that these include some of the earliest copies of the New Testament, written in the original Aramaic, the language of Jesus."

"And so how can we be of assistance?" Ambassador Hough asked.

This was something I had learned about Americans when I worked for Triple Shield. They liked to distill even the most obscure situation into a few action items, whereas we in the East were paralyzed by history, knowledge, the weight of generations of tragedy.

"We understand that you have direct, military flights between Amman and Erbil in northern Iraq," Father Francis said. "The passengers on these flights are given certain courtesies not available to ordinary travelers, such as not having to go through Customs. We would like you to allow an occasional delegation from the Curia to use these flights to go back and forth to Al Qosh so we can bring out those manuscripts and preserve them."

Ambassador Hough shot a questioning glance to Jasper Ganz, who gave a barely perceptible nod to indicate his disapproval.

"Why can't they simply take the commercial flights?" the ambassador asked.

Father Pacelli opened his arms out wide, and gave a big smile. "Mr. Ambassador, surely you don't think that the Kurdish authorities would give their blessing to the export of antiquities such as these? And then, of course, there is the question of security. If we go there in the open, everyone, including our enemies, will know our presence in northern Iraq. This will significantly increase the risk, both to us and to the local population. For this, we ask for your understanding and your assistance."

The Ambassador appeared to weigh this unusual request, looking toward his advisors for their input.

"Your wasting your time, father," said Gary Utz. "This embassy is more concerned with populating the United States with Muslim immigrants than with helping Christians. You heard the man yourself," he said, pointing to McGuinty. "They don't give a hoot about the church, or about Christians in general."

By then, the Consul General had arrived. She was in her early thirties, and wore a long Muslim-style *abaya* covering her wrists and ankles. She had a head of black, curly hair and large brown eyes and was carrying a stack of papers. She introduced herself as Samia Nabulsi. She wouldn't shake hands with the men.

"That's a Palestinian Muslim name," I whispered to Dona in Swadaya.

"I guessed as much."

She spoke about the UNHCR, the need for "additional infrastructure to process refugees" and "Direct Access programs" for Iraqis who had worked for the U.S. government. She probably would have kept talking for ten or twenty minutes if Gary Utz hadn't interrupted her.

"Why can't you do the refugee interviews here at the embassy?" he asked. "I mean, after all, you've only got something like two *thousand* employees here for a country of just six million. Unless, of course, Mr. Ganz and his folks are too busy to do normal embassy work."

The ambassador got up at that point. "Mr. Utz, I think you have a clear misperception of what this embassy is all about."

"No, Mr. Ambassador. I don't think I do," he said.

Governor Aiken tried to steer the meeting back onto friendlier territory. He extracted a promise from the ambassador that he would meet with Father Shemoun and visit his church to hear some of the refugee stories for himself, and that he would give serious consideration to the request made by Father Francis, even though it seemed clear that he had already made up his mind. When we finally broke for pictures in front of a rainbow-motif tapestry on the wall, the smiles were forced and the small talk non-existent. The ambassador instructed his aides to exchange business cards with the Governor and his delegation, and while that was going on, McGuinty got Father Francis in a corner and put his arm around his shoulder, kneading his large biceps, trying to make nice. I was sitting by myself, finishing the last few drops of cold coffee at the bottom of my cup, when Jasper C. Ganz sat down on the arm of my chair, one thumb hooked nonchalantly beneath his suspenders. After a quick look round the room, he leaned his face so close that his lips almost touched my ear.

"What is the matter with you, Bucko?" he said quietly, but with insistence. "You've been warned twice by very serious people. Just go and live your life and be happy. Don't mess with other people's business, and everything will be fine."

"What are you talking about? Who are you?" I asked.

He glanced back placidly toward Governor Aiken and Gary Utz, giving a friendly nod. "I met an old friend of yours a short while ago, and he is really pissed off with you. I mean, seriously, definitively, pissed off."

"You mean, Saddoun?"

"So you know his name. That's just great. I want you to forget that you saw him coming into this compound. You get that?"

"Sure," I said. "I was surprised—"

"Yeah, well look. I don't care. And maybe it was just a coincidence. But don't think for an instant that we can't find you. Any time. Any day. And that goes for everyone in your family, as well."

I must have turned white. Perhaps I closed my eyes, I don't know. But the next thing, I felt his hand on my shoulder, shaking me.

"And forget we had this conversation. Got that?"

"Yes. Yes, of course, sir," I stammered.

4

Amman

At the church the next morning I waited until I was thought Father Shemoun was alone, then I went in to see him in his office. I was surprised to find Dona standing behind him, leaning over, her arm draped across the back of his chair, her lips close to his check. She was pointing eagerly at something on his desk, and he was turning to say something to her when I opened the door. He reddened visibly when he saw me, but Dona hardly gave me a glance.

"Yohannes," he said, indicating that I should come in. "You should look at this, too. This is the reason why Miss Damreena is here. And, I believe, why you are, too."

Dark thoughts clouded my spirit, but it was impossible not to accept his invitation. Father Shemoun didn't get up, but pointed to the faded grey Photostat on his desk, the document he apparently had been deciphering when I discovered the two of them alone. The original had been written in the ornate calligraphy of earlier times, and I recognized it instantly. At the top of the page, it read, "Guardians of the Order of Saint Hormizd." Below that was an elaborate escutcheon, at the heart of which was a backwards Swastika, the most ancient form of Nestorian cross. There was some writing beneath, but the rest of the page had been destroyed by fire. My heart started pounding when I realized that they were holding another fragment of the document that had nearly gotten my brother and sister killed, and that had driven us from our homeland into exile.

"So you can read classical Aramaic?" Dona asked. She must have caught me looking at the document.

"Of course he can, my dear," Father Shemoun said gently. "That is why God has brought the two of you together here with me."

"Wh-where did you get this?" I stammered, incapable of hiding my emotion.

"So you know of it," Father Shemoun said. "It's as I thought."

Dona's great great uncle had belonged to an obscure religious order, known as the Guardians of the Order of St. Hormizd, Father Shemoun explained. This document was a fragment of the *Secret Book* of the Order, which the Guardians copied by hand and transmitted through a hereditary succession for over 12 centuries.

"Up until 1552, the Nestorian church allowed its priests to marry and have children, except for those chosen to become bishops," he said. "So until that time, you had hereditary orders, such as the Guardians. All the Patriarchs came from a single family named Abouna, through the descendants of the brothers and cousins. That is why to this day in Aramaic we call priests "abouna." It actually refers to the family of the first Patriarchs. This is also my family name."

"So your real name is Abouna Shemoun Abouna?" Dona said. She giggled.

"That's correct, my dear. Abouna Abouna."

Father Shemoun studied the *Secret Book* after he had completed his novitiate at al Qosh as a young man. As part of his training, he committed most of it to memory. "Until now, I never knew that copies of this manuscript existed outside of Iraq. Has your family ever shown it to anyone else?" he asked Dona.

"No. Mother said only that I should show it to you, that you would know what it was about."

"She was right," he said.

Uncle Andraos fled Al Qosh just before the genocide of 1915-1916 and came to America, she said. "No one ever talked about the manuscript until I told my mother I was coming over here. She said I should show you this copy, which was made before they had proper Xerox machines."

Father Shemoun nodded thoughtfully. "Even when I was in al Qosh, there were no copying machines of any sort. Everything was always copied by hand. We spent hours learning calligraphy from the Holy Fathers. A lost art in itself, I'm afraid."

The pages she had brought began during the siege of Rome in 846 AD.

"Read, Yohannes," Father Shemoun said, encouraging me with open palms. "This is your heritage, too."

Slowly, deciphering the ancient calligraphy and the elaborate syntax, I read:

'Three times the Saracen hordes breached the walls of the basilica, and three times we pushed them back. But the Holy Father, fearing eventually that they would succeed, ordered me, Hormizd VI Abouna, to carry the sacred relics to safety and to protect them through my descendants for as long as the Church was under siege.'

There were two more pages, or fragments of pages, since the originals had been partially destroyed by fire. The first described the narrator's perilous escape from Rome in the midst of the Saracen siege, along with a company of knights and several wagons carrying arms, provisions and the sacred relics the Pope had entrusted to him. The second described his onward journey by sea, threading the needle between Cyprus and Crete, both of which had fallen into Muslim hands early in the century, until he and his companions reached the Byzantine seaport of Iskenderun, the site of modern day Izmir, Turkey.

> '*From Iskenderun we pushed overland, crossing the Euphrates, until we reached the headlands of the Tigris. Using a portion of the gold given us by the Holy Father, we hired another ship and 36 oarsmen and made good speed for Mosul, whence we disguised ourselves as Muslim traders and journeyed by caravan on surly camels until we reached the monastery of al Qosh, then under the protection of the caliph of Baghdad, Harun al-Wathiq.*'

Dona was shaking her head in wonder when I finished reading.

"I can remember seeing pictures of Uncle Andraos when I was a child," she said. "He wore a brown priest's cloak, and a funny hat. And around his waist he had a sword with a jeweled handle. The grip was fashioned to look like an Orthodox cross."

Father Shemoun pointed to the wall between the bookcase and the corner of his office, where an identical sword had been affixed with thick iron rings, visible only to someone sitting behind his desk, as we were now.

"It is the symbol of the Guardians of the Order of St. Hormizd," he said. "Nowadays, we have other weapons, I can assure you."

My heart was full of trouble and incomprehension, and the more I understood of what Father Shemoun was saying, and what the fragments of the *Secret Book* revealed, the more I was filled with dread. I felt I was in the grip of something powerful, impersonal, inescapable, a dreadful force that was about to sweep me away from the life I had become comfortable with, just as a flash flood rumbling through a wadi rips shrubs and trees and rocks from the earth in its destructive journey to the desert floor.

"What were the sacred relics this monk Hormizd brought from Rome?" I asked.

"Search your heart, Yohannes. You know the answer," Father Shemoun replied.

"It can't be," I said.

"They were the bones of St. Peter, the Vicar of Christ."

Dona was thrilled, like a child that has been given a new toy. For her, Father Shemoun had just solved a riddle. But isn't it true that riddles were composed to hide a dark secret that would bring terror and dread if it were known? I feared that the secrets the Guardians were protecting were a curse, not a blessing, and that they were best left alone.

Father Shemoun read my thoughts, and plucked the words right out of my brain. It was uncanny. He spoke the precise words I had been thinking.

"Some believe these bones are a curse, not a blessing," he said. "But I believe the only curse is their secret. Certainly, men have died to protect it. And others have died, because they failed to do so."

I recalled what my mother had told me about why the sacred relics were in Iraq. "What about the story that St. Peter died in Babylon while proselytizing the Assyrian kings?" I asked.

"Just an old wives tale, a quaint story to allay suspicions. There is ample evidence that he died in Rome under Nero. And besides, if he really did come to Babylon, he would have come to preach to the Jews, I am sure."

He took Dona's hand, and mine, and holding them firmly, guided us over to the sofa.

"Yohannes, Damreena, *shawreh leh*, my children. There is much more that I must tell you, and so little time."

I couldn't believe what he was saying. My whole being rejected it. How could he know such things about my own family, things even I did not know? I had always been told that my grandfather had died a hero—or at least a fool—for standing up to Saddam Hussein and his thugs. No one had ever spoken about betrayal. But that is what Father Shemoun was saying.

"By the time I did my novitiate at the monastery at al Qosh, the Guardians no longer even hinted at the existence of the Sacred Relics to anyone who had not taken the holy vows. This was a lesson they learned from your grandfather, I am sorry to say, Yohannes. They initiated him into the mysteries of the Order, but ultimately he chose a secular life and left to attend the University of Mosul before taking his vows. Some time later, in a drunken bout, he spoke of the secret to a young Baathist we now refer to as Tariq Aziz. For you see, your grandfather, the brilliant polemicist and famous Arab nationalist poet, Issa Koriakos, had become fast friends with the rising Assyrian politician, Mikhail Yohanna. They were so close that Issa gave his only daughter to a relative of Tariq Aziz just to please him. These were your mother and father, Yohannes."

My head was spinning. What he was saying simply couldn't be true. "But grandfather Issa died for insulting that brute," I burst out.

"I am aware of that. But perhaps it was his guilt that was speaking."

My father's family were farmers and small landowners from Dawadiyah in the north, a mixed area where Kurds and Assyrians had lived side by side for generations, more or less in peace. My father was the fourth of six sons. His three older brothers were killed during the early campaigns of Saddam's Qaddissiyah—the dictator's bloody attempt to restore the caliphate of the Sunna, his holy war against the Shia of Iran. Because of this, my father was not drafted until 1983 when it became clear that the war would drag on for many years more. He was sent to officer's training school and earned a 2nd Lieutenant's commission in 1985, right after Marcos was born, eventually making Major by the time the war ended in July 1988. During the final campaign of the war, my father served on the staff of Lt. Gen. Maher Rashid, the national hero who struck the fatal blow that crushed the enemy at Fao and drove them out of Iraq, a success that ultimately proved fatal to him. (To prevent him from becoming a rival, Saddam had Gen. Rashid murdered not long afterwards). Father used to tell us that he could see the bodies of the Iranian soldiers killed by poison gas in his dreams for years afterwards. As far as I can tell, my father never gained any special privilege from his blood tie to Tariq Aziz. But it was this distant family bond that led to the shouting match between him and Grandfather Issa, just six months before Saddam's Qaddissiyah began.

By that time, Tariq Aziz had become a fixture in Saddam's regime. One day, when he was giving a speech at Baghdad University, a bomb went off nearby. He was shaken up, though not seriously hurt;

but Saddam called it an assassination attempt. He blamed the Islamic Dawa party for it, and rounded up all the Dawa members he could find.

My parents went to visit Grandfather Issa shortly after this event. "That thug is a shame on our family!" Issa shouted, referring to Tariq Aziz. My father protested that they were just barely second cousins. "Yes, but your grandfathers were brothers," Issa said, as if this were the most damning evidence of all. "You must disown that thug, or you will bring disgrace upon all of us. I'm willing to bet you there wasn't even a bomb—the whole thing was a put up job by Saddam and his Baathist criminals, just so they could start a war with Khomeini's Iran!"

Nana Soraya was there, and tried to quiet Issa. But as she would say later, she found the whole scene beguiling in a fatalistic way. No matter how much my father might try to be his own man, he was the product of his bloodline, for better or for worse. Just as Issa, her son, resembled his own father, murdered by the Kurds during the genocide for his mouth.

My mother protested that neither she nor my father had ever met Tariq Aziz. Because he was using another name, "no one even knows that he is a Yohanna," she said.

"Oh yes they do. Everyone in Dora knows. Everyone in Karada knows. Everyone in Mansur knows. And everyone in Tel Keif knows."[2]

Not long after this, Grandfather Issa took his insults public, and was arrested by the *Amn al-amn*,

---

[2] Dora, Karada, and Mansour were Baghdad neighborhoods where Christians lived; Tel Keif was the largest city of the Ninevah Plain, the unofficial capital of the Assyrian region of northern Iraq.

the Baath party secret police. His tormentors ordered him to recant and publicly apologize to Tariq Aziz. When he refused to do so, Saddam sentenced him to death and ordered Tariq Aziz to kill him personally, with a bullet in the back of his head.

Such were our close family ties to Tariq Aziz, the relationship Cory Reed cited as reason enough to fire me as an interpreter with Triple Shield.

And now, Father Shemoun was telling me that Grandfather Issa was a collaborator as well, whose youthful indiscretion had compromised a secret the church had kept quiet for more than 1200 years. A secret men were willing to die for. A secret men were willing to kill for. I just couldn't believe it. It shattered everything I thought I knew.

"You see," Father Shemoun was saying, "this is why the Holy Father was so outspoken against the American-led war to get rid of Saddam Hussein. It wasn't because he had any fondness for this dictator, but because the dictator had learned the most carefully guarded secret of the Church. We had no illusions about his motivation for keeping secret the knowledge he learned via Tariq Aziz from your grandfather. Saddam didn't help us out of fondness or compassion. He was no secret believer, no closet Christian. He did it because it served his purpose, which was to maintain his grasp on power.

"But for the Church, that was good enough."

Father Shemoun remained in the seclusion of the monastery carved out of the mountain above al Qosh for nearly ten years, until Monsignor Francis Pacelli spotted him while visiting from the Vatican in

1994. At his prompting, Father Shemoun traveled to Rome and took a doctorate degree at Lateran University, perfecting his French and learning Italian. While not a Guardian himself, Pacelli was among a select few of the Vatican Curia who had been instructed in the mysteries of the Order. He became a powerful supporter of the Church in Iraq. Father Shemoun became his protégé.

In 2002, sniffing the winds of the coming war, Pacelli dispatched Father Shemoun to Amman to head the Chaldean Eparchy and to be his eyes and ears in Iraq, his secret conduit to Saddam Hussein. Later that year, Pacelli himself made a visit to Baghdad and to northern Iraq. The Vatican's chief concern was not to prevent the war, although such pacifism provided a convenient and believable screen for their true activities to the outside world. Their concern was to ensure that the secret of the Sacred Relics preserved at al Qosh remained intact, or that the relics themselves be evacuated or destroyed.

"For you see, we had a problem at the Vatican," Father Shemoun was saying. "The bones on display in the Tomb beneath the High Altar have nothing to do with St. Peter. In the eyes of some, the whole church is founded on a myth."

Msg. Pacelli was acutely aware of the problem, since it was his uncle, known as Cardinal Eugenio Pacelli before he was elevated to become Pope Pius XII, who first leaked news of the discovery of St. Peter's bones to the press in 1949. In those dark days after the Holocaust and the devastation of World War II, such news should have been greeted as a sign that God once again had found favor in his church. Instead, as Pacelli told Father Shemoun, "that idiot Pope" allowed himself to become a subject of ridicule for having brought an urn containing bone fragments of a pig, a sheep, a cow, two men, a woman and a mouse into his private bedchamber, and venerating them as if they were the Sacred Relics of the Prince of Apostles himself.

The story, written by an Italian journalist, appeared on the front page of the New York Times on August 22, 1949.

Bones of Saint Peter Found Under Alter, Vatican Believes.

Reported to Be in Urn Guarded by Pontiff

By Camille M. Cianfarra, Special to the New York Times

Vatican City, The Vatican—The bones of Saint Peter, 'Prince of the Apostles,' who, according to Christian tradition, was crucified in Rome during the second half of the first century AD., are understood to have been found less than twenty feet below the pavement of St. Peter's Basilica.

Vatican archaeologists who directed the excavations have taken an oath of secrecy and are therefore forbidden to confirm or deny the discovery. However, statements made over a period of months by various persons in the Vatican are said to have supplied enough circumstantial evidence that

the remains of Saint Peter
have been recovered in the
hypogeum, or subterranean
cell, where tradition said he
was buried.

This crypt was unearthed two
years ago in the course of
secret excavations in the
Vatican Grottoes. The bones
are being preserved in an urn
closely guarded by Pope Pius
XII himself, in the private
chapel next to his study,
Vatican circles said.

Pius XII authenticated the relics as those
belonging to St. Peter in his Christmas radio address
on Dec. 23, 1950. He asserted that his personal
physician, Dr. Galeazzi-Lisi, and several medical
experts had examined the remains and found them to
belong to "a man, powerfully built, who had been
perhaps sixty-five or seventy years old at death."
Those facts "fitted well with the tradition regarding
Peter," the Pope added. "Beyond that, nothing can be
said."

Since the earliest days of the Church, the
crucifixion of St. Peter by Nero and his burial in
Rome had become the absolute bedrock of Rome's
claim to the apostolic succession. Whether it was
Tatian the Syrian, Tertullian, or St. Augustine, the
early Church Fathers took our Lord's call to St. Peter
quite literally.

And I tell you, you are Peter, and on this
rock I will build my church, and the gates

of Hades will not prevail against it.
(Matthew 16:18)

"If only that idiot Pope had left well enough alone, no one would have questioned this," Msg. Pacelli told Father Shemoun. "But he felt so guilty over the Holocaust and the Church's inaction that he had to go out and make those ridiculous claims and keep that stupid urn by his bed. Even Venerando Correnti, the anthropologist the Curia hired in 1956, shortly before Uncle Eugenio died, realized the truth once he pulled a *third fibula* out of the Pope's precious urn, when of course men and women have just two, one for each leg. Then he discovered five tibias, and concluded that the urn contained the remains of two men and one woman, at the very least."

And it got worse. One of Correnti's colleagues, Luigi Cardini, identified bones in the urn that belonged to pigs, sheep, and goats—even a chicken and a mouse! This was later explained by the fact that the place where St. Peter was laid to rest was in the Emperor's gardens, where animals regularly grazed and were occasionally slaughtered by the indigent after Nero's famously barbaric spectacles in the nearby arena.

"I've always wondered why the Vatican didn't simply announce that the Sacred Relics have been at al Qosh all along," Father Shemoun said. "But I guess that would only reignite the long-simmering dispute between the Eastern and the Western church, with our Eastern brothers claiming primacy because of St. Peter's presence. We in the Order have always refrained from any involvement in this dispute. You know, for centuries, the Monastery at St. Hormizd actually served as the Holy See for the Patriarchs of the Church of the East. It was also here that the Nestorian priest Youhanna Sulaqa, then Abbot of St. Hormizd, joined the Catholic Church and tried to dispel the hereditary Order in 1552. So if we've learned one great truth over the centuries, it is not to trust in temporal things."

I asked him if the Hormizd Abouna who brought the Sacred Relics from Rome to al Qosh was the first monk of the order to carry that name.

"No," he said, intrigued. "How did you know that, Yohannes? What have you been told?"

"Did they trace themselves back to a man named Bahira? Was he the father of the first Hormizd?"

"Yes, he was. But how—?"

"I've seen other portions of the *Secret Book*, father. Earlier portions," I said.

I told him about the arrest of Saddoun and the discovery of the manuscript pages. I told him about the threats I had received, and my surprise at encountering Saddoun at the U.S. embassy the day before. What I couldn't understand, I said, was why Saddoun would have portions of the manuscript, and why he would be meeting with Mr. Ganz at the embassy, when he had been a prisoner of the Americans just a year earlier.

"Does Pacelli know this?" Father Shemoun asked, suddenly worried.

"Ganz said I couldn't tell anyone. He threatened my family," I said. "My Mother and sister Rita are still in Karamlesh."

"I understand," said Father Shemoun. "But we must confide in Pacelli. I fear he has already told the Americans too much as it is, especially if this Ganz is in league with the jihadis. Islam has been seeking to destroy Christianity from the very beginning, ever since Mohammad denied the divinity of our Lord and cast out Bahira and the brothers from Medina."

Father Shemoun closed his eyes, and called up the words he had long ago committed to memory.

Mustafa is bent on going to war, and I fear that our days in this place of refuge are numbered. Ever since he came to Yathrib— that's what they called Medina at the time—*he has grown increasingly distant and argumentative. All his waking moments are now spent on horsemanship and women, expanding his armies, sharpening their swords. His seizures have become more violent, so that he now attributes his own excesses to others. Once, while preparing the wedding feast to marry his daughter, he awoke to find that someone had attacked the fattened she-camels of the dowry and cut off their hump, ripping open their haunches to extract the livers.'Who has done this?' the people cried. They brought him before Hamza bin Abdul Muttalib, who had fallen down drunk and was covered in blood, but no one was fooled. Staring into those bloodshot eyes, he vowed to never again share the bread and wine of fellowship with his companions, and pretended that this new command had been dictated to him by the Archangel.*

We have failed utterly, and the Lord will surely punish us for our hubris in believing we could use this man as a vehicle for spreading the Gospel. Mustafa could understand the God of the Quraysh, his enemies. He could understand the God of the Jews. But a God of love, a God of forgiveness and compassion, a God of self-sacrifice, is utterly beyond him.

Opening his eyes as if from a trance, Father Shemoun looked at us for a moment in silence, as if the question he wanted to ask was already in the air and he was waiting for us to answer. Finally, he spoke again. "They would do anything to destroy the Sacred Relics. And especially, all trace of the *Secret Book* of our order."

He hefted the faded Photostats Dona had brought to him and let them fall onto his desk. "Rome under the Popes had protectors," he said. "Who besides a handful of monks is protecting al Qosh?"

Suddenly anxious, he stood up, and pulled us up by the hands.

"We must hurry," he said. "We must find Pacelli. And you, *shawreh leh*, are going to Iraq."

5

Amman

Gary Utz and Governor Aiken spent two more days in Amman visiting refugees, hearing their stories. Father Shemoun asked me to accompany them, while he helped Msg. Pacelli with the last minute preparations for the aid mission to the Nineveh Plain in northern Iraq. There was money to be transferred, food supplies to be purchased locally, aid packages to be assembled for the distribution. Christian Witness, the conservative group run by Gary Utz, was footing the bill.

I sent an email to the Yahoo! account LTC Wilkens had given me, telling him that the person we had worked with during our last mission together was in town and was meeting with people at the Embassy. Did he know that this man had been released from Camp Cropper? If ever I needed the help he had promised me, it was now, I wrote. Saddoun knew my identity and the whereabouts of my family.

A few hours later, I saw that the email had bounced back. The account had been closed, it said.

Father Shemoun had arranged for the American delegation to meet a group of refugees at the Syriac Orthodox church, not far from where I lived in Jebel Ashrafiyeh. Emad, an aid to the Patriarch, greeted us at the top of the steps leading down to the parish hall that adjoined the church. He was around 40, and wore a working class cap like the kind you might see in some early Soviet movie. His thick rough hands showed dirt beneath the fingernails.

"Everyone is waiting for you," he said, addressing Gov. Aiken.

"Is the Patriarch here so we can pay our respects?"

"Unfortunately, he had to leave for a wedding," Emad said. "But he asked some of the refugees to stay so they could share their stories with you."

Dona gasped audibly when Emad opened the double doors and she saw how many people had packed into the small inner room. They sat in straight-backed metal chairs along the walls, Iraqi style, but there were so many of them that the chairs were packed three deep. The Patriarch's ornate desk and high-backed chair dominated the room from one end. Emad offered the seat of honor to Gov. Aiken, but he demurred. "This is your meeting, brother Emad," he said.

We found seats on a narrow, stiff-cushioned sofa by the desk. Dona sat next to the Governor, to translate for him, while Gary Utz took the armchair by the desk. I could feel the warmth from her legs through her long skirt, pressing lightly against me. Was it an accident that she sat so close to me? I dared not turn my head to seek an answer, so I just sat as still as I could, planting my foot into the dirty tiles of the floor, trying to feel any movement at all from her. But there was nothing.

No sooner had Emad introduced us as "the delegation from America," than a scene of utter pandemonium broke out. People jumped to their feet, waving their UN refugee documents, clamoring to tell their stories, to beg for help from the Americans. Emad pounded for order on the vast wooden desk, gesturing at a man hobbling toward us on crutches to sit down. He shouted, but no one seemed to pay any attention. It was the best he could do to take charge.

"We're not going to be able to hear individual stories like this," the Governor said.

"There are just too many people," said Mr. Utz. "Somebody should have screened them before we arrived."

The man on the crutches hobbled closer to us, forcing his way through the crowd, his voice rising above the generation commotion.

"This man says he was kidnapped by jihadis," Dona said, turning toward the Governor.

"Get his story—if you can hear it," the Governor said.

And so Dona asked what happened to him, and the man began to shout, waving his UNHCR refugee certificate. Gunmen wearing Ministry of Interior uniforms had burst into his office and kidnapped him. They blindfolded him and dumped him into the trunk of a car. For seven days, they hung him by his feet from the ceiling of a darkened room, somewhere outside Baghdad, beating him constantly. "This is why nearly a year later he is still walking on crutches," Dona said.

They told him that if his family didn't pay the ransom they would take his fifteen year-old daughter and marry her to a Muslim. He tried to smash his head against the wall in his grief, but they stopped him and beat him some more. I felt Dona's muscles tense as she listened to the man's story, and then I watched as tears welled in her eyes and she forced them back with a quick brush of her hand and transformed his personal agony into something comprehensible that the Governor and Mr. Utz could take with them. She was a fighter, and I was proud of her, proud of our Assyrian womanhood.

"Ask him if he worked for the coalition?" Mr. Utz said.

"He said he did," I answered. "He was an accountant for an American contractor in the Green zone."

Mr. Utz turned to Emad, who was trying to get everyone to sit down. "Ask them how many of them worked for the Coalition?"

Emad hardly needed to get out the question, when the room exploded with angry shouts of assent. "All of them," he said.

"And what happened when they went to the U.S. embassy and asked for resettlement?"

When Emad translated the question, the room erupted again and everyone held up the refugee papers they had been given with the familiar olive branches of the United Nations seal.

"The embassy told them to go to the UNHCR," Emad said.

"This is pathetic," Mr. Utz muttered, turning to the Governor. "I don't care what you think about this war, and whether it was justified or not. After Vietnam, we brought in 750,000 people in little more than a month. We have a responsibility toward these people."

I watched as Dona transformed herself right in front of my eyes. From being soft, feminine, overwhelmed by the suffering of so many people, she became efficient and orderly. Her mind engaged. She sorted through details, she navigated the pain, until she found the words that connected with Governor Aiken and Mr. Utz. She reminded me of my sister Rita, even a bit of my mother, but with a difference. She was not family, and I realized that the pride I felt toward her was something else.

At home, I would have found someone from her family and had one of my uncles speak to them.

But she had been brought up in America. She even bore an American name. How much had that changed her? I wondered in a flash of horror if she had adopted too many American ways, and like all those young women we saw on American television she too had become a harlot, a whore?

It couldn't be, I thought. It mustn't. Please, dear God, not her.

When we got back to the Eparchy later that afternoon, I used Father Shemoun's computer to search the Internet for LTC Wilkens. It turned out to be much easier than I had thought. He was listed as the deputy director of the Special Inspector General for Iraq Reconstruction, based in Arlington, Virginia. I didn't have a clue what that was or why Col. Wilkens was there. But it listed a DOT MIL email address for him, so I gave it a try.

Less than an hour later, I had a reply.

> *"I've been worried about you, little brother! This is much more serious than you might think. Will be at the airport Sheraton in Erbil one week from today. Get a fresh Korek SIM card and use it <u>once</u> to call this number: 914-360-2398. LTC Wilkens."*

All the Americans I had worked with used U.S. cellphone numbers in Iraq, since after the liberation this was the only telephone service available anywhere. Now, of course, there were three local cellphone companies, run by three rival clans, each of which had service in only the part of the country their clan controls. Korek was owned by Elias Korekjan, the wealthy Assyrian businessman and government minister close to the Barzani clan, which controlled Erbil and most of the Kurdish Regional Government. Mr. Elias, as everyone called him. The "benefactor" of the Christians of the North. Our collaborator in chief.

If I had any remaining doubts about accompanying the delegation led by Gov. Aiken and Monsignor Pacelli to northern Iraq, they were dispelled later that night. We had been discussing the trip, and Yousrah took the opportunity to make fun of me.

"From the way you talk about this Damreena woman, you would think she was God's perfect gift to man. She smart, she's beautiful, she's Assyrian, of course. But even better, she's got an American passport. I think I like that part," she said, mischievously.

"It's not what you think," I said.

"Oh that's alright. I don't mind going to America," Yousrah went on. "California sounds great––but please, let's go to the beach, not the desert."

Marcos was angry with me for leaving without offering to take him with me. He saw only the excitement of travel, not the dangers that we would encounter. He attacked the roast chicken Yousrah had baked in celebration of my imminent departure as if it were his enemy for life. "You're always just thinking of yourself," he said. "What about us? What am I supposed to do while you're gone?"

"What you always do, Marco," I said gently. "You haven't changed your life because of me. Continue working at the church."

I took my plate out to the tiny kitchen and set it in the sink to wash later when I heard my cellphone ring. I had left it on the table.

"I bet that's her!" Yousrah called.

I rushed back out to get the phone, but she had picked it up and was holding it away from me, pushing me away with the other hand.

"Hello?" she said, with an impish grin.

She held the phone out for a long instant, the grin stuck on her face, prolonging her gag, while whoever was calling spoke into her ear. Finally, her face fell, her expectations deceived. And then her eyes seemed to turn inwards and her look transformed into one of horror.

"It's Mama!" she said. "They've taken Rita!"

She handed me the phone.

"*Yimaa!*" I said. "Are you sure? Are you sure she just isn't late getting back from the ADM?"

"No, Yohannes. It was Jamal from the ADM headquarters who just phoned me. They stopped the car she was traveling in and shot the driver and took her."

"Is the driver dead?"

"Not yet. They shot him in the shoulder and the chest, but he's still alive. He saw the men who took her. He thinks they were Kurds. From the militia."

"Our protectors," I said ruefully.

"What should I do, Yohannes? They will surely want money."

"Let's hope that's all they want," I said. "I'm coming, Mama."

"Pray for her, Yohannes."

"Pray for her," I said, shaking my head. Surely there was more we could do than just that?

When she hung up, Marcos exploded.

"I'm coming with you!" he said. "There is no way I'm going to stay here when Rita's in the hands of those thugs. Come on, Yohannes. Besides, you're going to need me."

He was eager, and in a way he was right. At the very least, he could stay with Hannah and coordinate the ransom while I tried other methods to free her with Col Wilkens.

"What about you?" I said to Yousrah. "Perhaps I can ask Abouna if you can stay with one of the families from the church?"

"Yohannes, wake up," she said. "I'm not thirteen any longer. I'll be just fine here by myself."

I took a long look at her, and all of a sudden I realized that the little girl I had always known and protected had indeed grown up to be a sassy woman of twenty-one. She and Marco were the future of our Assyrian nation, and here I was trying to tell them they weren't adult enough to defend themselves, to defend us.

"Okay then," I said finally, proud of them both. "That's how it will be."

God help us as we drink the cup of suffering He has allotted us.

6

Erbil, northern Iraq

As our airplane made its descent in the pre-dawn light, the distant outlines of Erbil emerged from the desert like dull shadows upon the horizon. As we got closer to the ground, buildings emerged, and vast construction sites with innumerable cranes, and as we glided downwards on our final approach you could see the walls of the old Citadel and the wide empty streets, free of the dust that would soon envelop us.

Once we had landed and were taxiing to the terminal, the chief steward rushed down the aisle to fetch me and Marcos. "Governor Aiken has requested that you join him in the First Class cabin," he said in an urgent whisper. "Please get your things and follow me now before everyone gets up."

It soon became clear what was going on. Down on the tarmac, we could see the flashing lights of police cars and a half dozen black Suburbans, packed with Kurdish peshmergas who had come to officially welcome the Governor and his delegation. The other passengers were told to stay seated while we disembarked. The governor of Erbil, a short, bald-headed Kurd who spoke passable English, stood at the bottom of the jetway, at the head of a grimy stretch of red carpet that had been rolled out for the occasion. He was wearing an expensive dust-colored European suit, a white shirt, but perhaps because of the early hour, no tie. "Welcome to Kurdistan, Governor," he said.

Governor Aiken turned up all of his southern charm, as a handful of reporters and news cameras recorded his arrival. "Thank-you, Governor Rawandouz, for this warm welcome," he said. "It is my pleasure to be here in northern Iraq as a guest of the Kurdish Regional Government. I have come here along with Monsignor Francis Pacelli and Mr. Gary Utz and our interpreters to bring food aid to the suffering Christians of the Nineveh Plain, and let me just tell you how much we appreciate all you and your government are doing to help them."

The words came out in a gush of warmth as the two Governors smiled and pumped each other's hands for the cameras. I am certain that the subtle meaning of Gov. Aiken's message was totally lost on our Kurdish host. After all to the Kurds, we were no longer in Iraq but in Kurdistan. I was careful to make sure that I kept Marcos and myself well hidden in the crowd of Kurdish guards and politicians and airport personnel. We didn't need to see our pictures in the papers—or for that matter, in the hands of the thugs who had taken Rita.

They drove us at breakneck speed in the Suburbans to a small VIP pavilion on the other side of the terminal, while a minder from the Kurdish Foreign Ministry collected our passports and took them to get stamped. Waiters came with brass trays full of tea and small cups of sweet black coffee. "Don't ever refer to it as Turkish coffee," I hissed into Marcos's ear. Just as most Arabs did, we Assyrians referred to the traditional way of serving coffee by evoking the name of our former Ottoman masters. Here in Kurdistan, this was an insult that could have unforeseeable consequences.

It was still before 7 AM by the time our convoy raced down the highway to the Sheraton, sirens screaming to awaken anyone who was not yet aware of our presence. Still accompanied by the Governor of Erbil and his security detail, we were treated to another welcoming ceremony, this time with the hotel owner, an Assyrian named Hiram. He looked harried and overworked, his eyes drooping from a permanent state of fatigue, as if he had been up all night before we arrived. Gov. Aiken pumped his hand, and still smiling for the cameras, I heard him say, "Now tell me, ole' buddy. Are we going to have these goons with us the whole time that we're here?"

"It's the price of doing business, Governor, in the Land of the Kurds. They wouldn't want anything to happen to you."

The lavish entry pavilion of the hotel was fitted out like something from the Arabian nights, with soft couches and reclining chairs as wide as a single bed, with intricately carved wooden tables and brass trays and potted palm trees everywhere.

"Marcos and I will stay someplace else in town," I whispered to Dona. "The rooms here cost the equivalent of a month's wages for most people."

"Don't worry about that," she said. "The Monsignor has taken care of everything. Mr. Hiram is a personal friend. None of us are paying for anything while we are here. It's his way of fulfilling his duties toward the Church, I suppose."

She gave my hand a little squeeze, and I felt a thrill rush throughout my body until my cheeks were bursting with warmth. I turned away and pretended to busy myself with the baggage, hoping that Marcos hadn't seen.

A few hours later, after everyone had taken a nap, we met in Monsignor Pacelli's suite to map out a plan of action. The foreign ministry minder had insisted on setting up a series of meaningless interviews with various Kurdish officials.

"Look," said Gary Utz. "There's really only one official here in Kurdistan we want to see, and that's the Finance Minister, Elias Korekjan. We know what these other folks are going to tell us ahead of time."

"That may be true," Gov. Aiken said. "But you know what we always say down south. If you want to catch a fly, it's better to use honey than vinegar. I think we've got to go to those meetings and be polite, while we keep insisting on seeing Minister Elias."

"We have a much bigger problem than that," Msg. Pacelli said. "We've got to figure out a way of getting rid of the peshmergas so we can get up to al Qosh.

"I may be able to help," I said.

Of all the astonished looks that turned toward me, none was more surprised than my own brother, Marcos. He was about to see a side of my life that I had carefully kept hidden from him for years.

"I have a friend from Washington who will be arriving here in a few days," I said. "I think he will be able to help us."

"What about Rita?" Marcos said.

"Have you heard the ransom demand yet?" Gov. Aiken asked.

I shook my head in the negative. "It's better to discuss all that face to face when we go to Karamlesh tomorrow morning."

The logistics for the two hour drive to Karamlesh were as complex as any small-scale U.S. military operation. Msg. Pacelli had arranged for four cars and a team of bodyguards led by an Assyrian named Bassam. Each car took two members of the delegation, a driver, and an armed guard; Bassam followed with another guard in the fourth car and kept in constant contact with the other drivers via walkie talkies. Our Kurdish minders filled two black Suburbans, one at the head of our convoy, and one at the rear. In addition to the driver, each Suburban carried five armed peshmergas. As they had done at the airport, they drove at breakneck speed, sirens blaring. This became hazardous for the older, nondescript vehicles Msg. Pacelli had purposefully commandeered, which swerved wildly to avoid the giant potholes left from three decades of neglect and war.

Msg. Pacelli insisted that I accompany Dona. "Your brother is going to perfect his English with Mr. Utz," he said, a twinkle in his eye. "And I have many things to discuss with the Governor. I want you to make sure that Miss Hollinger can pass for a local with her accent," he said. "That's an order, my son."

Our driver and bodyguard were Christians from Karada, in Baghdad. As we soon found out, they didn't speak more than a few words of English, so Dona and I used that language to talk in private. My heart was heavy, as each moment took us closer to the terrible reality I knew I would soon have to face; and yet, I was filled with an unnatural gaiety. The many bumps in the road threw us easily together; each time our knees touched they felt like magnets we had to separate by force. Not knowing what to say, or how to say it, I found myself almost giddy, talking nonsense.

"You must be terribly worried about your sister," she said.

"It depends who has taken her. In Baghdad, kidnapping is a lucrative business. There are four or five gangs, and they have offices in the same building, just like companies. When someone from your family gets kidnapped, you go in to see a secretary and give her the name of the missing person, and she looks it up on a computer."

"You've got to be kidding," Dona said.

"No, seriously. If the first place doesn't have your relative on their list, they tell you to go down the hall and check with one of the other gangs. Nine times out of ten, it's all about money."

She pondered this information "But why do they always go after Christians?" she asked.

"They take Muslims, too. But the worst are not the kidnappings for ransom."

I found all of a sudden that I couldn't go on, because the worst is surely what had happened to Rita.

"Poor Yohannes," she said, taking my hand in her two hands and stroking it like a pet rabbit. "Will they abuse her—sexually?" she asked finally.

"It all depends," I said, turning away. "If the Kurds took her, they probably just want to teach her a lesson. She's been active with the Movement, the ADM. They'll rough her up a little, and warn her to stay out of politics. They'll dump her outside of town and that'll be the end of it."

"But you don't think it's the Kurds," Dona said.

"No, I don't."

I could feel the tears rushing to come out, and fought as hard as I could to keep them back.

"It's not a sign of weakness to cry, Yohannes," she said, taking her fingers and gently covering my eyes.

But I couldn't let go. Not in front of her. Not in front of our bodyguards. Not in front of God, who surely wanted me to be strong to confront the Evil that had seized my sister, and do battle against it, my life, for hers.

"You can't understand," I said finally. "You're lucky. Nobody should have to understand such things."

I wanted to know more about how she came upon the pages of the *Secret Book* of the Guardians she had shown to Father Shemoun in Amman, and so she told me a bit about her family. As a teenager, growing up in Modesto, California, she spent her afternoons at the shopping malls talking about clothes and boys, and her evenings around the dinner table hearing stories of massacres and pogroms. "I didn't know which was more real: the malls or the massacres. Or more unreal. I came here hoping to find out."

Her father was an evangelical pastor, a deputy in a mega church. He was open-hearted and open-minded, as his marriage to a Chaldo-Assyrian Catholic showed. What he liked about the Chaldeans was that they were Scripture-based, even though they accepted the authority of the Pope. "My mother always had a sense of longing about her; of something missing; of loss. It hung around her like the smell of a wood fire the morning after."

She went back to Turlock, where her mother's family still lived, to attend the State University, and on weekends volunteered at the local Chaldean church to practice the language. Once she graduated from university she went to work for a law firm in Los Angeles for a couple of years, while studying law at UCLA in the evenings. Eventually she passed the bar and joined a small law practice run by an Iranian Jewish woman who specialized in immigration cases. She looked at all her American friends, and all she saw was the malls: fresh and clean with piped in music, with no connection to the world beyond their doors. "The immigration practice was the only thing that connected me to the massacres, to my past," she said. "By the time I reached thirty and was ready to start a family, I wanted to know more."

Her father hooked her up with Gary Utz, who ran a large Christian political organization that had organized several mission trips to help Iraqi Christian refugees in Amman and Ankara. (They had wanted to go to Damascus, but the Syrians would never give them visas). This was the first time he had come to northern Iraq, and when she heard about his plans for the trip, she begged to come along.

"When I told my mother about it, she drove across central California the next day to see me before I left. That's when she brought me the pages from the book and told me about Uncle Andraos."

For her all this was a new adventure, a discovery of her heritage. I appreciated her spirit, and especially her strength. Was that how all women were brought up in America to be?

We flew through the checkpoint on the far side of the Greater Zab River without even having to stop. That was one advantage to having the peshmergas with us. They just opened their windows, stuck out the barrels of their rifles and showed their uniforms, and their brothers at the checkpoint waved us through.

The Kurds accelerated markedly after the checkpoint. There was a long straight section of road through the last portion of desert, and they wanted to put it behind us as quickly as possible. It was a no man's land between the official Kurdish region and the Nineveh Plain, which still belonged—at least in principle—to the Governorate of Nineveh, whose capital was Mosul. This was the most violent and ungovernable part of Iraq. The Kurds had extended their protection to the Christian towns and villages of the Nineveh Plain through paid guards, but they couldn't yet treat the whole area as a Kurdish domain. They knew the jihadis lurked just beyond the horizon. I could see that our driver and bodyguard had their eyes on the empty hard-scrabble desert to the South, hoping that some plume of dust in the distance tumbling across the desert didn't suddenly take the shape of a Toyota pickup full of armed men heading our way.

"Why are they driving so fast?" Dona asked.

"Maybe they're hungry," I said. There was no point in arousing her anxiety if we weren't facing some specific danger.

Our driver swerved violently to avoid a giant pothole that took up almost the entire right lane, throwing us together on the back seat. Playfully, she pushed me away.

"Maybe they can think of other people when they get *that* hungry," she said.

Just then, her cellphone rang in her bag.

"This is Dona," she said, once she had retrieved the phone.

There was silence on the other end, and then the caller shouted "BOOM!" so loud that she pulled the phone away from her ear. The voice on the other end burst into insane laughter. She held the phone out so I could hear it. "Dona! Dona! Damreena!" someone was saying lasciviously. And then they uttered a string of obscenities and sexual innuendos in Arabic.

"What are they saying?" she asked, covering the mouthpiece.

"Arabs," I muttered. "You don't want to know."

I took the phone from her and spoke into it harshly and then hung up.

"What did you say to them?"

"I told him that if he called this number again, I would find his sister and—"

"And what? Kidnap her? Violate her?"

She was disgusted, and I fear some of her disgust was turned toward me. I felt ashamed for my country, ashamed for the new Iraq. But somehow the idea of turning the other cheek and inviting another insult just didn't seem the right thing to do.

I took off the back of her phone, slipped out the battery, and examined the SIM card.

"Where did you get the Korek chip?" I asked her.

"I went out with one of the drivers to the market in Erbil," she said. "I bought one for the Governor as well, so we could call each other."

Opening the window a crack to let in the late springtime heat, I flicked the SIM card as far from the car as possible. Then I handed her the battery from her phone, and closing the back cover, gave her the phone.

"Keep it this way for now," I said. "As long as the battery is still in the phone, they can track you."

"Yohannes, they knew my *name*."

She grabbed my hand and I could feel the trembling just beneath her skin, as if the fear had

121

energized each individual molecule of her flesh. Her eyes implored me, wide and deeper blue than they had ever seemed before. She was beginning to share the fear that I had been living with ever since Saddoun's thug with the brass knuckles had cornered me in Karamlesh last year. The jihadis were everywhere, and they knew everything we were doing, at the very moment we were doing it. Sometimes I wondered if they could even read my thoughts, but I didn't want to frighten her more than she already was.

"For now, it's just a voice on the phone," I said.

I stroked her hand, and before I knew it, she buried her head into my shoulder.

"Tell me this can't be real," she whispered.

I held onto her, stroking her back, as she trembled silently like a bird with a broken wing. The massacres had just met the mall.

Out of deference to Msg. Pacelli and to Gov. Aiken, the peshmergas stayed at the checkpoint at the entry to Karamlesh and allowed us to continue on by ourselves. This didn't mean that we were out of their sight, because all the local guards handling security inside the town also worked for the Kurdish Regional Government, even if they were Assyrians. Such was the system set in place by Elias Korekjan for his Kurdish masters. We called him the Kurds' pet Christian.

Hannah, my mother, was at the ADM headquarters in the center of town when we arrived. With Rita gone, she wanted to help with the food distribution, and was pouring over lists of names with Jamal, the local ADM chief and the de facto mayor. I saw that her name was not on the list to receive a food package.

"Mama, this is not time to be proud," I said.

"What pride?" she said. "Your American friends have food packages for 80 needy families. There are surely 80 families here who have greater needs than I do, what with all of you down in Amman."

"You live in refugee housing. You don't even have your own house."

"But I have my widow's pension, Yohannes."

"Sure. That's $85 a month, and you think you live like royalty."

"I do," she said resolutely. "I praise the Lord every day for all that I have, and I say a prayer for all those who are less fortunate than I am."

There was no arguing with her. She was planning to sit next to Jamal when Gary Utz and Gov. Aiken announced the feeding program for the needy. And she fully intended to be among those who handed out the aid packages, not among the recipients. Such was my mother. She considered those who received to be blessed, but those who gave to be blessed more, although this was an un-Christian thought she would never admit to anyone.

"Yohannes, they came," she said, now that the others were out of earshot.

"Who came, Mama?"

"This man who said he was your former boss. Cory something."

"Cory Reed? The man from Triple Shield in Erbil?"

I couldn't believe that Cory Reed actually came to Karamlesh. He always considered the Nineveh Plain to be one of the least attractive places on earth. There was no money to be made, no nightclubs, and bad roads.

"He said that they were looking for Rita and thought they had identified her kidnappers. But that you had to stay away from al Qosh."

"Why would I go to al Qosh, Mama, unless they are holding Rita there?"

"That's not what he meant, Yohannes."

"What if I have to go to al Qosh?" I said. "What if that's the real reason we are here? The most important reason, the reason Rita was kidnapped? The reason grandfather Issa was murdered?"

"Don't say that," she said, turning away, holding up her hands to supplicate God, a little ritual I had seen her perform countless times whenever someone broached a particularly sensitive subject. "Just watch over Marcos. Why in the world did you bring him back here?"

"He's no longer a baby, *Yimaa*. He will be able to help. Lieutenant Colonel Wilkens will arrange to give him proper weapons training."

"You have more powerful weapons than the ones you can shoot, Yohannes."

"Show them to me, Mama. I will gladly take them up."

I found Marcos a bit later and asked him to come with me.

"I have something for you," I said.

We walked in silence through the narrow dirt streets leading into the heart of the old town, until we reached the pock-marked asphalt road that formed the border with the litter-strewn fields and led to

Hope in Our Savior, the refugee housing complex where Mama lived.

"What are we doing here?" he said.

"You'll see."

Once we reached the small housing unit *Yimaa* called home, I lifted up the narrow bed reserved for me when I lived there. Rita had taken over the room that Marcos and I once shared, now that we had moved down to Amman. Strapped beneath the bedframe, near the top, were the slim black boxes, made of Armalite, just where I had left them more than a year ago. I undid the rubber straps and laid the two of them on top of the bed.

"Col. Wilkens gave me these when I worked at Triple Shield," I said. "You may need them."

I opened the boxes, revealing a pair of Glock 19s set in foam casing. The Glock 19 is a 9mm pistol sometimes carried by USAF pilots because of its reliability and compact size. I took one of them in my hands and rammed in a magazine, pulled back the slide and let it snap forward to chamber a round. Then I removed the magazine and charged the weapon again to expel the round, so Marcos could see how to clear the chamber.

"Have you ever fired one of these?" I asked my brother.

"You don't really think this is the first time I've seen a handgun, do you? Papa taught me how to shoot in Baghdad."

"Marco, this is not a game. You need to know everything about this weapon, how it works, how to take it apart, how to load a fresh magazine with your eyes closed."

Each case had a foam cutout for an extra magazine, cleaning tools, and a box of ammunition. I showed him how to load the cartridges into the magazine, then emptied them out and passed the magazine and the ammo to my brother.

"I think I get it, Yohannes."

"It's not a test, Marco. Each weapon is different. Just put your hands on it to get the feel of it."

Reluctantly, he practiced loading the magazine, ramming the magazine into the pistol, chambering a round, and popping it out, as I coached him. One particularity of the Glock was that it had no positive safety mechanism; instead, a triple action trigger deactivated the safety when pulled and reactivated it when released. I insisted that he safe the weapon by removing the magazine and emptying the chamber. Then we repacked everything in the foam boxes and secured them beneath the bedframe with the bungee straps.

"Now you know," I said. "Just don't play games and try to bring them to Erbil. The Kurds have strict controls at the checkpoints."

For two days, back in Erbil, our foreign ministry minder played games with us, setting up endless meetings with Kurdish officials while avoiding insistent questions from Gary Utz and Gov. Aiken about getting an appointment to see Finance Minister Elias Korekjan. One day, they told us he was in Baghdad, meeting with the Prime Minister. Another day, they said he was out of the country. The officials we met all told us the same story: how happy they were for the U.S. invasion of Iraq, and how wonderful things were in Kurdistan, the Land of the Kurds.

"If things are so wonderful," Mr. Utz said to the Interior Minister, "why are Christians so desperate to leave?"

Through Monsignor Pacelli's sources, we learned that Minister Korekjan used a number of "private" offices in addition to the Finance Ministry to conduct his business. Late one afternoon, Msg. Pacelli arranged with our team of drivers and bodyguards to pay an impromptu visit to one of these. It was nothing more than an anonymous two-storey villa, on a closed side street not far from a newly-erected government complex, with no visible security other than the closed metal shutters on the main ground floor window, and of course the Kurdish security guards at the barricade a hundred meters away who controlled access to the entire neighborhood.

"Who's taking bets that we find Mr. Korekjan at home?" the prelate said, once we all had gotten out of our cars.

Gov. Aiken gave a look round to the dusty street, the quiet houses, the shuttered window, and shook his head. "If I've learned one thing with you, padre, it's to take nothing for granted. You are a man of many surprises."

"Let's hope so, Governor."

A man in his early forties, wearing a white shirt and a dark tie, answered the door. Bassam, the head of our private security detail, could speak Kurdish. He told the man we had an appointment with Mr. Elias.

"He's not here," the man said, eyeing us warily.

"When do you expect him?"

"Maybe a bit later, I'm not sure."

"That's okay, we'll wait," Bassam said.

Nodding to us to follow him, Bassam pushed gently but with insistence past the man into a tiny hallway that was empty except for a coffee table and a half dozen open boxes of books. They all had the same cover, a picture of Jesus in a brightly colored robe welcoming a group of children to sit at his feet. Apparently it was some kind of church school primer.

The man, whose name was Wissam, led us into the next room and took a seat at the chair behind the desk, where he had been working at the computer before we arrived.

"Oh my," Mr. Utz said, with a curt nod to the giant safes that lined the walls of the room. They were stacked two high, and reached nearly up to the ceiling. "I imagine one could buy a few villages with that. Maybe a few priests. Hell, even a bishop!"

"Why don't you call Mr. Elias at the Ministry and see when he will come back here?" Msg. Pacelli said. "Here's the number they gave us for his private secretary."

When Wissam understood, he just shrugged. "Nobody answers that line."

"So is there a better one?" Msg. Pacelli asked.

"No. They don't answer the phone."

"So why do they have the bloody phones anyway?" Mr. Utz said.

Wissam just shrugged again, as if to say, that's just the way it is.

Finally, the next morning, our minder appeared as we were having breakfast beneath potted palm trees in the glassed-in buffet at the Sheraton.

"His Excellency Mr. Elias Korekjan has granted your request for an interview," he said. "Please come with me."

He spoke loudly enough to attract the attention of the middle-aged Austrian man who had been conversing quietly with a local contact at the next table. He had a large briefcase full of promotional materials he was showing the other man, emblazoned with the letters "OMV," the Austrian state oil company.

Outside, a half-dozen black Suburbans were waiting for us, packed with very nervous Kurdish security guards. A ministry official took Governor Aiken, Mr. Utz, and Monsignor Pacelli, and ushered them into the second vehicle. The foreign ministry minder grabbed me by the arm and nodded to Dona to get into the last car. No sooner had the doors closed than we set off, sirens wailing. I could see the Austrian from the next table watching us through the glass walls of the breakfast room.

The finance ministry was part of the prime minister's office complex, but we came in through a separate entrance, without any security checks other than the sirens and the assault rifles of the Kurdish guards. The building itself was a mix of Italian marble, unpainted iron bars, and rough cement. We were whisked upstairs into a large antechamber with traditional Iraqi sofas along the walls, where servants in bedslippers and traditional Kurdish pantaloons offered us tea and coffee and dried pastries. After a few minutes, the ministry official who had fetched us at the hotel rejoined us and told us that the minister was ready to see us. He escorted us down another corridor into another antechamber, this time with large upholstered chairs of cheap imitation Damascus cloth. More trays of tea and coffee emerged, but before we could refuse them, an official wearing an impeccable European suit appeared and beckoned us through leather-padded doors into Mr. Korekjan's ministerial office.

"Gentlemen, I understand you've been trying to see me," Mr. Korekjan said.

He was standing in front of a gigantic desk that was remarkable not just for its size but for a polish so high you could see your face in it. And there was absolutely nothing on it; not a paper, not a telephone, not even a paperclip. Like Mr. Korekjan himself, it seemed to have been produced at some unseen factory and been plopped down in front of us, untouched by human hands.

He was older than I had expected from the rare newspaper photographs I had seen, which regularly showed him from a distance, entering the parliament building, or getting out of an official car. His black hair was streaked with white, especially just above the ears, giving you the impression that it had just been dyed. Close up, you could see that the sallow skin of his face was so thin and tight that the web of veins showed through, like the veins of an autumn leaf before it loses its color. His hands were small, even for a man of his slight stature. He spoke hesitant English with a slight American accent, perhaps the distant imprint of the Presbyterian school he was rumored to have attended as a child in Iran.

"We understand you are a very busy man," said Governor Aiken. "So we will be brief."

Being a politician, however, Gov. Aiken was anything but brief. He described the conditions of the refugees his delegation had met in Amman, and the hopelessness of the Christians who had been forced to leave their homes in Baghdad for the relative safety of the Nineveh Plain. Minister Korekjan listened impassively, trying to divine the Governor's intent more than the meaning of his words.

"You may not know this, Governor, if you listen to certain people in Washington" he said finally. "But the Kurds have been very good to the Christians. They have even allowed certain Protestant sects to evangelize. Do you know of any country in the Muslim world that has granted such freedom to Christians? That has treated our Christian faith with such respect?

"Everywhere there are Kurds, there is security. With security comes development. With development comes jobs, and with jobs come prosperity. These are the basic building blocks of happiness, of God's will. Without the Kurds, there is chaos. No foreign investment, no development, no prosperity, no happiness, for Christian and Muslim alike.

"Let me tell you a secret, Governor. I am not married. I have no children. But I consider all of these people you have mentioned as my children, and I have spent a great deal of money, a great deal of money, trying to help them."

Mr. Utz cut in. "With all due respect, Mr. Minister. The complaint we have heard in the Nineveh Plain and elsewhere is that you've spent millions of dollars of U.S. aid money to build churches and cemeteries, but you are not building schools or helping small businesses so they can create jobs. People who have come here from Baghdad can't even get a work permit from the Kurdish Regional Government!"

The minister listened, his hands poised on the shiny desk as if it were a piano, and when he finally replied it was with a time lag, as if he was translating the words in his mind. Despite his impeccable European-cut suit, his tailored shirt, his manicured nails, his sensitive skin, I had the feeling he would leave wet footprints if he walked out of the room.

"Mr. Utz," he said. "You run a Christian organization, am I right? Jesus says that man does not live by bread alone. We need the church. We need all the earthly benefits it can bring, the jobs, the prosperity, the protection. Don't we, father?" he said, turning to Msg. Pacelli.

"Indeed, your Excellency. Indeed," Msg. Pacelli said, with all the unctuousness of a priest saying the benediction. "And the Church needs men of faith such as yourself to defend Her. And that is why we are here."

Msg. Pacelli was the real politician, I was discovering. He could be bullying or conciliatory, hard-nosed, coy, provocative or ingratiating, all depending on whom he was addressing and what he sought to get from them.

There had been threats against the Monastery in al Qosh, he confided to the minister. "This is a site of great historic value to the Church, and its preservation is a matter that has come to the preoccupy the Holy Father himself—which is why I am here, of course. We have learned that a certain jihadi organization, in league with former Baathists, is planning to destroy this monastery, and with it, certain invaluable manuscripts that date from the earliest days of the Church. We very much need your help, Mr. Minister. The Church itself is calling on you."

The notion that the Church, with a big C, would call on Elias Korekjan was something that the Minister found not only natural, but expected. He gave a regal wave of his hand, as one might to a loyal subject who has just paid him a compliment. Modesty was not a quality he seemed to possess in great abundance.

"We have peshmerga forces protecting the town," he said, with the time lag.

"I understand. But I am speaking of an imminent threat, an extraordinary threat, one that requires extraordinary precautions." "I will look into it," he said, with another little wave of his hand. Then he got up, our audience clearly over.

As we were leaving, he placed a hand on Msg. Pacelli's shoulder, tentatively, clearly uncomfortable with the physical contact.

"I wouldn't worry about that old pile of rocks, father," he said. "If they destroy the monastery, I will build a new one. It will be bigger, better. You will see!"

7

Northern Iraq

The evening of the 7th day after my brief email exchange with Col. Wilkens, I asked Bassam, the chief of the small personal protection team hired by Msg. Pacelli, to buy ten fresh Korek SIM cards from different street vendors in the market. I explained to him that Dona's mobile phone had been compromised, and that every number she had called was probably being monitored. I held out a hundred dollar bill to pay for the chips, but Bassam shook a finger. "Monsignor," he said, with a slight tilt of his head. I understood what he meant and nodded in return. Bassam was a man of few words.

When he came back to the hotel an hour later, we sat down and went over the numbers. There were two sets of five SIM cards, so if one of the phones got compromised, we all could switch over to the second set of numbers with a reasonable chance of maintaining security. Bassam took a felt pen and marked the back of each chip with the number 1 or 2. He wrote out all ten numbers on six separate pieces of notepaper, one for each of us and a master for himself. Bassam and his guards all had U.S. cellphones, issued by friends down in Baghdad who worked with the Coalition. These were much harder to crack than the Korek phones.

After I took my leave from Bassam, I went back up to my room and dialed the number Col. Wilkens had given me. Had he actually come, I wondered? I hadn't seen him arrive, but then again the Sheraton was a big place and it wasn't as if we had been hanging out down in the lobby. I prayed quietly as the telephone seemed to go dead, sifting through hundreds of millions of distant electronic locks and keys, searching for a match, for the one man who could help me and save our heritage at al Qosh, our 21st century Hormizd. Even as the phone started to ring, I realized that I had invested too much in this call, too much in Wilkens, and that salvation never came from human hands but from the Lord who delivered it in his own time, in his own way. And yet...

He answered after the fifth ring.

"That you, little brother?"

He spoke casually, and I could hear other people talking behind him. "You ever make it to Echo City?"

I searched my memory for instant, then made the connection: Echo, E, Erbil. "Yes, I'm there now."

"Well okay then," he said. "Meet me at the place we mentioned in one hour."

Exactly fifty-seven minutes later, I went down to the main lobby and found a seat beneath one of the potted palms, close to where a man in Bedouin clothes was kneeling on a cushion, using fire tongs to pile up coals in a small brazier beneath a pair of brass coffee pots. When Arabs came here, they all stopped to taste the thin cardamom coffee he brewed, each time sipping scarcely more than a teaspoon of the hot bitter drink. After each swallow, they would jiggle the small cup and he would refill it until they had enough. He cast his eyes downward as I took my seat, almost making a point of not looking at me, tending to his coals, and then it dawned on me that the coffee-master was the perfect spy who could see everyone who came and went at the hotel. What better way for the jihadis to have eyes on the foreigners who came to Erbil than through this seemingly meek mock Bedouin? I was about to get up and move to a more secluded part of the lobby when someone tapped my shoulder from behind. "Mr. Yohanna?" he said quietly. I turned around, but it wasn't Col. Wilkens. Instead, there was an older American I had never seen before, wearing tan chinos and a blue and white checkered shirt, his graying blonde hair pulled up in a pony tail. "Please come with me," he said. When I didn't move, he gave me a wink. "It's okay. Big Brother has arrived."

The elevator opened on the fourth floor, and I was surprised to see Deron and Mojo, one at either end of the long corridor, dressed in civvies, arms folded against their chest so you could see their well-developed muscles even through the loose-fitting bush jackets they wore. We turned toward Mojo, I saw that his ear was fitted with some kind of communications device and that the bush jacket scarcely concealed what must have been considerable firepower. He pointed up to the ceiling as I approached the door to Room 430. "Smile for the camera," he said, his reddish-blonde beard cracked into one of his crazy grins. "Don't worry. We get the tapes," he added.

LTC Wilkens was seated at the sofa, with binders and documents and hard cases of equipment spread out everywhere. There were communications devices, computers, a few hand-held video cameras. A Glock 19, identical to the ones he had given me, sat on the coffee table. He got up as I came in and wrapped an arm around my shoulder as he pumped my hand. I thought I detected a hint of grey in the short hair at his temples.

"How you making out, little brother?" he said.

"They took my sister," I blurted out.

It just came out without thinking, and I immediately regretted it, as the words unleashed a flood of tears I had been holding back for the past week. I turned away and squeezed my eyes and managed to push the tears back, but I know he saw it and I was ashamed.

"I'm sorry, sir. It's just—"

"It's okay, Johnny. Hey, the cavalry has arrived."

He punched me on the shoulder and smiled.

Wilkens never thought he could be happy back in Washington, DC working an administrative job. The last time he had been stationed there, just before we worked together in Baghdad and Mosul, the political rivalries of the various U.S. intelligence services drove him crazy—and allowed the Iranians to smuggle a nuclear weapon into the United States, despite warnings from an Iranian defector who risked his life to bring out photographic evidence. Only God's grace had prevented the weapon from going off on the 4th of July right in front of the White House, he said. That, and a little skill from his wife, who worked as a demolitions expert with the Department of Energy's Nuclear Emergency Search Team. His wife was now working at the White House in the new administration. "She's Hispanic, and minorities are now the in thing," he said. "But I won't bore you with American politics. Besides, there are things these guys aren't cleared to know."

He picked up the spare magazine that lay on the coffee table and pointed to the man with the pony tail who had come downstairs to get me, and to another colleague, a younger officer, with whom he had been going over some papers when I came in.

"Richie is what we call a forensic accountant," he said, indicating the man with the pony tail. "That's a fancy term for somebody who spends most of his time pouring over ledgers and spread sheets, looking for numbers that don't match up. I sent him down to get you so he could get some fresh air."

"Yeah," Richie laughed. "If you call air with Arabs fresh."

"Kurds, Richie. Kurds," Wilkens corrected him. "We are in Kurdistan, Land of the Kurds."

The other man, sitting across from him, was Capt. Jed Stewart, and he was a Defense Department procurement expert who also served as Wilkens' logistic officer. With his wife's new-found political clout, Wilkens had landed a job as deputy director of the Special Inspector General for Iraq Reconstruction, SIGIR, a watchdog agency established by Congress to investigate waste, fraud and abuse.

"We're a creation of Democrats who were just out to get Bush," Wilkens explained. "But that doesn't mean there isn't plenty for us to do. Whenever the U.S. government starts spending tens of billions of dollars, you can bet a good portion of it gets lost. Our job is to find out where this is just incompetence and correct it; or where it is criminal, and then everyone duck."

Richie bent over, hand shielding his eyes, and made a whistling sound and then a mock explosion.

"I think your sister is being held by Kurds who are in league with the people we are investigating," Wilkens said. "If you hadn't reached out to me with that email, Jed would be tracking you down as we speak."

Procurement fraud was a common thing in the United States, and government contractors were regularly fined millions of dollars, sometimes even hundreds of millions of dollars, he said. "Imagine what happens when they are operating outside of the United States, where they think no one can touch them?"

Richie began to sing.

"Too many fish in the se-ea.

"Surely there is one for me-ee."

Captain Stewart rolled his eyes in exasperation.

"It's what we call a target-rich environment," Wilkens went on, ignoring the two of them. "So to make my job fun I try to find the biggest target, the dirtiest players. And I think we're pretty close. If I can help a good friend along the way, then that's a blessing."

"Who are you going after?" I asked.

"Sit down, little brother. It's quite a story."

What initially sparked his curiosity, Wilkens said, was what happened down at Camp Cropper where he had brought Saddoun al-Adnan for CIA interrogation more than a year ago. "I kept plugging his name into classified government data bases, and it kept coming back, 'Access denied.' And then, a few days later, the Baghdad station chief, a man named Jasper C. Ganz, stormed into my office and pulled me off the case."

I must have grimaced or shown my fear because Wilkens gave me a look of concern.

"I know that you've already paid a high price for this idiocy," he said. "We're going to get your sister back."

I shook my head. "This man, Ganz. I met him down in Amman just last week. He threatened me and my family. You think he knows where Rita is?"

"Without a doubt," Wilkens said. "He believes that you convinced me to fast-track the money to train a local police force up in al Qosh. But that money was going to get released anyway. There were huge political pressures back in Washington to allow the Assyrian Christians to control their own towns and villages and to move the various Kurdish forces out. But Jasper Ganz and his outside man, Cory Reed—your former boss at Triple Shield—were pissed off big time, because they had all the contracts to train and equip the *peshmerga* and their local goon squads, and now we were replacing them with Christians who reported to the mayors, not to Minister Korekjan. Basically, we are eating his lunch."

I was stunned, but not sure what to make of this. "You mean, it's just about money?"

Richie circled a finger around his temple. "What else would it be about, nitwit?"

"Enough, Richie," Wilkens said. "We don't need friendly fire."

"Finally!" said Capt. Stewart, relieved.

Wilkens and his team had been going through all the U.S. military sales contracts to the Kurds, and started to detect anomalies. Triple Shield had one set of contracts to buy military equipment from the Pentagon, and a second set of contracts to sell the same equipment to the Kurdish Regional Government (KRG). At most, they should have been charging transportation, warehousing, and overhead, giving them a net profit of somewhere between ten and fifteen percent. "But we obtained through a source one of their invoices to the KRG, and found they were charging the Kurds four times what they paid the Pentagon for the same equipment."

"Why would the Kurds go along with that?" I asked. "And why would they want to buy through Triple Shield anyway? Can't they buy military equipment directly from the Pentagon?"

Wilkens nodded to Richie, who was just itching to talk. "Alright, Richie. You can do Corruption 101."

The whole point of buying weapons through a front company, Richie explained, was to transform someone else's money into your own personal profit, *ta-da*, just like that. In the case of the Kurds, they were using KRG funds, some of which came from the central government in Baghdad, and some from the United States. Using the cozy relationship they had with Triple Shield, they agreed to pay inflated prices for the weapons on condition that Cory Reed and his buds kick back 85% of the excess to a series of numbered accounts with a bank in that mountain swamp called Lichtenstein, from which distributions were made on a 60/40 basis to the two leading Kurdish governing parties. "So if Triple Shield was normally making a 15% profit on these transactions, now they were making four times that amount while still appearing to take a 15% commission, should anyone on the Kurdish side bother to have a look," he said.

The scheme probably would have remained secret if SIGIR hadn't obtained the Triple Shield invoice to the KRG, since the Finance Ministry refused to provide any accounting of the state budget, Richie went on. That was how finance minister Elias Korekjan could get away with claiming that he was using his own personal funds to build churches and refugee housing in the Nineveh Plain. "What little money he actually spends on these things comes from

USAID[3], but nobody around here would ever know it," Richie said. "This is a man who came out of nowhere, who never had a job except as a party hack, and who suddenly claims the day after the war that he made a fortune as a financial wiz kid. If you believe that one, I've got a convent to sell you in Las Vegas. Call him the Great Gatsby of Kurdistan."

"But why Saddoun?" I asked. "He's a Tikriti. He's Saddam's nephew. We caught him in the thick of the jihadi networks."

"And much more than that, actually," Wilkens added.

What little information he had been able to gather on Saddoun down at Camp Cropper showed that he was getting money through couriers from Saddam's daughter, who now controlled the secret billions Saddam had managed to hide in the final years of his rule through bearer bonds and front companies operating in Qatar. "There is no doubt that Saddoun was financing and controlling one of the largest al Qaeda networks operating in Iraq. But he was also playing a double game," Wilkens said.

He opened his hands and looked at Capt. Stewart and then at Richie, as if asking their permission to continue.

"The rest of this is just a working hypothesis for the moment," he said finally. "That's what we're here to prove, or disprove eventually. So obviously, you need to keep this to yourself."

"Of course," I said.

Once Wilkens returned to Washington and joined SIGIR, he tasked a couple of analysts to comb

---

[3] The U.S. Agency for International Development, USAID, is a federal government agency that distributes foreign aid money appropriated by Congress.

through the DoD terrorist incident reporting data bases, to see if he could get a handle on the types of attacks Saddoun's jihadi network was committing. What he found out didn't surprise him. "Not a single attack against a U.S. military installation that could be attributed to Saddoun ever succeeded. Not one. Either the bomb didn't go off, or the suicider blew himself up by accident, or they were intercepted by our guys, or something. All of his successes were against Kurds or Christians. In the last year before we captured him, Saddoun and his goons were single-handedly responsible for turning Mosul in the capital of Jihad. His men kidnapped and assassinated the Archbishop last year, even as we had Saddoun himself in custody at FOB Tiger."

Their goal, Wilkens believed, was to generate a climate of instability in the north that would have two distinct results. First, the attacks would prompt the Kurds to expand their security services, thus generating more business for Triple Shield and their Kurdish partners. Second, the tension would provide political cover for the Kurds to annex Mosul and especially Kirkuk, where the overwhelming majority of the oil fields in the north were located.

"No attacks means no need for Kurdish protection," Wilkens said. "That has been the KRG's trump card in arguing with Baghdad that they should be the masters of all of northern Iraq. That, and of course, the Anfal. Righting the evils of the Anfal gives them the moral high ground, or so they think.[4]"

---

[4] Confident of his victory against Iran in August 1988, Saddam immediately turned his forces against the Kurds in the north, massacring tens of thousands of civilians and massively deporting Kurds and Assyrians from their historic lands, including Dohuk, Mosul and Kirkuk. Saddam gave their properties to his Sunni Arab supporters. With Saddam

I found myself just shaking my head as all the pieces started to fall in place. So this meant that Saddoun was actually being protected by the Americans, or at least the CIA? That the CIA itself was corrupt and paying kickbacks to the Kurds? That Elias Korekjan, the man we called the Kurds' pet Christian, was knowingly party to terrorist attacks against Christians and Kurds in the north? I felt like a man who has just been thrown overboard into a stormy sea at night, with no guiding lights, no solid footing, and death in every direction.

"Consider our friend Saddoun as armed, dangerous, and protected," Wilkens said. "The only way to stop him is to cut him off from his godfathers. For that, we're going to need your help."

"And Rita?" I said.

"She's the bait."

I didn't like the sound of that, and let my skepticism show.

"I know it's not much consolation, but think of it this way," Wilkens said. "That means they've got to keep her alive until we bite."

Wilkens asked me to continue doing what I would normally do for the time being and to stay with the Governor's delegation. He gave me a 914 cellphone that had been modified to override the GPS locator and that provided the local network with a constant address, showing that the handset was located in Pleasantville, New York. He would call or text with instructions.

---

gone, the Kurds now were seeking to reverse the impact of the Anfal campaign by expelling Sunnis and bringing back the Kurdish deportees, while allowing Assyrian Christian refugees such as my family to resettle in the Ninevah Plain—as long as they supported the Kurdish government.

The next day passed in a haze, as if I had drunk too much the night before and was wading through the fog of an immense hangover. We drove out with the Kurdish security detail to Baghdeda, one of the larger towns of the Nineveh Plain. With the bad roads, it took us nearly two hours. We went from the desert around Erbil, across the checkpoint along the Greater Zab river to the greening hills of the Nineveh Plain, then back into a pre-industrial wasteland of ruined and half-finished houses, piles of rubble, broken cars, gigantic potholes caused by broken sewage pipes eating away at the roadbed. Blue plastic bags were fluttering everywhere in the breeze like windsocks caught on the fences.

As before, the Kurds escorted us to the checkpoint at the entrance to the town, where a man was selling jerrycans of diesel fuel off the back of a pickup truck, our version of a gas station. There, the local guards took over. Governor Aiken and Gary Utz had a meeting with the mayor, one of the key politicians in our community. Monsignor Pacelli had stayed behind in Erbil, along with Bassam and half of our private security detail.

I had set the American cell phone to vibrate and clipped it in the front of my jeans, but as we walked from the cars to the ADM headquarters it felt conspicuous since I was carrying my Korek phone in one hand. I felt the local guards were staring at me. Why did the interpreter have two phones, they seemed to be thinking. Mr. Utz also thought something about them was unusual. "Are the goons our friends? Or do they belong to Minister Korekjan?" he asked.

"He has his eyes and ears everywhere," I said. Dona picked up on my tension and gave me a look of concern. Looking around to make sure no one was watching, she grasped my hand quickly and gave it a squeeze.

"You seem distracted," she said.

"Ssh. We're not among friends. Not here. Not yet."

I was beginning to understand better the system that the Kurds had put in place. They had their militia, the *peshmerga*, who wore uniforms and were trained and equipped by Triple Shield. They were responsible for overall security, not just in the KRG, but also here in the Nineveh Plain, which was still in a kind of administrative no-man's land. Then there were the local guards bought and paid for by Minister Korekjan, who patrolled inside the towns and villages and reported back to him and the KRG. We might think we were safe around them, because they were Assyrians like us; but in reality they were agents of the Kurds. In al Qosh, the local guards had been replaced by an Assyrian police force, trained and equipped directly by the U.S. military. If successful, the al Qosh experiment was supposed to serve as a model for all of the Nineveh Plain. That's what made the Kurds—and Cory Reed—so angry.

The mayor, Shadrack Dhia, had put together a whole program for our benefit, and swept us into the assembly hall before I could say anything to him. I was sure he must have news about Rita, since the ADM had people just about everywhere, but he was totally focused on his guests. When Governor Aiken saw the men and women lining the walls of the large meeting room and the long table at the far end bursting with sunlight and soft drinks and food, he hesitated.

"Whoa," he said, taking the Mayor's arm. "This is too much. You shouldn't have put all these people out on our behalf, especially on a Saturday."

The Mayor just looked at him, perplexed.

"*Yohannes, ayit msukera ellukh*—pay attention," Dona whispered urgently in Swadaya. She then proceeded to translate the Governor's comments. The Mayor apparently didn't understand a word of English.

"I wanted you to see the capacity of our Assyrian people, not just their suffering," Mayor Shadrack said. "We have doctors and lawyers, civil engineers and computer experts, teachers, administrators and businessmen. Our young women have university degrees. I want you to hear some of their stories and take them back with you to America."

There must have been twenty-five people waiting for us, all sitting Iraqi-fashion in straight-backed chairs lining the walls of the assembly hall. Springtime sunlight flooded through thin curtains that were once yellow. At the far end of the room, near the dais where Mayor Shadrack was directing us, was the flag of the ADM party, with a geometric blue sun at its center set against a field of white, with exuberant waves of red white and blue light streaking out toward the four corners.

Mayor Shadrack introduced his distinguished guests from America and everyone sat forward, each man and woman with a story to tell but waiting respectfully to hear what the Americans would say first.

"We come to you as Christians," Governor Aiken began. "That is our main reason for being here, because we believe in the teaching of St. Paul, who said in 1st Corinthians chapter 12 that Christians throughout the world form one body of Christ. 'When one part of the body suffers, every part suffers with it; if one part is honored, every part rejoices in it.' Verse 26. We are here because your community is on the verge of extinction, and we in America have a duty to reverse that. I'm here to tell you that we are suffering with you, and we plan to rejoice with you."

He spoke quickly and passionately, and through the haze of my inner turmoil I had difficulty keeping up with the translation.

"Amen," Gary Utz said in a quiet voice.

Mayor Shadrack went around the room, and asked everyone to give their profession and level of education. One man was a geologist who used to work for the Northern Oil Company under Saddam. Another was a researcher at the Education ministry. One of the women ran a kindergarten; two others were teachers. A fourth, like Rita, was an activist with the Assyrian Women's Union. Almost all of them were 40 years old or younger.

"How many of you today have jobs?" he asked. Only five of the twenty-five people in the room raised their hands.

"These people are grown men and women," he went on, turning to Governor Aiken. "Among our youth, almost 100% are unemployed."

A man named Matti joined the conversation. "It's only Christian youths who have problems," he said. "Muslim youths get jobs no problem."

The Mayor went on. "We have always lived under one form of discrimination of another. Today, the persecution is expressed in many ways—at the political level, the cultural level, the administrative level, even the religious level. Decree 117 of the previous regime transferred this area to Muslim control."

An older man named Isha jumped in. "In 1977, there were only three Muslim families in all of

Baghdeda. Today, nearly 50% are Muslims, and they are building housing projects on Christian land to bring in more Muslims."

"This is true," the Mayor said.

Most of this conversation was in Arabic, and I was doing my best to give Governor Aiken and Mr. Utz and Dona the gist of their comments, but I'm sure I must have lost at least half of it.

"We are between the hammer and the hard iron," a man said in English. "What do you call it—"

"The anvil," I said.

"Yes, we Christians are between the hammer and the anvil, between the Arabs and the Kurds."

"What's you're name?" the Governor asked, pleased to find someone who could speak to him directly in English.

"Just call me Morning," he said with a giant grin.

"I don't get it," Mr. Utz whispered to me.

"His name is Saba. That means morning in Arabic," I told them. "Saddam tried to force all of us to adopt Arabic names."

"Oh."

Although they had taken part in many meetings like this, I could sensed that Mr. Utz and Governor Aiken were started to get overwhelmed by the unending procession of misery of my Assyrian people. Why were we always the victims? When will we start to fight back, I wondered.

"How many of you want to leave Iraq?" Governor Aiken asked.

Nearly everyone shot up their hand, except for Mayor Shadrack. When he saw the reaction of his own hand-selected Greek chorus, he got angry and started to berate them in Swadaya.

"*Ma brele gawukh!* How can you say that you want to leave?" he said. "These people have come

149

here to help you so you can stay. Men and women
have died for you. Priests have been martyred for you.
The Movement has bled for you. Our blood has
watered the ground. Are you cowards that you now
want to leave?"

"*Ay hesanila talukh d'amritla*—That's easy for
you to say," a woman at the far end of the room said.
Everyone went quiet and looked down at their hands
or the floor.

"I know what happened to your husband,"
Mayor Shadrack said defensively.

"So what do you want, for us all to stay here to
become widows?" she said angrily. "Do you want our
children to be orphans? Who will take care of them
when we are killed? Your friend, Mr. Korekjan?"

Mr. Utz turned to me

"What was that all about?" he asked.

I threw up my hands. "They're just arguing."

"I can see that."

"It's complicated," Dona said, coming to my
rescue. "But you should ask him what he thinks about
Elias Korekjan."

Governor Aiken leaned toward the Mayor
confidentially, and turned on all of his southern
charm. "If I understand right, there seems to be one
name on everybody's lips," he said. "Mayor Shadrack,
what do you think of Elias Korekjan?"

I translated into Arabic, and the whole room
burst into angry shouts.

Mayor Shadrack gave a contemptuous shrug.
"What benefits have we seen from Minister
Korekjan? You've seen our young people; they are
unemployed. We have taken in refugees from all over
Iraq, who have come here martyred and broken. Our
infrastructure is bad. Our cultural and scientific
institutions don't exist. We have no services, no
electricity, bad water, broken streets. We've asked

Mr. Elias to build schools, not churches. We've asked him to help create jobs, not cemeteries. We say the dead can take care of themselves. We want him to pay attention to the living. His money is encouraging our young people to leave Iraq, because they have lost all hope of building a future here. This is not good."

I translated as best I could, and when I had finished Mr. Utz looked over his reading glasses at the Governor. "Well, that was pretty unambiguous."

"Careful, now. The walls have ears," the Governor replied, indicating the door that had just opened at the back of the room.

Two of the village guards came in, but Mayor Shadrack was undeterred. "And I say to Minister Korekjan: don't make us choose between the Arabs and the Kurds," he went on. "The Arabs in Mosul are 20 kilometers away. If we take sides with the Kurds, we will make problems with the Arabs. And if we take sides with the Arabs, we will have problems with the Kurds. This is not our conflict. We are just the victims of their struggle. We are the sandwich meat between Arabs and Kurds. Without us, there is no sandwich."

I noticed then that another man had come into the room behind the guards, and I recognized him. We had worked together as interpreters at Triple Shield, and now I remembered that he had told me he came originally from Baghdeda. He tried to get my attention and pointed with his eyes in the direction of the courtyard, wanting to talk. I gave a slight nod to acknowledge that I had understood.

But I never got a chance to have a long conversation with him, and Mayor Shadrack didn't get the opportunity of hosting the lunch he had organized for his guests, because one of the village guards was now whispering urgently into his ear and he was motioning to me to come over to hear what the man was saying.

"They have to leave. Now. This minute," the guard was saying. "The *peshmerga* are getting nervous."

The Mayor got indignant when he heard that. "Why do I care if the *peshmerga* are nervous? The *peshmerga* are always nervous because they are just itching to use their guns."

"Mr. Mayor," the guard said, with more deference this time. "If these people are not out in their cars in about five minutes the *peshmerga* are going to come into town. And then who will be responsible for what happens?"

The Mayor rolled his eyes, but he gave in. The *peshmerga* were so hated by the townspeople all over the Nineveh Plain that their presence alone was enough to start a riot. No one could forget what had happened during the last elections, when *peshmerga* troops controlled all the polling places and simply stole the blank ballot forms before Christians could vote. Thousands of people came out onto the streets to protest. Hundreds were beaten to a pulp and scores arrested, including Mayor Shadrack himself.

It was past three o'clock. While the sun was still high in the sky it was early spring, and in another two hours dusk would begin to gather and with it the dangers along the road back to Erbil would multiply. Perhaps it was just the advancing hour that made the Kurds nervous, I suggested to the Governor and to Mr. Utz. "We really should be heading back," I said.

Out in the courtyard, I caught up with Boutros, my friend from Triple Shield. We called him Paulo, but with the Americans it always came out "Polo," so someone nicknamed him "Pony" and it stuck. We had worked together down at the Big Snake two years earlier. He was a big tall gangly kid, who wore his hair long like a pop star.

"I don't know what you've done, my brother. But you are in their bad book."

"What have you heard about Rita?" I asked him.

He ignored my question. "Mr. Reed, he is gunning for you. If he sees you, I think he will kill you with his bare hands."

"Why would I go to see him? He fired me."

"Just some friendly advice. I would stay away from him if I were you."

"What have you heard about Rita?" I asked again. "What does the Movement know?"

"She's alive," he whispered.

Samir, one of our Assyrian drivers, rushed up to me, the sweat clearly visible on his forehead and cammo t-shirt. He was moving his hand like paddling water out toward the street. "Let's go-go-go," he said.

The Governor and Mr. Utz and Dona were still talking to the Mayor.

"So the *peshmergas* are nervous. They can stew for another two minutes," I said.

"*La, rabi.* They have picked up something. We must leave now. Now," he said, louder this time.

Samir was not one to get excited over nothing. That's one thing that made him a good driver and bodyguard. He was level-headed, calm, and always on the look-out for danger. And that's what he saw now.

"Governor, Mr. Utz, it's for real," I said. "We've got to go now. Right this minute."

I made hasty apologies to the Mayor, who clearly was disappointed, and ushered the three of them out to the cars, which were waiting outside, doors open, engines running.

"What's going on?" Dona asked as I put up the window and tried to convince our driver to get the air conditioner on our battered old BMW to work. "I'm not sure. The *peshmerga* apparently think there's a security threat. Personally, I think they just want to get back to Erbil before dark. Eh, Faraj, what do you think?" I said, switching to Swadaya. "*Kul mindi lele tawa*—It's not okay," he said. "*Et qinta*—there is danger."

When we reached the checkpoint at the edge of town, the peshmerga were already in their black Suburbans, racing the engines to keep them from overheating, their M-4 carbines pointing out the windows. They saw us coming, and popped on blue flashing lights and sirens. One of the Suburbans pulled out in front of Governor Aiken's car, the other waited until we passed then swung in behind us. We made it to the main highway in less than ten minutes, and then we were flying, swerving crazily to avoid potholes, slamming on the brakes when the road surface suddenly gave out entirely. The least of our worries was traffic. There were no other cars in sight.

"Any news?" Dona said once the road got a bit better. We had reached the long straight away through the heart of jihadi land by this point. Dona read my mind.

"Some," I said. "She's alive, at least. I'm pretty certain of that. I've heard it now from two different sources. You know, the Movement has people all over the place. When it comes to intelligence, they are as good as the Kurds."

A voice crackled on the walkie-talkie Faraj had clipped to the harness holding the spare cartridges for the AK-47 he had jammed in between the front seats. I couldn't hear what it said through the static, but Faraj understood and pointed off toward the desert to the south, on our right-hand side.

"Look, *rabi*. That's what the Kurds were worried about."

Dona saw the pick-up truck in the distance as soon as I did and gripped my hand. It was following our trajectory, kicking up dust, light from the waning sun glinting off windows and bits of chrome as it matched our speed across the hard dirt.

"Does Faraj have another weapon?" she asked.

"I think the Kurds have got them out-gunned."

"No, look!" she said then. "There are more of them."

She was right. Emerging out of the distance to the south were three more vehicles. I watched in disbelief as they gradually reached the pick-up that had been following us and fell into formation with it. It looked like a sandstorm in miniature, a tornado of fire, their side windows lit a brilliant orange by the setting sun. They were moving in a straight line at breakneck speed on an intersect course with us. And then I heard Samir's voice, and all of a sudden Faraj was braking wildly, trying to keep our car from spinning as he swerved to avoid the wrecked vehicle just ahead of us. It hadn't been there when came past here this morning. Car bomb, probably.

Fifty meters later, we came to a halt. Samir, who had stopped just ahead of us, came running toward our car, motioning to Faraj to open the window. He was holding his own talkie-walkie in one hand, a black pistol in the other. He spoke in short, clipped phrases, telling Faraj to change the channel on the talkie-walkie and to speak only in Swadaya from now on. They checked comm, then Samir ran back to his car, jumped in, and threw it in gear.

"What was that all about?" Dona asked.

"They were hearing Arabic chatter on the other frequency. Samir thinks there may be more jihadis to the north of us as well. The Kurds should be able to deal with them, but you never know. Do you know how to use this?"

I took the BHP pistol Faraj handed back to me and held it out to her.

"Are you kidding? Where would I learn to shoot growing up in southern California surrounded by anti-gun nuts?"

Next, he handed me his AK 47.

"Look. Nothing is going to happen," I said. "But just in case, all you do is point and squeeze hard. This is a Browning 9 mm automatic pistol. You move the safety like this with your thumb."

I put the weapon in her hands and maneuvered her thumb so it activated and deactivated the safety at the top of the grip. Then I pulled back the slide gently and saw there was no cartridge in the chamber, so I took the pistol and charged it by pulling the slide back fully and releasing it, stripping the top round from the magazine. I checked again to see if the cartridge was chambered properly, then held the weapon out to her, grip first. She took it uncertainly, holding it with both hands as if it were a newborn child.

"It's not fragile," I said. "Just point it that way, please. And only use it if they get really close."

It was a similar drill with the AK 47. Seeing no brass in the chamber, I pulled back the bolt then let it fly forward, slamming a round into the chamber, all the while I kept my eyes on the jihadis. They seemed to be playing with us, one instant charging forward as if they were about to attack, and the next pulling back slightly and keeping parallel to us.

"It was only a matter of time before they figured out what we were up to," I said. "You can only go back and forth in a convoy on this road so many times. With our Kurdish escort, we stick out."

"Monday is the last day," Dona said. "The food distribution at Karamlesh."

"I know."

Suddenly, an idea occurred to Dona that made her smile. She leaned closer to me and whispered conspiratorially. "Will your brother and your mother be there?"

"Lord, I hope not," I said.

It wasn't what I meant to say, and it wasn't what Dona had hoped to hear. But it came out without thinking.

"You *are* worried, Yohannes," she said, pulling away, whatever idea she had been toying with now discarded.

"This is Iraq."

A few minutes later, the lead Suburban put on its flashers then came to a sudden halt, and two men jumped out from the rear doors. One man carried a large weapon with a long black scope and a small bipod beneath the barrel, and ran to the side of the road. The other man carried an M4 carbine with a large optical device attached to the top of the barrel.

"They've got a Barrett, an M82," Faraj said.

"What's that?"

"A Light Fifty. Sniper rifle. Big one," he said.

In the distance, the jihadis kept going for another ten seconds or so until they had gone beyond us by a few hundred meters, then two of them veered off into the desert and were lost in a cloud of dust. The other two made slow wide turns in our direction so they could come about, apparently intending to see what we were doing. That turned out to be a fatal mistake.

The spotter took aim at the pickups through the laser ranging binoculars attached to his M4, and called out the distance to the shooter. The peshmerga who had fallen to the ground behind the Light Fifty adjusted his aim, led his targets carefully, then fired off three rounds in rapid succession and the lead pickup truck burst into flames. The second pickup careened crazily, trying to avoid a collision, and then the Kurd fired off two more rounds and must have hit it in the fuel tank because it leapt sideways into the air and started rolling, leaving a trail of burning gasoline behind it. The burning wrecks must have been a good 500 meters away, so the sound of the impacting shells and the explosions hit us with a second or two delay. Gary Utz jumped out of the car in front of us and peered over the roof at the spectacle.

"Holy Mother of God," he said. "These guys sure don't play by Washington rules. Did you see that?" he called to me.

"Yes, sir. I think that should keep them away for now."

"I should say so. Unless the ragheads have got one of those pick-ups with a Douchka mounted on the rear. That could get spicy."

The next twenty minutes seemed like hours as we raced along the final piece of straightaway leading to the checkpoint at the entry of KRG territory. Dona kept watch to the south, where the jihadis had shadowed us, while I surveyed the horizon to the north, looking for telltale wisps of dust in the distance.

"We're assuming, of course, that these guys don't have more sophisticated weapons that can hit us before we can see them," Dona said.

"What else do you want to do? Pray?"

Dona looked at me strangely, and for the second time that afternoon I immediately regretted what I had just said. Aren't we supposed to believe in the power of prayer, especially here, in the face of immediate danger? Isn't this when our trust in God's mercy should be strongest? My doubt was an insult to the Lord, a provocation, as bad as an Asharah pole on a hilltop. That's what her look was telling me.

I felt my face going red and turned away to watch the horizon.

8

Sunday

The next day was Sunday, a working day in Iraq. We all gathered for breakfast at 8:30 am downstairs in the hotel. Apparently Msg. Pacelli had used the opportunity of our trip to Baghdeda to make a discrete trip of his own up to al Qosh, just taking the head of our security detail and a chase car.

"First, I visited the seminary at St. Joseph's to see if the Kurds had any interest in me whatsoever," he said. "And then, Bassam just drove me straight up to Al Qosh—if you could call the road we took straight! We used to go there directly from Mosul. Now it's a two hour drive. Oh well. Father Charbel sends his greetings and is looking forward to meeting you."

His joviality vanished when Governor Aiken described the shooting incident with the Kurds.

"My, my, they are trigger happy, aren't they? I think I had rather have a word with Minister Korekjan."

"Father, it was Minister Korekjan who gave them the shooting orders to begin with," Gary Utz said.

My American cellphone beeped twice, and I saw that I had a text message. Everyone stopped talking and turned to me expectantly as I called up the message. It was simple and direct. "Please come join me ASAP," it read.

"Someone who may have news about my sister," I said, getting up. "Do you mind?"

The Governor was gracious, as always. "Brother Yohannes, you don't need to ask. We've all been praying for her, and for you."

I got out of the elevator on the 4th floor, and saw Mojo and Deron, guarding the corridor as before. Col. Wilkens greeted me at the door of his suite.

"Show time, Johnny," he said.

Mojo and Deron suited up in field dress, and were carrying their M-4 carbines and a full web kit when we arrived at the gate house of the U.S. embassy in Ainkawa. Wilkens showed his DoD ID, and the guard waved us through. Richie, the accountant, was carrying two thick binders. Captain Stewart, the logistics officer, had only a notebook and a Beretta M9 in a shoulder holster underneath his sports coat, as did Wilkens. I was terrified of the encounter we were about to face, but Col. Wilkens had insisted that I come.

"You are an interested party, Johnny. You're not a bystander in this."

"But, sir. What if he gets so angry that they kill Rita?"

"He might like to, but he won't," Wilkens said. "We've got paper on him up the yin-yang. He'd spend the rest of his life in the slammer."

As I suspected, Cory Reed was not at all happy to see us, and was visibly taken aback when I came into his office behind the others.

"You didn't tell me you were bringing him," he said, jerking his thumb at me. "He was terminated for cause. Or is that what this is about? You goody two-shoes are now the Labor Department or something?"

"Please sit down, Mr. Reed," Wilkens said.

"You got a lot of nerve bringing your heavies in here," he went on, indicating Deron and Mojo. "You want to have a contest for who's got the most firepower? I'm in."

"No contest, Mr. Reed. Just prudence. Now please. Have a seat."

"Don't mind if I do," he said sullenly.

He fished for the leather thong holding the pair of brass balls he kept on his desk, but Wilkens held out his hand gently, asking him to put them down.

"I don't want anyone misinterpreting your movements, Mr. Reed," he said.

"Whoa, soldier. We're the good guys here, remember? We're the ones riding the white horse."

"Let's hope you're right. Because we have a problem, and we'd like your help."

He explained about my sister's kidnapping, and said that he was hoping that Mr. Reed, with his network of contacts, could help to get her released.

"What's this girl to you, soldier?"

Wilkens didn't take the bait. Reed shifted his eyes to Capt. Stewart, then to Deron and Mojo, and made a decision. He wouldn't look at me and I thought beneath his bluster he was getting nervous.

"Okay, so look," Reed went on. "Let's say my sources have been telling me something about her. Let's say, for example, they think this is not a jihadi job, that maybe the Kurds did it. Why would the Kurds do such a thing? I'm asking myself this question. What interest do the Kurds have in the sister of Johnny the ex-terp?"

"She's politically active with the Movement," I said.

"Nobody asked you," Reed said sharply, his finger popping out like a switchblade to point at me.

"So what do you think, soldier? I'll tell you what I think. I think the Kurds suspect Johnny-boy and Sister and their buddies in the ADM of doing a nasty on them up in al Qosh. Convinced you and a bunch of politicos to push the peshmergas to the edge of town so that ridiculous police force could move in."

"The police force proposal has been in the works for three years," Wilkens said quietly. "It's an Assyrian town."

"Oh, puh-lease. Al Qosh is part of Kurdistan. Always has been, always will."

"So you... can't help us," Wilkens said carefully.

"I didn't say that," Reed countered. "But you're in way over your head, soldier. That I can tell you."

"You know, Mr. Reed, I have a lot of confidence in your abilities," Wilkens said, changing tack. "I used some of your reporting—at least, it went out under your name. I know that you can help us if you want to."

Reed nodded, never one to resist flattery. "Maybe I can."

"So here's your chance to tell me what you need," Wilkens went on. "I'm sure you'd always blame yourself if something bad happened to the girl."

Reed guffawed at that, and pushed himself back in his chair until he knocked against the file cabinet with the huge cipher lock behind his desk.

"You think I'm some kind of bleeding heart or something? This ain't southern California, and you're no Arnold Schwarzenegger. You wanna know my price?"

Wilkens narrowed his eyes and rolled his left shoulder slightly, the one with the titanium joint.

"Yes," he said finally.

"Dump the Christian cops. Let Minister Elias put his people back into al Qosh."

Wilkens sighed. "That's not going to happen, Mr. Reed. It's an act of Congress—not the kind of thing that can be signed away by someone like me. I was hoping to find at least one altruistic bone in your body. But I guess I was wrong."

He turned around and glanced at Richie, who was grinning from ear to ear. He had been waiting for this moment.

"I'd like you to meet Mr. Armitage, one of our forensic accounts," Wilkens said.

"Forensic accountants?"

"That's correct. Richie, I think you've found something that Mr. Reed might be interested in seeing."

Richie hefted the two black binders as if weighing them in his hands, trying to decide which one to give him first.

"You're joking," Reed said.

"Actually, he's not," Richie said.

He opened the top binder, unclipped the hasp, and took out a single sheet of paper. He passed to Wilkens, who examined at it for a long moment, as if pondering whether or not he was actually going to show it to Reed.

"I think you'll recognize this, Mr. Reed," he said, laying the sheet of paper on the desk.

The paper had the familiar logo of Triple Shield, like some kind of medieval heraldic blazon, and beneath it had columns and figures. Reed blanched when he saw it.

"Where'd you get this? This is proprietary information. Client privilege." Then he turned and stared at me with a flash of hatred. It lasted just an instant, but it was chilling, murderous. It was clear he suspected me of having provided the documents.

"You know the rules, Mr. Reed. You are a U.S. government contractor, and you are subject to U.S. laws. I have the authority to bring my guys in here and camp out for weeks if I want to, going through your books."

Reed got up and planted his two hands squarely on the desk, glaring at Wilkens. "Be my guest," he said. "I'll make sure the air-conditioning breaks down. You want my invoices? Go ask the Kurds. You want my help? Ask nicely."

When Wilkens didn't budge, and Deron and Mojo stayed at their posts by the door, cradling their rifles, he collapsed into his chair and grabbed his forehead.

"Okay. Okay. I'll tell you what," he said, not looking at us. "I'll make some calls. Give me a call back today by five o'clock and I'll let you know what I found out."

Wilkens shook his head sadly. "Not good enough, Mr. Reed. That gives you all the time in the world to use that giant shredder you've got behind your desk."

The idea seemed to amuse Reed, who for instant regained his composure. "That would be cheating," he said.

"And illegal," Wilkens said. "Especially when our forensic accountants are unable to find your copies of the invoices they already have."

Richie held up the two black binders, and smiled innocently.

"Okay. Leave one of your guys here, if you like. But I'll need until 5. We got a deal?"

"That's going to depend on the results, Mr. Reed."

They agreed that Capt. Stewart would remain behind on the premises, while Reed went outside to use his cellphone. No one bothered to tell Reed that the single sheet of paper that Wilkens handed him was the only documentary evidence he possessed. But neither did they tell him that I was not the source of the leak.

A few hours later, around noontime, Capt. Stewart phoned us back at the hotel.

"He's on the move," he said. "What should I do?"

"Stay put," Wilkens said. "It's not like he's about to flee the country. Let's hope he's meeting a contact. Give him some leash."

Mojo ordered food, and we snacked on hummus and mouttabal and tabbouleh and small skewers of grilled meat while we waited. I didn't have much appetite. All I could think about was Rita's broken lips, her bloody eyes, the gauzy pulp where her ear had once been.

"So what do you think, boss?" Richie asked after awhile, wiping small pieces of parsley and dried fat from his lips with the back of a hand. "Did he fall for the binder trick?"

"Oh, absolutely," Wilkens said. "That's not what worries me."

He looked at me grimly, and I knew he didn't want to say what was on his mind.

"They don't have her," I said, completing his thought. "They sold her to the jihadis.

Two hours later, Stewart phoned us again to tell us that Reed had returned to his office, alone. Then he put Reed on the line and Wilkens turned on the speakerphone.

"This is going to be slightly more complicated than I had thought," he said. "The good news is, we know who's got her, and she is alive. The bad news is, they aren't friendlies, so we've got to go through intermediaries."

"Five o'clock, Mr. Reed," Wilkens said.

"What, you think you can put a deadline on this? This is Iraq, soldier."

"I thought it was Kurdistan, Mr. Reed. The *other* Iraq."

"Ha-ha. Not funny," he said and hung up.

The Kurds ran quite a publicity operation in the United States, bringing church leaders and members of Congress to Erbil and taking them around the countryside, far from Kirkuk and Mosul, to show them the "other" Iraq. This was a land of security and well-being, a land of smiling children and church spires and crowded markets where people shopped without fear of car bombs. It was a land of normality, where Americans were revered. It was the Land of the Kurds. Their message was simple and direct: invest in us, invest in our security, our separateness from Baghdad, and you can have all of this. There is an alternative to the Iraq you know and fear. Why should Americans care how the Kurds achieved the relative stability they enjoyed in their enclave? Triple Shield arranged tours for these groups, and I translated occasionally when they took them up to the new villages Minister Korekjan had built for Christian refugees in isolated parts of the north near Dohuk. They never took the American visitors to the Nineveh Plain. "Too dangerous," they said. "Not under our control." Cory Reed and the Kurds only wanted their guests to see the Fairy Tale.

At 4:45 pm when we still had no word, Wilkens ordered Deron and Mojo to suit up again so we could head back to Cory Reed's office in the embassy complex. Besides the clipped telephone calls back and forth with Capt. Stewart, no one said a word as we drove over there. The sun hung low in the sky but the air was still hot, dry, and full of dust. Erbil seemed to live and breathe in a giant dust cloud. Dust kicked up by the buildings going up all over the city; dust kicked up by the buildings going down. Ashes to ashes, I thought.

"Now it's time to pray," Wilkens said, seeing the look on my face.

"I've been trying, sir. Nobody seems to be listening."

"That's just the way it seems to you, Johnny. None of us can know God's plan. Miracles happen here. I've seen it with my own eyes."

When we reached the embassy complex, the bells of St. Joseph's started to ring, calling parishioners for the Sunday evening service. Cory Reed was waiting for us in the gate house along with Capt. Stewart, an ironic smile on his fat lips.

"Good news, soldier. The Kurds raided the safe house an hour ago and rescued her. The Governor himself got involved. He's waiting for us at his office. I think some kind words would be in order."

"It is always right to give him thanks and praise," Wilkens said, with a wink to me. "We'll follow you."

The Governor's Palace is the most imposing public building left over from Saddam's era in all of Erbil. Built to demonstrate the power of Saddam's authority, the broad inelegant façade, built more like a blockhouse than a palace, faced a large inner courtyard that doubled as a parking lot for important visitors and was surrounded by a high cement wall along the street. The peshmergas at the main gate waved Cory Reed through without even stopping. He indicated to the guards our two cars and they waved us through as well. On the broad ceremonial steps, a half dozen television camera crews had set up.

"Who are the creeps?" Deron muttered when he saw them.

"Everything has its price," Wilkens said.

At the top of the stairs, just before the main entryway to the palace, stood Msg. Pacelli, Governor Aiken, Gary Utz, and Dona, caught in the rich orange glow of the expiring sun. We went up to join them.

"What are you doing here?" I asked Dona in Swadaya.

"We got a call a half hour ago from our minder, asking us to come meet the Governor. He wouldn't say what it was about."

I told her briefly what we had learned, and her whole face transformed, the muscles of her cheeks twitching slightly as she fought her emotions, somewhere between tears and joy. She said, "Yohannes, I am so happy for you. See? You must have faith. God answers prayers from the faithful."

"We don't know what shape she's in yet," I said quietly.

And then the ceremonial doors opened and from inside the palace a small crowd was moving toward us, cameramen attached to soundmen carrying large blue bags backing toward us, checking frantically over their shoulders to make sure they didn't knock into a pillar or fall down the steps. Beyond them, walking briskly, was the familiar face of Governor Rawandouz holding forth to the reporters, flanked by aides who gently pushed them toward the doors. And then I saw her: wide-eyed, blinking wildly, cringing with the brightness of the late afternoon light, unsure of herself, on the verge of tears.

"Rita!" I called. "*Enee tawta wan!*—You're ok!"

But she said nothing, bustled forward, clutching the arm of the Governor as if it was the only solid thing left in her universe.

I didn't know what they had done to her, but as I looked upon her hollow cheeks and her cringing eyes, she broke my heart.

After the ceremony, where the Governor explained how his peshmergas had acted swiftly on a piece of intelligence they had received anonymously that very afternoon, LTC Wilkens went down to Cory Reed, who had remained in the back seat of his white Jeep Cherokee the whole time, engine running. The TV cameras were gone by then. Reed put down the window and stuck out his hand, almost as if asking for a tip.

"See?" he said. "Promise made, promise kept."

"Why all the reporters?" Wilkens said."

"The Governor likes a little public recognition for his good deeds."

"They didn't miss one of us. I was watching them when they were shooting."

"Hey, nothing's free in this life, soldier. Think of it this way: now you're a star of the small screen."

Wilkens leaned closer to him, and I had to strain to hear what he said next.

"Why was Saddoun al-Adnan meeting with your inside man in Amman?"

All the feigned amusement and jollity that had molded his face into a moon-shaped grin suddenly left him, and the folds of fat collapsed and seemed to quiver. He said, "I don't know what you're talking about."

"Jasper C. Ganz."

He stiffened on hearing the name. "That identity is classified, soldier." He indicated me with his eyes, but Wilkens shook his head.

"Johnny saw them together, so I guess Mr. Suspenders blew his own cover."

Reed ducked back inside and the door opened. "Get in. Let's go for a ride," he said.

Wilkens nodded, then pulled out the Beretta M9 from his shoulder holster and slowly chambered a round.

"What's this?" Reed shook his head in mock disapproval. "I keep on telling you, we're the good guys in this story."

"Maybe you are. But I'll have my guys keep right on our tail."

Reed sighed in exasperation. "When are you military Buckos going to learn to roll over?"

That evening, Hiram, the hotel owner, hosted the Governor's delegation to dinner. We sat railroad style at the narrow trestle table covered with heavily-starched white linen, as waiters brought platter after platter of *mezzeh* dishes until they couldn't find room to put them down. Besides us and another half dozen more conventional tables, the vast dining room was

171

empty. With its floor-to-ceiling windows, its giant chandeliers draped with garlands of fresh-cut flowers, its centerpiece buffet flowing with a fountain of grape juice lit to make it look like wine, the expense and lavishness of the setting seemed wasted on so few people. But Hiram, an Assyrian-Christian doing business under the tutelage of the Kurds, was living on borrowed time, and tonight he let us know all about it. Normally he never opened his mouth in public, but tonight, after three stiff *araks*, he couldn't stop talking, and he entertained the Governor, Mr. Utz Msg. Pacelli, and Dona for hours.

"You can't do business here without a Kurdish partner," he said at one point. "But so what? The only time you see them is when you get your bank statement and you see how much they have stolen. There's a price to doing business wherever you go. It's like the Mafia."

At one point, Msg. Pacelli tried to convince him to give more money to the local Chaldean church so they could open schools and day care centers in the Nineveh Plain.

"If I did anything so openly they'd shut me down the next day. I give lots of money—but always through Minister Elias. He is the only conduit the Kurds will allow."

"So you're helping him to build empty churches and cemeteries," Gary Utz said.

"What would you have me do, Mr. Utz? If I supported the Movement, they'd simply kill me."

Throughout the meal and the entertainment that followed, Rita kept quiet, looking down at her plate. But I noticed that every time a serving platter was passed her way, she took a soup spoon and shoveled an extra helping onto her plate. She ate and ate until I was sure she would burst. When the giant platters of *masgouf* came, she ate some more. Four huge platters of the Tigris river fish appeared, stuffed with Tamarind and topped with chopped onions and tomato, and I am certain she had a good portion of each one of them. She was a handsome woman, tall but well-proportioned and with elegant bones. I had never seen her eat like that in my life.

"So who is your military friend?" Mr. Utz asked me, as the others were caught up in some epic story Mr. Hiram was telling to fend off the skulking beast of his natural loneliness.

"He used to be my CO when I worked at Triple Shield."

"He's got juice. You can see that."

"He's a good man."

"I think that's right. Do you think I should ask him to join us tomorrow?"

I must have looked horrified because he didn't insist and didn't bring up the subject again that night. But my guess is that the former Marine recognized a fellow officer and instinctively understood what he was about.

It was nearly midnight when we went back upstairs. Dona had offered to share her room with Rita, but went up separately in the elevator with me.

"Don't worry about her," she said. "She just needs time. We're going to spend some quality time together, just the two of us. Girl talk, you know? Just trust me, and get a good night's sleep."

"We shouldn't meet in elevators," I said.

I tried to make it sound like a joke, but instead of laughing, Dona put her hands on my shoulders and looked me straight in the eyes. Her grey-blue eyes had gone almost black and seemed to swallow me up, knowing me from the inside in that place before words ever form.

"Dear, dear Yohannes," she said as the elevator came to our floor. Then she reached up and kissed me quickly on the forehead and went out.

Instead of going to my room, I went back down in the elevator to the 4th floor to meet with LTC Wilkens, who had sent me a text message asking me to join him after dinner. Even though it was late, they were expecting me. Mojo opened the door quickly and pulled me inside, even before I knocked. He had a finger up to his lips and pointed with the other hand to Capt. Stewart, who was passing some kind of metallic wand over the walls, the lamps, under the coffee table, and along the picture frames.

"Those two seem to be it," Capt. Stewart said quietly. Mojo understood my bewilderment, and motioned for me to follow him into the bedroom, where he pointed at a pair heavy crystal ashtrays set in burgundy leather that were now sitting on the made bed. The radio was playing, and he turned it up a notch then closed the door. Here in the 'other Iraq,' I thought, trust runs as thick as water.

"Are you sure we're clean, Jed?" Wilkens asked.

"Never 100% certain, but I'd say so, yes."

"Well, let me tell you all what our friend Mr. Reed told me on the way back from the Governor's palace. I'd like to get your take on this."

Mojo motioned me to keep still, then wrote something on a piece of paper and handed it to me.

"You're not here," it said. "So don't talk."

Reed claimed that the CIA had recruited Saddoun down at Camp Cropper, which was why they took Wilkens off the interrogation team. After they turned him, his Agency handlers orchestrated a spectacular escape that became the talk of the detainees for weeks. "We made him into a hero," Reed said. "He was already big. We made him a star."

Saddoun al-Adnan was the biggest catch the Agency had ever made in Iraq, their most reliable, high-level point of entry into the structure and activities of the jihadi and Baathist stay-behind networks. Ganz had to jump through all kinds of hoops back in Washington to get his recruitment approved, but eventually he did.

"We give him money and protection. He gives us bodies. That's how things work in the real world," Reed said.

Of course, the CIA Director used more obtuse language when he explained the reasoning behind the recruitment to the eight Cardinals of the Senate and House intelligence committees. Until now, the Agency had been unable to penetrate the jihadi networks at a level high enough to thwart attacks that were killing American soldiers, the Director told the esteemed Senators and Congressmen. With Saddoun on board, the number of successful attacks had dropped like a rock. "He was our nuclear weapon, our deus ex machina," Reed said. Saddoun was providing the cover the new administration needed in order to successfully pull out of Iraq without giving the appearance of a rout.

Of course, they suspected Saddoun's motives. Only a fool would fail to do so. But if the Agency was only allowed to deal with Boy Scouts, they might earn Merit Badges but they wouldn't catch any terrorists.

"Thanks to Brother Saddoun, we now know the entire organization chart of al Qaeda in Iraq. The whole nine yards," Reed said. "So now we can play with them, disrupt their operations, arrest key members of the network, and keep them from killing Americans."

"And the price of that is letting them continue to kill Christians and Kurds," Wilkens said.

"You're being a Boy Scout!" Reed scolded. "Look, this is Sensitive Compartmented Information. You're not read into the Compartment, but what the hell, I wrote the box to begin with, so I'm reading you in right now. This is the single biggest successful operation we've ever run in this country, soldier. And you want to jeopardize it to theoretically save the taxpayers a couple of million bucks? Hell, your average Member of Congress wastes as much money every half hour of every day! So stand down."

Wilkens asked him why Saddoun was going after his interpreter and had kidnapped his sister.

"Hell if I know. It's some religious thing. As far as I'm concerned, they're all nuts. Shias, Sunnis, Yazbekis, Shabaks, Chaldeans, Syriacs, Evangelicals, Catholics, the whole writhing snake pit of them, all nut cases as far as I'm concerned."

The important thing was that they were finally closing in on the big one, the Emir of Jihad himself, Abd-al Hadi al-Masri, the right hand man of Osama bin Laden. This is the man who was parachuted into Iraq by bin Laden, with help from the Iranians, after the U.S. killed al-Zarkawi in 2006.

"If we get the Emir, we sever the spinal cord leading back to Bin Laden. Then we can roll up Saddoun and all his stay-behind networks in an afternoon," Reed said.

One thing was missing from this story, and I'm sure that Col. Wilkens caught it as well. In fact, I'm sure he told the story in this way to make it obvious. Why would Saddoun give up the Emir of Jihad knowing that by doing so his usefulness to the Americans would be over? If Saddoun was smart—and he was—he would play them for all they were worth, string it out as long as possible, then flee the country for a comfortable retirement in Singapore just before everything blew up.

"So what do you guys think" Wilkens asked, once he had finished.

Mojo caught my arm and motioned again for me to keep quiet, pointing to the sprinkler overhead.

Capt. Stewart played it straight. "It sounds plausible enough to me, boss. The bit about the drop in jihadi attacks certainly coincides with what we know."

"What about you, Richie?"

The accountant pretended to pout. "You're giving my Kurds a-way."

Capt. Stewart groaned.

Before tonight, I had thought I had no illusions. Iraq was an ugly, violent place, where brutal men killed each other on a whim and God's almond eye remained closed to injustice. But I had never realized the extent to which the Americans were fighting first against themselves. Perhaps that is why it took them so long to beat the insurgents. They first had to beat their allies at home.

At least now I knew for sure that Saddoun was behind Rita's kidnapping, and that the whole Kurdish "rescue" had just been a show.

It was not a comforting thought.

9

Monday

Rita smiled when she came down for breakfast. It wasn't a great big gap-toothed smile, a child's smile, or a smile of victory. To most people who saw her, she probably just looked bashful. The cringing was still there, the hesitation. But there was something new—or rather, something old, something of the Rita I had known before the kidnapping, a flicker of light in her eyes.

She came up to our table with Dona, holding hands, and made a slight curtsey to Governor Aiken. It was what Assyrian girls were taught to do in the church schools, but I can't remember the last time I saw Rita do this.

"*Basima raba wali*—Thank-you, Governor, for everything you are doing for my people," she said quietly. Dona translated for her. "Men like you truly can change the world."

"Young lady, it is so little," he said. "But that smile of yours brings joy to my heart."

Gary Utz turned to me. "Do you think she's ready to go back to Karamlesh? She could come with us for the food distribution today?"

Rita understood what he said, and shook her head. "Please," she said hesitantly in English. "I prefer to stay here. Dona say I can spend the day in the spa—*w'mkhallanna kulla ay shikhta*," she added in Swadaya. And wash away all the filth.

We all looked at her as she stood there, her eyes fighting back tears, trying to smile, to appear normal. I was proud of her, and moved down a seat so she and Dona could sit next to each other.

"You must be hungry," I said.

"I could eat a she-camel!"

She gave a little laugh at her own words, and started to help her plate from platters of ham and tomatoes and olives and soft cheeses and bread. "I think I just want to eat and eat until I get fat and then sit in a hot bath for hours." Dona nodded and smiled at me.

When breakfast was over, the Governor stood up and came over to our side of the table and took her two hands in his own. "You're a brave young woman," he said. "We'll say hello to your mother and brother. I know how happy they must be."

Rita looked down, the cringe momentarily returning to her shy smile.

"I spoke to them last night by telephone," she said finally. "They understand. Karamlesh will still be there tomorrow."

If she had known what was going to happen, would she have said something different? Would her presence in Karamlesh have changed anything, made her more than just a mute witness to one more atrocity, one more personal tragedy, to be carried in the flesh and memory of our family for generations?

I know she will never forget those words and will always regret them. Because she never got a chance to see Marcos again alive.

The Kurds weren't taking any chances with us today, and threw on to our convoy two HUMVEEs fitted out as gun trucks when we crossed the final KRG checkpoint into no man's land. If the jihadis tried to attack us this time, they would need a significant force. The open-topped HUMVEEs had .50 caliber machine-guns mounted at the rear that were effective against light armor at a considerable distance. Although the desert was abloom with delicate springtime flowers and tufts of fresh grass, the flat terrain provided no cover for someone hoping to detonate a roadside bomb. The Kurds would see anyone coming close enough to the road to do us harm and could neutralize them well before we came in range.

"I'm feeling quite comfortable, actually," Msg. Pacelli said as I described the added security to him and Dona as we left the checkpoint. He had squeezed in with us in the back of our ageing BMW so we didn't have to add another car to the convoy. After awhile, he told us more about his trip to al Qosh two days earlier.

"You realize that both of you, by blood, have the right to become Guardians of the Secret Order of St. Hormizd? I may well be the nephew of a former Pope, but that is one thing that will always be beyond me. I am condemned to be just a minor actor in these momentous events—although I happen to believe my small part has its importance. How much do the two of you actually know about the Guardians? About the Secret Book?"

Dona looked at me and shrugged. "We know about St. Peter's Bones. That was in the burnt pages Uncle Andraos left my mother."

"A bit of an embarrassment, that bit," he said. "But I presume Father Shemoun shared my feelings with you in Amman?"

Dona couldn't help giggling, then caught herself. "Yes, he said that you referred to your uncle as 'that idiot Pope.'"

"Ah-hah," Pacelli said, raising his eyebrows. "I fear Shemoun's memory is rather too sharp for his own good."

When Pope Leo IV dispatched the Sacred Relics to the small monastery in al Qosh for safekeeping during the sack of Rome in 846 AD, he knew this was the one place in the world where they would escape the predations of the Muslim empire, because the monks of the Order of St. Hormizd knew dark secrets about the Muslims that gave them power and made them feared. "Besides," he said, "they paid the *jizya* regularly to the Caliph of Baghdad."

There were times when those payments were the only significant revenues of the State Treasury, so the stature of the monks of al Qosh grew. They and the Caliph agreed to keep each other's secrets, and the Order thrived as an island of learning and peace at the very heart of the Muslim empire. Over the centuries, the Muslim memory of the secrets of the Order of St. Hormizd grew dim and eventually vanished. But the monks enshrined their knowledge in the pages of the *Secret Book of the Order of St. Hormizd*, which all members of the Guardians committed to memory. "Remember: the monks' diary is the only real certificate of authenticity that the relics preserved in the monastery at al Qosh are actually the bones of the Prince of Apostles," he said. "Without the chronicle to authenticate the evacuation of the Sacred Relics and their continued care and custodianship, the bones are just those of a man, powerfully built, aged between 65 to 70 at the time of his death—perhaps some local shepherd. Without the diary, the bones are just... well, bones."

But beyond this, the greatest of the secrets contained in the monks' diary—and this was a view Msg. Pacelli insisted was shared by the current Pope—was the account of the true origins of Islam, an experiment in proselytizing by an expanding Church that went dramatically and tragically wrong.

"One doesn't want to insult the legitimate and very sincere faith of hundreds of millions of people," he said. "Indeed, that was what prompted the early Brothers to spread the Gospel into Araby. But what emerged as a result of their good-hearted efforts was a monstrosity, and they recorded in great detail how this happened, as well as their regret. Many of them we are told committed suicide, dying in sin, away from the Lord. That's how deeply they regretted their actions. They felt they deserved to suffer the eternal fires of Hell to atone for what they had done."

There has always been a dialogue between Muslims and Christians, he said. Sometimes that dialogue breaks down, and you have the Crusades. At other times, such as today, a violent sect of Islam attempts a power grab, claiming with some justice that they are merely imitating the actions and original intentions of Mohammad, the self-appointed apostle of Allah. "Remember: Christ exhorted his disciples to keep his true identity secret, so that his actions alone would stir the hearts of men to faith. Mohammad demanded that his followers proclaim him a Prophet. Is that how a true prophet behaves?"

Hundreds of Muslim scholars have pondered the Christian influences on their faith, the "borrowings," they call them at times. And there are many early sources, starting with the great Ibn Ishaq, whose *Life of Muhammad* was based on the living memories of some of the original companions, who acknowledge the first meeting between the Nestorian monk, Bahira, and Muhammad as a young man. Ibn

Ishaq states unequivocally that Muhammad received instruction from his wife's cousin, Waraqa bin Naufal, although he tries to downplay this. "So these things are known and have been a subject of great debate within Islam itself from the very beginning," he said.

On both sides of the Muslim-Christian divide there have always been ecumenists, so-called "moderates" seeking commonalities between these powerful systems of faith and dogma. They would point to the influence of Bahira and Waraqa, and note the many references in the Koran to Abraham and Isaac, Jesus and Mary. But no matter how hard they tried, the ecumenists always ran aground against the hard reality of the Koran itself, which rejects in absolute terms the moral foundations of our faith and the divinity of Our Land. "These differences were recorded in great detail in the early chapters of the Secret Book, which is why the Holy Father and I are so determined to ensure that it be removed safely from al Qosh, where the dangers are great."

Dona asked, "And the Sacred Relics? St. Peter's bones? Don't you want to get them back?"

Msg. Pacelli had been leaning toward us as he was speaking, gesturing with his hands, and now he collapsed back into his seat and folded his hands across his ample belly, encased as it was in the black short-sleeved shirt with the clerical collar. The wiry black hairs of his forearms glistened with sweat. Bassam had given up on the air conditioner and the windows were open.

"Ah yes, the Sacred Relics. It would be nice, I suppose. We'd have some explaining to do, but I imagine the Holy Father could manage it.

Dona persisted. "So I take it, that's not your priority."

Msg. Pacelli sighed. "My dear, what are bones? The Prophet Ezekiel spoke famously of the

Valley of Dry Bones coming back to life, and look at all the trouble that has given us! Who knows what Schisms within the Church would be reopened should we ever admit that the Sacred Relics had not been in Rome all these years? I care much more about these scrolls, it is true. Why? Because the Word is the living breath of God in all its power and glory. This is what St. Paul was alluding to in his letter to the Ephesians, chapter 5, when he talked about 'the sword of the spirit, which is the word of God.' These words, I can assure you, have more power than a thousand swords, than a thousand armies. They are legions of light crafted to defeat the darkness."

As they had done before, the peshmerga left us at the checkpoint leading into Karamlesh and parked their vehicles to await our return. Three of the village guards jumped into a ramshackle Suzuki jeep, and in a whirl of dust led us into the center of town where Jamal, the ADM chief and defacto mayor, was waiting to welcome us with a crowd of notables just beyond the broken Jersey barriers that blocked the street. Jamal was wearing a cheap Turkish suit of some indiscriminate color that seemed to blend in with the dust, and was giving orders to a small crowd of young men who scurried off in different directions as we pulled up. Just down the street, people were milling around before the tall green doors of St. Paul's cathedral, their magnificent crosses in filigreed iron work guarding the entry like sentinels. Jamal waved for the village guards in front of the ADM office to open the doors of our vehicles, and when he saw Governor Aiken he came to greet him. I was never reassured by the village guards, and even less so today. Most of them carried their AK-47s by the stock of the barrel, as if they had just picked it up in haste. Those who used the shoulder strap had their fingers curled on the trigger. Most of them wore sandals and carried extra magazines in web gear dangling from their shoulders, unbuckled.

"This is the protection Minister Korekjan gives us," I said to Msg. Pacelli. "Even the Jersey barriers are second-hand. We get what was blown up some place else. We need a professional police force like we have up in al Qosh. Not these jokers."

"Patience, young man. Everything in its own time," he said. Then he adjusted his collar and got out.

I did the interpretation between Jamal and the Governor, with Dona whispering to Mr. Utz and Msg. Pacelli the bits they didn't hear, then we moved across the street to where a large metal-ribbed tent had been set up to protect people from the midday sun during the food distribution. The dingy grey tent was long and narrow, like an aircraft hanger. Already there were so many people that the spillover crowd was seated on cheap plastic chairs out in the direct sun in the rock-strewn lot beyond the tent. Behind them, the broken stone walls of Sargon's ancient fortress jutted up like the rubble of a bombed out house, a reminder of our glorious Assyrian past and the misery of our present condition.

"Why has the town never restored the fortress," Dona whispered, "with so many people unemployed?"

Only an American could ask such a question, and I admired Dona for it. In so many ways she was like Rita, always looking forward, always the optimist, whereas we were mired in the swamp of history and oppression.

"Look, there's Marco!"

My brother was standing near the official entrance to the tent, where a makeshift sign handwritten in red and blue block letters announced the feeding program jointly sponsored by the ADM and Christians United, Mr. Utz's group.

"*B'shena, Rabi,*" Dona said, holding out her hand.

She could have kissed him on both cheeks, because he was that much younger, but I saw that she was authenticating him, showing her recognition of his adulthood, his manhood. As he reached forward to take her hand, his faded denim shirt rose slightly and I could see that he had tucked a Glock 19 beneath his belt. So Marco was working for the Mayor.

"Keep your eyes out, Marco," I said. "You'll be the only one who sees anything with these *qahbuta*...."

He nodded curtly, showing no sign of emotion, and continued to survey the gathering crowd coolly from behind his sunglasses, but I could sense his pride and I was happy for him. Marco had found his place as a guardian, just like Baba, protector of the innocent, sentinel against the evil one.

My mother, Hannah, was running the registration table inside, checking off people as they arrived and giving each one a large red circular stick-on badge, their ticket for the food distribution. She had on her reading glasses and her cheeks seemed hollow, a visible blemish of Rita's kidnapping.

"*Yimaa!*" I shouted and waved.

She stood up when she saw us and burst into a smile, and we pushed through the crowd pressing in on us on all sides until we reached the table. "This is Damreena—the one I have been telling you about."

I said that for Dona's benefit, of course, but my mother just rolled her eyes playfully and beckoned for Dona to embrace her.

"Look at you, brata. A lawyer, brought up in America! Coming back here to the gates of Hell to help your people. Thank-you," she said.

She was holding Dona's two hands in her own and looking at her, and smiling, as if the crowd with the jostling and the shouting and the crying babies and the barked orders simply ceased to exist. I saw a tear well up in Dona's eye, and automatically she raised a hand to brush it away. But Mama caught her hand and brushed it away herself.

"Now, let's go to work. Yohannes, you need to handle the rice," she said.

She pointed to a stack of 12 kilogram sacks of basmati rice piled on the ground at the end of the table, next to large plastic bags packed with canned food, oil, and pasta. I looked for Mr. Utz, to ask him how he wanted to handle the distribution, but he and Governor Aiken were leaning over an old woman at the far end of the tent, apparently praying.

"I don't know what her story is," Mr. Utz said when we joined them. "I can't understand a word she is saying. But you really don't need to, do you?"

Governor Aiken had taken the old woman's gnarled hands in his own and was praying with her quietly. But she was looking up at us and at Mr. Utz, imploring, wisps of grey hair escaping from beneath her black shawl, her eyes gone red from weeping. She was mumbling and I had to lean close to her to understand what she was saying.

"See how my eyes are closed from weeping," she said. "I cannot see because I am crying all day, from the moment the sun comes up until it goes down at night. All of them are dead. All of them are dead.

There's only me. Where can I go? I have no one. Help me, dear sir. Please help me."

They prayed with her, and Dona asked her questions to learn her story. Her name was Noneh Toma. She was 74, but looked at least ten years older than that. She came from the Hay al Amil district in Baghdad. The terrorists kidnapped her son and then her husband and killed both of them when she couldn't raise the ransom money they demanded. Then they came to her house, carried off her possessions, and forced her to leave. She had wanted to stay because she was old, but the Americans told her she had to leave because they couldn't protect her.

"Governor, I think it's time," Mr. Utz said, standing up. He pointed back toward the registration table, where Jamal was testing a microphone.

We all went back up to the head table, and Jamal made a brief presentation, welcoming our guests from America and thanking them for their generous help. "Everyone in this tent is a proud Iraqi, a proud Assyrian," he said. "We don't take handouts. We can take care of ourselves. You all know this. But this is special. This is sharing from the people of America to the people of Iraq. This comes from Americans who want to give something back to us for all we have suffered."

Most of the hundred or so people inside the tent were women. Many had small children on their laps. There were proud faces, desperate faces, joyous faces, and souls that were shrouded in darkness. I looked for the village guards outside, but I couldn't see them, perhaps because of the crowd. But Marcos was on point, guarding the entryway. His hands were crossed in front of him, pointing to the ground, and I could see that he had taken out the Glock 19. Careful.

Cautious. Respectful of the weapon and of the people in the crowd.

Now it was the turn of Governor Aiken to speak, and I had to translate. He explained that he and Mr. Utz had made an earlier trip to Iraq last fall, then returned to America where they told the story of how Iraqi Christians were suffering and persecuted. This allowed them to raise the money they needed for the food parcels they would be distributing today.

"The Bible tells us that as believers in Jesus we are all part of the body of Christ. So even though we live far away and you may not have seen us before, we are closely attached to you as one spiritual body," he said. It was a repeat of the speech he had given in Baghdeda, but as I listened to him and translated this time, I felt there was a difference. After hearing the story of the old woman, and his prayers over her, his words had a new meaning, even for me.

"St. Paul teaches us that when one part of the body suffers, the rest of the body suffers with it. So there are people in far away countries like the United States who have felt your suffering and have provided funds for us so we can come here and provide these food parcels. And when we leave here, we will share the news of your sufferings with them. And we hope that the body of Christ will respond as a healthy body and come to your assistance, not just with humanitarian aid, but with political help, to create the conditions that will enable you to go back to your homes or to live in peace and security in some other part of Iraq where you have friends and relatives."

People never stopped talking as the Governor was speaking, but he spoke evenly, sentence by sentence so I could translate his words, and didn't seem to mind the general commotion. I guess he knew that his words would be heard where it was important. A few people applauded politely when he finished, and then we all moved to the food distribution area, and people started lining up to get their parcels.

Just then, I heard Marcos shouting outside. "*Enee, tamewat!*" he called out to some woman. "You there! Go around. *Tlup m'tama!*"

I turned my head just in time to see a woman dressed all in black, wearing a very un-Christian veil, about twenty meters away from Marcos. She had been approaching across the now-empty dirt lot, and when he shouted she started to run in his direction. My mother was seated behind the registration table, and Dona was leaning over her, checking the names. I shouted "Bomb!" and lifted the edge of the table and threw it on top of them and pushed them toward the far wall. I shouted "Get down!" in English and Swadaya, and threw myself at the Governor and Mr. Utz. Just as the three of us were tumbling over the mountain of rice into the cans of food and oil, I heard Marcos firing the Glock 19 and an instant later the explosion hit with a blinding flash that seemed to come from everywhere all at once. The blast deafened me momentarily. My hands gripped something wet and I felt bits of rock and dirt slam into my back and then heavy pieces of hot metal as the armature of the tent came down on top of us. In the next instant, I felt Governor Aiken and Mr. Utz start to move. "Stay down!" I shouted, or at least, I think I shouted. I still couldn't hear anything. "There could be another one."

Although it was midday, the cloud of dust kicked up by the bomb was so thick I could barely see the Governor or Mr. Utz, let alone anything beyond them. But a few moments later, my hearing started to come back and I heard Bassam's voice calling my name. Bits of tenting caught on the remains of the metal armature were burning all around us.

"Are you okay?" I asked the Governor. He rolled over, and blood was streaming down from his nose and forehead, apparently from where I had pushed him into the food tins on the ground.

"Oh, Lordy," he said. "What was that?"

Mr. Utz groped forward with his hands, and finding something solid, pushed himself up and rolled over. And then he sat up quickly and peered an instant into the dust cloud and bounded to his feet. "Somebody's got to help these people," he said, and rushed off and began pulling people from under tables and metal beams and burning canvas. I shouted out to Bassam, and he found us and got the Governor to his feet and started to rush him outside.

"What about Marcos?" I asked him.

"He went down. *Bas qtille masilana*—But he shot the bomber. It couldn't have been a woman."

By now, people were screaming. I saw the hole outside in the lot where the suicider dressed as a woman had blown himself up, but no sign of the bomber—or of Marcos. I ran back inside, pushing against coughing and screaming people, frantic to get out, until I saw the table I had upended on my mother and Dona, the legs shorn off but otherwise intact.

"Yimaa?" I shouted "Dona?"

Hearing nothing, I grabbed both sides of the table and pulled, gently at first, trying to lift it away. Mr. Utz saw me and came over and helped me clear it away. I recognized Dona from her tunic, but her hair had gone completely white and her face was caked in a thick white paste. Beneath her I saw pieces of my mother. Dona opened her eyes and looked up at me, but she seemed only half-conscious and barely registered my presence.

"Flour," Mr. Utz said, as he pulled gently on her arms, trying to free them from the debris.

"What"?

"Flour. We had sacks of flour in the food parcels."

Mr. Utz got her legs free and then started to lift her up. I could feel the heat from the burning canvas all around us. "Look, I don't know if she's got internal injuries, but if we don't get her out of here now we might not have enough time to find out."

He cradled Dona's limp body in his arms and started to back out of the wreckage, finding his way outside.

Now I could see Yimaa. She was lying on her side, hands covering her face, and now, with the weight of the table and Dona's body off her, she began gasping for breath and coughing violently. Her hands went out to her sides, groping. She tried to move, and groaned.

I managed to roll her over onto her back. She opened her eyes for an instant, then began wiping feverishly at the dust. Finally she looked at me.

"Marco?" she said.

"He did it, Mama. He shot the bomber. Marco did it."

She knew that he was dead, I am sure, for she said nothing more. She just stared up at the burning canvas as tears filled her eyes and began to run down her face.

"I'm going to carry you outside, Mama," I said. "Don't try to move until we get you outside."

People were rushing in all directions. Some were pushing their way into the wreckage, looking for loved ones, while the survivors who could still move were struggling past them to get away. I heard sirens rend the air in the distance like helicopter blades and start to come our way, punctuated by bursts of heavy machine-gun fire. That must be our peshmerga escort, I thought. Where were they when we needed them?

Bassam was herding everyone from our delegation into the cars. His men had cleared the street and were now guarding it in full battle dress, their AK-47s at the ready, but like the peshmerga, they were too late. No one had noticed the black-clothed woman emerge from the back street from inside the town, merge with the crowd, then break free into the open lot by the tent. The woman who was of course a man.

A pair of ambulances arrived, and medics jumped out with stretchers. Men from the village had already begun laying out the dead in a row by Sargon's fortress. Most of them had been seated in the open area outside the tent. The medics tried to find the living and triage those with major wounds who could still be saved. I got Yimaa onto one of the stretchers and said goodbye. I couldn't believe how thin she had become. Her body felt like wadded paper through her clothes.

"They will take care of you, Yimaa. You're going to be fine."

I gave her a kiss and brushed her cheek with the back of my hand.

"Come back for the funeral, Yohannes. Promise?"

"Yes, Yimaa. I will."

"Yohannes?" She closed her eyes for an instant, fighting either pain or emotion, I don't know.

"What, Mama?"

"The angel of death passes at his will. We can never know when. So you must always be prepared."

10

Tuesday

Before heading back to Karamlesh for the funeral, I met with LTC Wilkens in his suite at the Erbil Sheraton early on Tuesday morning. My ears were still ringing from the explosion, but worse than that was the burning in my heart. It licked at my insides with a fiery tongue, it hollowed me out as with a dragon's breath. Col. Wilkens wrapped his arm around my shoulder and offered his condolences for my brother's death.

"Your brother was a good shot," he said. "Our guys saw the police report from Mosul. They found a piece of ceramic body armor. We've never seen the jihadis use body armor before. By coincidence, it's the same type that Triple Shield has been selling the Kurds."

"A .45 would have knocked him to the ground."

"Correct. But your brother hit the bomber four times. Even with a 9 mm, four hits to the chest will take any man down."

"I should have gotten him a .45."

"You can't blame yourself, Johnny. Be proud of your brother. Honor his memory. Without him, dozens more people would have died."

Wilkens asked if he could join us for the funeral.

"What about your security?" I asked.

"I don't think we'll have much to worry about
on that score today," he said. "I understand that Task
Force Lightning, 25h Infantry, Mosul is going to
button things up tight."

At the KRG checkpoint into no-man's land, I
understood what he meant. A half-dozen HUMVEE
gun trucks were waiting for us, manned by U.S. troops
from the 2-27th Infantry, not peshmerga. Armed OH-
58D Kiowa Warrior helicopters were patrolling the
road from overhead. They accompanied us all the way
to Karamlesh, which had been cordoned off by several
dozen more U.S. troops. The Americans with their
body armor and ceramic knee pads and helmet mikes
were patrolling the streets of the town as well.

I traveled with Rita and Dona in the BMW,
and we were silent for most of the two hour drive.
Rita just stared out the window the whole way, and I
could not read her thoughts. Dona held her hand and
smiled at me whenever I caught her eye. Without
Dona's presence, I think both of us would have been
lost, numb with the pain, silenced by the inner voices
whose whispering roamed from guilt to revenge to
despair.

The entire town was in the street for the
funeral procession to St. Paul's. The only on-lookers
were the TV crews and the U.S. soldiers posted at
every cross street and alleyway and on rooftops
overhead. The broken yellow Jersey barriers had been
removed. We filed past the bomb site in silence, a
priest waving a censor full of smoking incense that
mingled with the pungent odor of burning garbage
that blew in from the edge of town. People had

strewn flowers all over the vacant lot that were already wilting in the midday heat. The wind had blown some of them into the wreckage of the tent and across the alleyway into the ruins of Sargon's fortress. A single bell from St. Paul's rang eighteen times, once for the soul of each victim.

Inside the church, the eighteen coffins were closed, because many of them did not contain complete bodies. I'm not even sure how much of Marcos they eventually found, but his coffin was the only one draped in the Assyrian flag. The others were covered in white or yellow linen. Col. Wilkens went ahead of me in the line of mourners, and I watched as he took something from his pocket, kissed it, and pinned it to the flag on Marco's coffin. It was a golden star suspended from a v-shaped ribbon of red, white and blue. The star was stamped with a laurel wreath, at the center of which was a raised silver star.

"I earned it here in your country a few years ago," Col. Wilkens told me when we returned to our pew. "It's called the Silver Star. Marco may not have been a member of the U.S. military, but he earned it. Believe me."

I translated for Hannah, who was waiting for us in the aisle in a wheelchair. She had broken her lower leg and was bruised all over, but other than that, she was okay.

"You are a good man," she said to Col. Wilkens, taking his hands in hers. "Marcos wanted to become like you."

Now came the time for the speeches. I wasn't sure I was ready for them, but translating them for Col. Wilkens and Msg. Pacelli took my mind off what was being said. Dona did as best she could for Mr. Utz and Governor Aiken, who were sitting right behind us. A large bandage covered the lacerations on the Governor's right cheek where I had pushed him into the food tins. Many people in the pews also had fresh bandages.

After the priest bade eternal rest upon their souls, Mayor Jamal addressed the townspeople.

"Eighteen of our brothers and sisters have been taken from us. Eighteen of our flesh and blood. Father Raymond wants you to believe that God has called them back to him. But you know that I don't know very much about that."

At the back of the church someone chuckled quietly, then caught themselves. Jamal gave them a dirty look, then went on.

"But I do know what happened yesterday. "The peshmerga who oppress us every day with their presence, who steal our ballot boxes, who harass our young people, where were they? They say they must occupy our towns and villages for our security. So where were they when we needed protection? I'll tell you where they were. They were sitting in their air-conditioned Suburbans drinking tea with their lackeys, the so-called village guards."

He cited the discovery by the police from Mosul yesterday of the ceramic body armor from the bomber, and demanded that the central government open an investigation into the bombing to determine if the Kurds had foreknowledge of the attack. The church erupted with murmurs of agreement and shuffling feet.

Then Rita got up to speak.

She began quietly, remembering Marcos as a child, her hands folded in front of her, looking down at the stone tiles. She remembered his laughter; she remembered his pranks. When he was just one year old, during the war with Iran, he got into the kitchen in the house in Dora and discovered Nana Soraya's cache of chocolates. When Rita discovered him, he was sitting on the brick tiles, a huge grin on his face, his face and hands and even his clothes covered in the gooey mess, as he sucked his fingers to get that last bit of chocolate before she snatched him away.

As a teenager, he always wanted to be older than his years and to fight for his people. "When the Americans liberated our country, Marcos was just 18. But he was one of the first men from Karamlesh who volunteered to help them discover where the Baathist strongholds were located in the Mosul area. Baba and Yimaa were terrified, because he disappeared for nearly a week."

So that's what he had been doing, I thought. I hadn't known that, and he never explained where he had gone in those heady early days of the Liberation when the rest of us were down in Dora.

"Now Marcos has shown us what it means to be an Assyrian man," she said.

She looked out at the townspeople defiantly, no longer broken by her own pain. Some of the old fire had returned to her eyes.

"Where are you, my Assyrian manhood!" she said, her voice rising now. "Will you stand up right here, right now, to defend your mothers and sisters? We need dozens of Marco's, in every Assyrian town and village. Will you stand up and defend us?"

She dared us. That's what she was doing. She was actually daring us to stand up right there in the church, shaming us if we did not. I looked back to Dona and she encouraged me. I stood up.

For a moment, the church remained entirely silent. Then gradually, as I stood there, feeling the stares of the entire town at my back, I heard shuffling in the pews behind me as other men rose to their feet.

"Let Marco's death be the beginning, not the end," Rita said.

She fell silent, holding on to the moment, and turned her gaze toward each man who had come to his feet, nodding, approving, encouraging. We were her Legion. We were her Warriors.

"O my Assyrian manhood," she said finally. "Show me your valor! Show me what you are worth!"

I caught a glimpse of Hannah next to me in her wheelchair. She had buried her face in her hands.

By the time we got back to Erbil, it was almost dark. Rita had stayed behind in Karamlesh to take care of Hannah, and I am sure the two of them had words over Rita's fiery speech in the church. I knew the arguments, because I had heard them so many times. We must accept our lot of suffering and prepare for the rewards in the Kingdom of Heaven. How could our suffering begin to compare to that of the Savior who had died to redeem our sins? But Rita would have none of it. She was all here and now. Will and determination. Courage, strength, struggle. Turning the other cheek might be fine as a matter of personal ethics, but not as an expression of political will.

Col. Wilkens texted me awhile later to join him in his suite. When I arrived, Mojo and Deron were adjusting their combat gear and Col. Wilkens was checking the laser aiming device he had attached onto the slide of a Beretta M9. Capt. Stewart shut the door behind me. Wilkens handed me the pistol and a shoulder holster.

"Put this on under your jacket," he said. "Hopefully, we're not going to need it, but better be prepared."

"Where are we going?" I asked him.

"Cory Reed has set up a rendezvous in the desert. I want to make sure we have insurance coverage."

Richie, the accountant, was seated in the sofa, toying with a pair of Beretta handguns. He was going to remain behind. "I'm going to blast anything that comes through that door," he said.

"Keep the safeties on so you don't hurt yourself," Capt. Stewart said.

We piled into two dark blue Suburbans. I rode with LTC Wilkens in the first car, with Mojo riding shotgun up front, while Capt. Stewart rode in the second Suburban with Deron. Mr. Reed was waiting for us in his white Jeep Cherokee on Government road. They had pulled up on the sidewalk by the Finance ministry. I recognized his driver, Dindar, from when I worked at Triple Shield. He was my age, and came from a formerly Christian village about an hour to the north. He had a thick black moustache and an easy, shy grin. He was chatting with the ministry guards when we drove up.

Our driver flashed his lights, and Dindar and the Triple Shield chase car pulled out in front of us. At the intersection they turned west toward the amusement park, taking the main road into the desert. Around forty-five minutes later we reached the final KRG checkpoint and the beginning of no man's land. I was nervous.

"It's dark," I said to Col. Wilkens. "How much further are we going?"

He turned around, and together we watched the lights from the checkpoint grow smaller in the distance.

"We're stopping here," he said.

He had the driver flash his lights, but Mr. Reed apparently had the same idea and was already pulling over to the side of the road. We could just barely see the light from the checkpoint behind us. We all got out and went up to Reed's car.

"Phone your guy," Col. Wilkens said. "One car, that's it."

Dindar took out the walkie-talkie strapped to his web gear, adjusted the frequency, and said something into it in Kurdish.

A few seconds later the set crackled, and I heard a familiar voice speaking Arabic through the static. "*Ya Kurdi, sharmouta*! I will cut off the tips of your fingers and grind them into hummus."

Involuntarily, I clenched my fists and ground my teeth. When I turned to Col. Wilkens I could tell that he had recognized the voice as well. "It's him," I said.

"What did he say?" Mr. Reed asked nervously, since Dindar didn't speak Arabic.

"It wasn't very polite. He murdered my brother."

"What are you talking about?"

"Yesterday. In Karamlesh."

"I thought your brother was in Amman."

"Yeah, well I was there, too. So were Governor Aiken and the Americans."

"Enough," Col. Wilkens said. "Tell him to flash his lights and come forward in one car."

Dindar handed me the walkie-talkie and I was tempted to throw it out into the cold desert night. If I did anything with Saddoun, it should be to place the bead of the laser on his forehead and shoot him.

"Translate, please," Wilkens said softly.

A few seconds later we saw a pair of headlights flash out in the desert to the south, and then we heard the sound of a vehicle approaching us in the darkness. Deron and Mojo had shouldered their M-4 carbines and switched on their night vision scopes. Capt. Stewart scanned the desert to our north with a pair of night vision goggles just in case.

"Turn the cars around," Col. Wilkens told our driver.

A sliver of moon provided just enough light to see the outline of objects at about thirty meters. The night had cooled quickly, and the wind was blowing dust and plastic bags across the desert. A Toyota pick-up emerged from the darkness and came to a halt. Despite the cold, I unbuttoned my denim jacket and slipped my hand inside so I could feel the butt of the pistol. Col. Wilkens saw me, and laid a hand gently but firmly on my forearm.

"Tell him to come forward," he said. "Anyone with him?" he asked Mojo.

"Not that I can see, sir."

A lone figure began walking toward us across the desert. He was dressed like a Bedouin in a long dirty *dishdash* and checkered *keffiyeh*. He was holding his hands in front of him so we could see he was not carrying a weapon, although he wore a revolver in a holster slung from a belt at his waist and carried AK magazines in a web harness slung over his shoulders. Col. Wilkens nodded to Deron and he moved forward in a crouch toward the approaching figure. The man stopped, smirking as Deron unholstered his pistol and patted him down. I could now see his narrow reptilian eyes, and they bore into me for an instant, recognizing me. I returned his gaze, and he must have seen the hatred in my eyes, because he cocked his head, as if noting something new. Deron stood up and nodded to us. "All clear, sir," he said.

"We meet again, Colonel," Saddoun al-Adnan said. "You come to my country with your men in arms and yet you still fear the darkness. Look at me: I thrive in the dark. I will be here long after you leave."

"Cut the speeches and talk to us," Cory Reed said nervously. "You're the one who wanted this meeting."

"That's correct. I wanted to tell you that my men were not responsible for what happened yesterday at Karamlesh."

He looked at me cautiously, noting the bulge of the M9 beneath my jacket, then squatted down on his haunches and began smoothing away the desert dust with a hand. Col. Wilkens knew this was a gesture not of submission but of parlay, and squatted down as well. The rest of us remained standing.

"I had my men investigate," Saddoun went on, glancing up at me. "You know about the ceramic plate?"

Col. Wilkens nodded.

"The Resistance doesn't have such things. I believe you know this. I have brought you a list of names."

He pointed to a pocket inside his clothing, and Wilkens nodded his assent. He fished for the paper and extended it to Wilkens, who looked at it momentarily then handed it to me. The names were written in Arabic, but they were all Kurds. I started to read them out and then I exploded.

"You!" I bellowed at Mr. Reed.

The flesh of Mr. Reed's face fell into folds of denial, quivering with fear. "They can't be Kurds," he said.

"You killed my brother!"

The anger swept over me as I have never felt it in my life, filling my veins and my muscles with raw energy. I swung my fist at him and connected with the soft flesh of his jaw, sending him skittering into the darkness. Reed's Kurdish bodyguards went for their weapons, but Dindar gave a slight shake of his head and they backed off. I haven't done something like that since I was eighteen and a gang of Muslim toughs cornered Marco one day after school in Dora, demanding that he give them money.

Col. Wilkens put his hand on my shoulder. "Stay focused."

"I swear I didn't know," Reed said, getting up, nursing his jaw.

All of a sudden he appeared pitiful to me, and I saw him for the first time: overweight, pretentious, protected all of his life, ordering other people to do his dirty work, hiding behind veils of secrecy and denial. He was a maggot, feeding on dead flesh. He deserved a maggot's end.

Wilkens gave me a hard look, but he didn't try to stop me. I don't know what he would have done if I had hit Reed again, but as I looked at him I felt the anger begin to drain away. I dropped my fists and turned back to Saddoun, who was drawing lines in the desert with a finger, watching us carefully. Wilkens crouched down again and met his eyes.

"Why?" he said finally.

"I could give you other names if you prefer. But those are the real ones. Hasn't Mr. Reed told you about our arrangement."

Reed looked terrified now, but there was nowhere for him to escape. He came toward us slowly, wedged between the two Kurdish bodyguards, staying as far away from me as he could, and handed Saddoun a large manila envelope that had been folded over several times. Saddoun unfolded it, bent back the metal tabs and looked inside. I could see a wad of U.S. currency. Saddoun judged his payment by its thickness, then folded it back up and stuffed it inside his *dishdash*.

"There's something else," he said, tracing a long curving line in dust. "The Emir of Jihad is determined to destroy Mar Hormizd. He has become obsessed with this. Some days it is all he will talk about. I told him that manuscript was a forgery and it put him off for awhile. But three weeks ago he returned from a lengthy visit to Mashhad, where he met with a senior Iranian religious authority. This ayatollah, this *mullah*"—he spoke the words with derision—"told him that it was authentic, and that scholars had known since the beginning that Mohammad had received instruction from a Christian monk. This knowledge was shared only with the *marjah*, the highest religious authorities. It was not for ordinary Muslims to know."

Wilkens was looking him in the eyes, trying to gauge whether he was telling the truth. "When?" he asked finally.

"We have learned there will be an announcement this Sunday. Our sources tell us that the Abbot plans to make a public declaration. The attack will happen before then."

Wilkens looked at him coldly. He said, "You're lying. You know exactly when it will happen."

Saddoun was now crossing the lines he had drawn in the sand and continued as if he hadn't heard what Wilkens had just said.

"The Emir of the so-called Islamic State of Iraq has chosen only foreign jihadis for this operation. He suspects that Iraqis will not agree to destroy such a target. It is part of our history, our heritage." A note of contempt crept into his voice. "We are not like those donkeys in Afghanistan who blew up the Bamyan Buddhas."

He erased the lines he had been drawing and got up. "That is the best I can tell you," he said.

Wilkens nodded to Mojo to return his pistol, and with just a nod—no shaking of hands—Saddoun left us and merged back into the night.

Without waiting for him to reach the pick-up, Wilkens ordered us all to mount up. Cory Reed tried to take Wilkens by the arm. "I didn't know about the Kurds," he was blubbering. "Honest. I didn't know." Wilkens shrugged him off and got into the idling Suburban.

"Punch it," he told the driver.

11

Wednesday

Our KRG Foreign Ministry minder, Nijyar, was not pleased when Governor Aiken informed him at breakfast that the delegation had decided to extend its stay for a few days because of the bombing in Karamlesh. He was even less pleased when he learned of our plans for the day. I sympathized with him; he was just doing his job, which was to make sure that these Americans came and went without making waves. While I couldn't understand more than a few words of Kurdish, it was clear that his bosses back at the Ministry were furious.

"Your Excellency," he said to Gov. Aiken, holding out the phone and letting his boss vent. "It is much too dangerous for you to go to al Qosh. We tried to discourage you from the beginning from going to the Nineveh Plain, but you insisted on the food distribution."

He heard something that made him put the phone back to his ear. Then he held it away again. "We don't control al Qosh. They've got some kind of local police force. We can give no guarantee for your safety."

Governor Aiken rubbed his cheek just below the bandage. "With all due respect, Nijyar, it seems to me your guarantees aren't worth a whole heck of a lot."

Nijyar went into full damage control mode. "Governor, you can't say that. It's not fair. The bomber was dressed as a woman. We've never seen this before. We don't have suicide bombers here in Kurdistan."

Gary Utz turned to the Governor and shook his head. "Well, you do now," he muttered beneath his breath.

Msg. Pacelli jumped in, the diplomat. "Our security team has already checked the route up to the north. If you could just coordinate with the peshmerga, I'm sure everything will be fine. We'll stay in KRG territory right up until the outskirts of town."

Nijyar was doing his best, but realized he was losing this battle. "Really, Governor," he protested again.

"You're not trying to tell me, Brother Nijyar, that the KRG doesn't even control its own territory."

"No no, of course not."

At the next table, the Austrians from the state-owned oil company were just finishing their breakfast and didn't look up as we left.

As promised, we took a different road into the Nineveh Plain. Instead of driving west toward Mosul, we headed due north on the road to Alqrah and Dohuk, crossing the Greater Zab River at a point far to the north of the danger zone. It added about an hour to our journey, but this route took us out of the desert into the empty rolling hills of the Nineveh Plain. There was not a tree in sight all the way up to the rock-strewn mountains that formed the beginnings of the border with Turkey. Just a vast expanse of fertile land tinged with rich waves of green and yellow, the beginnings of early wheat. It was so peaceful you could almost forget the evil beast biding its time just a few miles away.

We had a full convoy. The Kurds led in one Suburban, followed by Bassam, the head of our security team, and a car full of armed guards. Msg. Pacelli followed in a separate car, then the Governor and Gary Utz. I rode with Dona. Behind us was another Suburban full of peshmergas. We had ten guards of our own, all Assyrian Christians, mostly from Baghdad. Some of them had mounted M203 grenade launchers on the rail beneath the barrel of their M4 carbines, giving them added firepower. I felt less apprehensive than on other days because we had told no one about our route.

"You've changed, Yohannes," Dona said. "Something in you has—hardened, I'd say. I don't know if I like you more, or less."

We were in the back seat, each sitting by a window, lost in thought, gazing at the landscape. Now I saw that she had been looking at me, trying to read my soul. I forced a smile.

"It's been a hard week."

Her fingers reached across the seat and took my hand. "I didn't mean it like that. I'm sorry. You and Marco were so close."

"We weren't, really. At least, I didn't think so."

"Rita was magnificent in the church. So strong."

"It's not enough to be strong. We also need to be armed. Force is the only thing that counts in this God-forsaken country. Force and the money to corrupt weak souls."

"You know that's not true, Yohannes."

"Do I?"

"There is also love. Love carries no ledger of wrongs. That's what St. Paul said."

"You're not going to get me to forgive my enemy."

"I'm asking you to forgive your friends."

I looked at her questioningly, unsure of what she meant.

"I can't always follow you on your journey. I don't know what you are thinking. But try me," she said. "Share a little. Open your heart. I feel it closing."

I should have felt joy at what she was saying. But she was right: a certain hardness had come over me. How could I open my heart when the future only brought pain? Even though we shared a similar heritage, Dona came from a different world from the one that I inhabited. She could always disengage and return to America and pretend that none of this had ever happened. Increasingly I felt the distance between our two worlds, as wide as the real ocean that separated them.

"Remember what you said about your mother? How she carried loss around with her like the stench of an old wood fire?"

She bit her lip and nodded.

"Is that really what you want me to share with you?"

"Try me, Yohannes."

She leaned closer to me and brushed my lips with her own, then kissed me fully until our tongues met and danced with eager delight.

"Try me."

The road snaked lazily through the lush farmland leading to the entry of al Qosh at the foot of the barren mountain, which loomed above us almost white in the midday sun. The checkpoint was patrolled by men in Iraqi police uniforms. They spoke Aramaic to the Kurds, and then Arabic, which made the Kurds furious. Hajyar had to calm the head of the peshmerga security detail, who had gotten out of the lead Suburban and drawn his sidearm. He was shouting in Kurdish and making gestures of insult to the police, waving his pistol, shaking it at them, stomping around. Finally, he got back in and the two Suburbans full of peshmerga sped off down the road, sirens blazing and blue lights flashing.

Bassam was chuckling as the Kurds drove away. He introduced me to Captain Al-Mekdesi, the head of the al Qosh police detail.

"B'sheyna rabi," he said, extending his hand to me. "Welcome to the Nineveh Plain."

We chatted for a few minutes, then got directions from him to the Monastery. I was thrilled to see Assyrian Christians manning the checkpoint, wearing the Iraqi uniform. It gave me a feeling of pride I hadn't felt for a long time. "This is what we need," I said to Dona emphatically.

The road circled around the outskirts of town, and then began to climb up the barren rock cliffs in a series of switchbacks, gradually narrowing as we climbed higher above the vast green plains and approached the ancient fortress of Mar Hormizd. You could understand the thinking of the monks who initially built this place in the 7th century, hollowing the first chapel out of solid rock. With the mountain at their back, and a view over the plain that extended for tens of kilometers, they could see danger approaching in time to prepare their defense. While their isolation didn't always protect them, and the Monastery had been attacked many times over the centuries, it did ensure their survival. You could see ruins from earlier parts of the complex crumbling into the hillside beneath the tall, imposing fortifications that protected the prayer cells and chapels inside. The open windows looked like cave openings dug out of the cliff.

The heavy wooden gates in the outer wall stood open and gave onto a large courtyard paved with diamond-shaped tiles that formed a washboard pattern leading to the archways of the graceful colonnade of the main building. Father Charbel was expecting our arrival, and was waiting for us. He was a great wild boar of a man, dressed in the simple brown cassock of the Order, his closely-cropped white hair standing straight up like bristles. He towered over the other monks with him, and wore the great sword of the Guardians with its jeweled handle in the form of an Orthodox cross. Despite the grisly beard and the forearms that seemed as solid as another man's thigh, he reminded me a bit of Father Shemoun. He had the same thick nose and low forehead, and the same dark blue eyes that sparkled with humor. He and Msg. Pacelli exchanged greetings in Latin, then embraced. The Monsignor stroked his cheek, prickled by Father Charbel's whiskers.

"My Italian fuzz," he said, addressing all of us. And then he gave a great laugh and stuck out his hand, which was large and rough from labor, to Governor Aiken and Mr. Utz. When he came to me and Dona, he addressed us in Aramaic. "Welcome to you, children of the Order. Consider this your home."

A narrow, tall archway led through the first set of buildings into an open-roofed cloister. We followed Father Charbel beneath the arches, which were cool and a bit damp in contrast to the hot sun out in the courtyard. A fountain in the center of the cloister reinforced the coolness with the sound of running water. At the far end, Father Charbel stooped and inserted a large iron key into a massive lock. We all had to stoop to make it through the low door. This was his office, and we crowded in to sit on simple wooden chairs to take refreshments while he told us about the Monastery and himself.

"Some of you may have heard of the Prophet Nahum," he said, as a brother brought in trays of coffee and sweet tea and dry cookies. "He was an al-Qoshite, said to be among the first Hebrews brought out of Israel by the Assyrians, well before the fall of Jerusalem. Although he prophesied against them, the Assyrians left him and his brethren in peace. Today, of course, the tables have turned and the woes Nahum predicted have indeed befallen the children of Assyria. We don't believe that our oppressors will behave toward us with the same equanimity the Assyrians showed the Hebrews in Nahum's time. And that is why I am so pleased to welcome all of you here today."

Father Charbel's family emigrated to Lebanon from Al Qosh during the Genocide and remained there for three generations. They were of the Abouna clan, which explained the resemblance I thought I had detected between him and Father Shemoun.

"You know, the British joke that their royals must beget an heir and a spare," he said. "With us, given the rules of our semi-hereditary Order, it's the same. There must be a male heir to supply the Abouna family line, and a spare who is eligible to become Abbot of the Guardians of the Order of St. Hormizd. I did my best as a young man in Lebanon to break the succession, but apparently the Good Lord had other plans for me. Because the two of you are descended from Guardians through the female line, you cannot become Abbot. But you can join the Order."

Dona was thrilled when she heard this, but I couldn't help thinking of what Father Shemoun had told me about my grandfather, Issa. The Abbot must have noticed my doubts.

"I'm not talking about that grandfather of yours who never took the vows," he said quietly. "His mother, Soraya, didn't seek shelter in al Qosh by accident after her husband was murdered in Tabriz during the Genocide. Her uncle, whose name was Marcos, was a Guardian here at the time. I believe you had a brother who carried the same name, did you not?"

I didn't know what to say. Obviously, Father Charbel had done his homework on me. But why? Was he trying to recruit me—to become a monk? The idea was absurd. It didn't have the same novelty appeal to me as it apparently did with Dona. I gritted my teeth and said nothing.

"It is our lot as Christians of the East to endure tragedy and persecution," he went on. "But nothing in our faith says that we must go like lambs to the slaughter. St. Augustine was the first to lay out the criteria requisite for a Christian people to wage war. In more than fifteen hundred years, those precepts haven't changed and we include them in the Catechism of the Church. Evil *should* provoke a righteous anger. What makes war "just" is the order we impose onto that anger and the spirit of love that ultimately motivates us—love of each other, love of life, love of God—and forgiveness for our enemy, once he has been *thoroughly* crushed."

In Lebanon, Father Charbel joined the Christian Phalange in the mid-1970s and became a comrade-in-arms to Bashir Gemayel, the phalangist leader who was elected president in August 1982 and was murdered just one month later before taking office. "I fought side by side with Sheikh Bashir in the Qarantina, in Ashrafiyeh, in Tel el-Zaatar," he said. "I accompanied him on the infamous raid deep into Fakhani in West Beirut, where we slaughtered more than two dozen Fatah and as-Saiqa leaders in their beds at night to avenge the 582 martyrs they had murdered in Damour, when they locked women and children inside the Maronite church and set it on fire. That was hard... When Bashir was murdered, I felt that hope itself had been slaughtered. That's when I took the vows and joined this order."

Since he first came to Al Qosh, many changes had been made. The war with Iran convinced the Abbot at the time to raise money to build a new ring of fortifications, which we had driven through to enter the courtyard where Father Charbel had welcomed us. Since becoming Abbot himself in 1998, Father Charbel had made additional modifications to enhance the security of the complex and its precious holdings.

"I don't know how much Father Pacelli told you about the Guardians of the Order of St. Hormizd," he said to Governor Aiken. "But today, I am going to reveal secrets to you that generations of my Order have fought and died to keep. So first, I want you to hear the reason why."

Msg. Pacelli jumped up out of his chair with a celerity I didn't think he was capable of, and planted himself squarely in front of the Abbot. "Charbel!" he said forcefully, and spoke again in Latin. The Abbot stood up slowly—he towered a full head taller than Msg. Pacelli—and spoke over him to Governor Aiken and to Mr. Utz.

"Father Francis and I have a slight disagreement," he said. "But I have reminded him that while the Vatican may have ultimate authority over this Order, we have been enjoined by the Pope himself as Guardians of the treasures of this Monastery. And it is my judgment, as Abbot, that we can no longer guarantee the security of our holdings." He looked down to Msg. Pacelli, "Francis, we have to face facts. The Americans are leaving. The jihadis are coming back. In a way, what we are planning to do is no different than what we did under Saddam."

"No," Pacelli said icily. "Saddam came to you *after* he learned your secret. You're planning to reveal your secret to the Prime Minister *before* he even suspects it. This is something you cannot do."

Governor Aiken was watching them argue back and forth, and scratched his head.

"Whoa, now," he said. "What is it that we're really talking about here? I understand you've got a crypt with priceless early manuscripts. What's the problem with telling the Prime Minister about that?"

"You haven't told him," the Abbot said. It was a statement, not a question. Msg. Pacelli shrugged.

"Governor, we are sitting—almost literally—atop the Sacred Relics of St. Peter, the Prince of Apostles. We are the Guardians of St. Peter's bones."

When Governor Aiken's shock had subsided, Father Charbel told him the story of the Order. "In 570 AD, a young man from Ahwaz, in southern Persia, decided to become a monk and at the age of twenty made a pilgrimage to the Holy Land. On his way home, he met three brothers from a Nestorian monastery near Damascus, who invited him to join their Order. He stayed with them for many years. At the time, Damascus was a hub of the caravan trade, where wealthy merchants bought and sold goods from all over the world. It was also a den of iniquity, so there were many souls to save. Over the years, the young monk, whose name was Bahira, started to frequent the camel drivers and traders who came from central Arabia. He became convinced that their vibrant pagan beliefs could be harnessed and with the right teaching, transformed. Remember: this came at a time when the Church was in full expansion and the proselytizing mission was still new.

"And so he booked passage with a trader bound for Mecca. During a stop one evening, he met a 12-year old boy named Ubul Kassim, who was known to familiars as Mustapha. The boy was an orphan, and had been put under the care of an uncle named Abu Talib, who was a merchant from Mecca. Abu Talib used him as a camel driver on his caravans, and in the evenings the boy, who was prone to seizures, would entertain the men as they sat around the fire drinking tea with stories of momentous battles and celestial confrontations. Bahira was intrigued by the boy and wondered if his somewhat overwrought and untrained imagination could somehow be molded into a vehicle for spreading the Gospel. And so he learned everything he could about the boy and his family, and eventually moved to Mecca so he could become the boy's teacher.

"At the age of forty, the grown-up boy, who now called himself Mohammad, declared himself a Prophet, a Messenger of God. Bahira continued to give him religious instruction; indeed, many of the passages of what later came to be known as the Koran are direct borrowings from the Gospel or from the Old Testament. But as Mohammad built his movement and his fortune, he ran into trouble with his own tribe, the Quraysh, and eventually was forced to flee Mecca for nearby Medina. By this time, Bahira was an old

man, and had begun to have doubts as to the wisdom
of his life's work.

"The Nestorian sect allowed priests and
monks to marry. Indeed, that was one of the
differences that ultimately drove Rome to declare
them a heresy. So Bahira was succeeded by his son,
Hormizd, who was two years older than the Prophet
of Islam. Hormizd didn't have the same authority over
Mohammad as his father had, and before long the two
men had a falling out and Mohammad expelled
Hormizd and his fellow monks from Medina. That's
when they came up to Nineveh and eventually
settled here in al Qosh, following in the footsteps of
St. Thomas and, some believe, St. Peter."

Mr. Utz shot a glance at Msg. Pacelli, who was
looking urgently at his hands. "Are you saying that St.
Peter died here and not in Rome? After all, in his
letter to the Church, he did send greetings from
Babylon."

Msg. Pacelli shot back. "We settled that
dispute centuries ago. When he said Babylon, he
meant Rome. It was just a metaphor. A code, if you
wish, to keep the Romans off guard."

"What, and so when he wrote Jerusalem, he
actually meant New York? They knew where Babylon
was. Heck, we know the apostles came here to preach
to the Jews."

"To answer your question: no," the Abbot
said. "We accept the traditional version that St. Peter
was crucified upside down by the Emperor Nero, and
was buried by believers in secret in Rome. "

"So how did his bones get up here?"

"Let me continue the story of St. Hormizd
bint Bahira, and you will understand," Father Charbel
said.

Hormizd was clearly a holy man and
performed many miracles. His fame spread out before

him across the entire region and people made pilgrimage to this Monastery, which he built, to seek his blessing. The story is told that the Mayor of Nineveh, which by this time had been conquered by the invading Muslim armies, was encouraged to bring his ailing son up to Hormizd to be healed, even though the two of them were Muslims. On the road up to the monastery, the son died. The Mayor tore his hair and swore vengeance against the monks, but the people of al Qosh implored him to take the son's body up to the monk anyway. So he did, and Hormizd prayed over the body, and behold, the son rose up from his deathbed just like Lazarus. "And so, over the years, the Order of St. Hormizd grew in fame and fortune. And since it was a violent time, what with the expansion of the Muslim empire, they became a military order, a bit like the Templars many centuries later. Hence the suits of armor you see preserved here," he said, gesturing to a pair of gleaming medieval knights, faint red crosses still visible on their battered shields, standing guard behind his desk.

As the Muslim empire expanded northwards into Europe, Rome came under attack repeatedly, Father Charbel went on. While Charles Martel managed to stop the Muslim expansion into continental Europe in 732 AD at Poitiers, the Saracens—as they were then called—stormed across the Mediterranean. In 826 AD, they occupied Crete. Shortly afterwards, they began the conquest of Sicily, then a Byzantine possession. Saracen raiding parties went up and down the Italian coast, raping and pillaging towns and villages, up to the outskirts of Rome itself. Then in 846 AD, the unthinkable happened, and an Arab army landed at Ostia and sailed up the Tiber to launch a surprise attack against the Vatican. "That is when the Pope transferred custody of the Sacred Relics and numerous other treasures of the Vatican to the Guardians of St. Hormizd," Father Charbel said.

"And-uh-how would we know this?" said Gary Utz.

"That's what I propose to show you now," said Father Charbel.

As Father Charbel got up, there was a knock at the door. Bassam came in, a worried look on his face, and went up to Msg. Pacelli.

"The Kurds are gone," he whispered urgently. "My men saw them driving off toward Dohuk."

"I dare say that's a relief."

"Your escort?" Father Charbel said. "There's a lot of friction between them and our local police. Still, I will alert our security people."

He pressed a button on his desk and the wooden panels separated and slid back, revealing a bank of small flat-screen monitors.

"I mentioned that I had made some modifications to our security when I took over as Abbot," he said. "Closed Circuit TV is just one of them."

One of the monitors showed a darkened room with large metal lockers. Two others were completely dark. A fourth revealed a brother sitting before an entire wall of video monitors, apparently dozing. Charbel pressed a button beneath the monitor, activating a microphone. "Awake, brother Ishoo. There's always time to sleep when you die." He chuckled as the brother sat bolt upright, startled awake. "Some of them tell me they woke up because God was speaking to them in a dream." He depressed the microphone button again. "Proceed to alert Code Mark," he ordered.

I felt my American cellphone vibrating in the pocket of my jeans, and saw that I had a text message from LTC Wilkens. "Slow going," it read. "Combat units don't like to take orders from accountants. ETA early evening." After the meeting with Saddoun, Wilkens had thought it prudent to request that a deterrent force be positioned around the Monastery before Sunday's announcement, but I hadn't realized they would be coming so soon.

It was around 2 pm, and Father Charbel had prepared a luncheon for his guests. But first, he planned to show us the rooms that were completely dark on the CCTV monitors.

He pressed a hidden button beneath his desk, and the magnificent tapestry hanging between the two suits of armor behind him began to move upwards in folds like a curtain, revealing a vault door with a great combination lock and a spoked wheel. Father Charbel dialed in the combination, grasped the wheel with both hands and turned, and with a gasp of compressed air a dozen solid tungsten plungers released and the door popped open an inch or two.

"This is a real bank vault door," Father Charbel said. "It took the Swiss specialists the Vatican brought in nearly two weeks to install this thing. It's a good twenty-five centimeters thick—nearly a foot."

"It was enough to protect you from Saddam," Msg. Pacelli grumbled. "Don't you think it's enough to protect you now?"

But Father Charbel just waved him off, and started heading down the dark stone staircase. "Follow me!"

"Hey, I'm game," said Mr. Utz. "I've got my camera. After you, Governor."

The steep, narrow staircase was dimly lit by a series of ancient electric lamps, connected by black cable attached to the stone with metal spikes that had been bent over—clearly one thing Father Charbel hadn't gotten around to modernizing. On the right-hand side was a braided metal rail, curiously free of rust. The air got much cooler as we descended into the rock of the mountain itself, but remained remarkably dry.

The staircase emptied into a small circular room, lit dramatically by a pair of halogen spotlights that highlighted the chalk-white keystone in the archway at the far end. A pair of small wooden doors covered a recessed cupboard, similar to the one used to store the elements at the rear of the alter in most churches. The doors had been ornately painted, and the scene they depicted made immediate sense now that we had all heard the story of the Sack of Rome from Father Charbel. On the left-hand panel was the Pope, dressed in his pontifical robes, making the sign of the cross. Behind him, flames were licking at a nearby window and the Tiber was visible in the distance beneath the burning arches of a bridge. The right-hand panel showed a knight in full armor, kneeling to receive the blessing. In one hand, he clutched a scroll sealed with red wax; his other hand lay atop a simple chest made of dark wood, its top inlaid with the sign of the fish.

"This is the Ledger of our Order," Father Charbel explained as he undid the simple clasp of the cupboard. He took out a leather-bound book and set it on a small table before us. Opening to a fresh page, he wrote the date, then turned to Governor Aiken.

"Governor, would you like to be the first to sign?

We all wrote our names beneath that of Governor Aiken, including Msg. Pacelli. "Boy, what I wouldn't give to see some of the earlier pages of that guest book," Mr. Utz said.

"Ha!" Father Charbel laughed, good-naturedly. "Father Francis, show him your last visit."

Sighing, Msg. Pacelli started flipping back through the pages.

"Whoa-whoa-whoa," said the Governor. "Didn't I just see George W. Bush? That must have been Thanksgiving 2006."

"That's correct," said Father Charbel, turning back to the page. "They flew Air Force One up to Mosul, then choppered up here. They landed right in the middle of the courtyard where I met you today."

"What I don't understand then," said Governor Aiken, "is why he didn't do more to help the Christians?"

"It wasn't yet time," Father Charbel said. "But he gave us the cipher locks and other help with our security."

Mr. Utz got out a palm-size camera. "May I father?"

"Certainly."

Father Charbel then opened to a page with the header December 2002, with Msg. Pacelli's florid signature and that of another person. Msg. Pacelli said nothing, staring glumly at the page.

"So that was when you came here just before the war," Mr. Utz said. "Who was the other person—Joseph something?"

"Ratzinger," Father Charbel said in a whisper.

"Why, that's the Pope," Governor Aiken said.

"He was dean of the College of Cardinals at that point," said Msg. Pacelli. "Our mission was to determine if Saddam Hussein had kept his word and had not disturbed the Sacred Relics. He did, and he hadn't."

"So did Hitler come here?" Governor Aiken asked.

Father Charbel laughed. "No, no, no. Neither did Mussolini, or the Kaiser, or the King or Queen of England. But many centuries ago, we did get a visit from Michelangelo. He was sent as a secret emissary by Pope Paul III some years after the Sack of Rome in 1527 in hopes of reuniting the Vatican with the Church of the East. The Pope realized that no alliance of kings or princes could help him to resist the Hapsburgs so he was seeking greater pastoral authority to use as a trump card against the Holy Roman Emperor. While the Great Schism was not fully healed until the 20th century, Michelangelo's visit brought some modest gains to the Pope since History tells us that my predecessor as Abbot, Mar Yohanna Sulaqa, pledged fealty to Rome and made a public visit to the Vatican in 1552, just before he was assassinated."

"Sounds like it didn't do him much good," Mr. Utz said.

Father Charbel laughed again, and clapped Mr. Utz on the back with his large rough hand. "I like your sense of humor, Mr. Utz. Actually, it was Sulaqa who abolished the hereditary priesthood at Rome's request and forced the Abouna clan to produce all those spares."

He replaced the ledger in its cabinet, then turned to the metal door behind him. It was attached to the rock wall by invisible hinges and secured by a cipher lock such as I had seen in the U.S. embassy complex in Amman and in Erbil. Father Charbel punched in the combination, the hidden bolts released and he pulled open the door.

"And now we go down to view our Holy of Holies," he said.

Msg. Pacelli was right behind him.

We descended another six steps into the mountain, and then went down a long, low corridor for perhaps fifty meters until we entered a large room hollowed out of the bare rock. The ceiling was surprisingly high—perhaps twenty feet or more —and from an upper corner a single shaft of natural light descended to the floor. A long refectory-style table cut the room in half, and along the walls were shelves that had been cut out of the rock and lined with dark wood. Most of them were filled with ancient books; others contained what appeared to be small chests.

"This is what we call the Scribe's Room, where for centuries our brothers have studied these manuscripts and copied them. It is a naturally dust-free, humidity-free environment," Father Charbel said.

He went over to one of the shelves, and carefully took down a chest the size of a telephone book, whose cover was made entirely of gold. The top was fixed with hinges, and opened like a book. Inside were pages covered with writing. Carefully, using both his large hands, he took out the top page and set it on a stone slab set in the center of the long table.

"This may be the oldest copy of the Book of Matthew in existence," he said. "It was brought to Nineveh by St. Thomas himself when he went to proselytize India and the East. As you can see, it is written in Aramaic, not Greek like most of the manuscripts in your museums in Europe and America. And unlike the papyrus texts found in Egypt, this one is written on animal skin, like the scrolls discovered in jars in Qumran along the Dead Sea. We believe it was originally a scroll that was cut into pages to make its transport more commodious. When we return to my office I will show you a copy made by one of our brothers in the 12th century and an English language translation we did just before I became Abbot. You will find few differences with the text you are familiar with, except for the end of the Lord's Prayer. Originally, this prayer ended:

'And lead us not into temptation,

but deliver us from the Evil One'

"Only later, apparently, were the last lines now familiar to us added."

Governor Aiken recited: "For yours is the Kingdom and the power and the glory for ever."

"Amen," said Father Charbel.

Dona was clutching my hand and just stood there, speechless, shaking her head in disbelief at what she saw. Mr. Utz had his camera, but Father Charbel held out his hand.

"No picture here, Mr. Utz. The flash could have an effect on the manuscript."

"How about if I try one without the flash?"

"Be my guest."

Msg. Pacelli was fidgeting, clearly unhappy about something. Several times I saw him reach for his stomach, patting it as if he had indigestion.

"We have hundreds of ancient manuscripts," Father Charbel went on. "We have never even compiled a catalogue of them, for fear it would be stolen and our secrets revealed. Father Frances probably knows more about our holdings than most of my monks. My hope is that the Prime Minister will recognize the priceless treasures we have and agree to petition UNESCO to declare Mar Hormizd a world heritage site and give us protection. That is the purpose of my meeting with him this Sunday."

He went to a large cabinet set in among the bookcases. It stood as high as he did, its dark wooden doors unadorned except for two large swords—the Swords of the Guardians—hung from the top corners, their tips crossed midway down the doors to hold them closed.

"I know you didn't come down here with me just to look at old books," Father Charbel said, with laughter in his small, close-set eyes.

He reached beneath the handles of the two swords and they swiveled away from each other, freeing the cabinet doors. He pulled them open, stood aside, and Dona gasped. Staring at us was a giant bearded face, the troubled forehead rendered in bright gold as if catching the rising sun, the eyes the color of a sandy sea. The gold was obviously gold leaf, and a golden halo sat aslant St. Peter's head. The icon had been carved into the front panel of a large vertical chest that sat beneath a stone altar, from which rose a simple wooden crucifix. "'Blessed are you Simon son of Jonah... And I tell you that you are Peter, and on this rock I will build my church, and the gates of Hell will not overcome it.'"[5]

He extracted a brass cylinder from a recess above the chest containing the Sacred Relics and unscrewed the top. Inside was another cylinder, in glass, which he took out and set on the table. "You can still see the red sealing wax of the Pope's seal," he said. "This is the Pope's missile designating the Order of St. Hormizd as the Guardians of St. Peter's bones."

Gary Utz had placed his camera on the table, and was trying to set the timer so it would automatically take a picture without the flash when I

---

[5] Matthew 16: 17-18

heard a rustling of fabric just behind me and felt Dona's hand suddenly clutch mine hard. I turned around and saw that Msg. Pacelli had pulled out a gun, a small snub-nosed revolver, and was now pointing it at Father Charbel. With his free hand, he pushed Dona and me out of the way.

"You can't do this, Charbel. All week long I have tried to reason with you. The books we can take out one by one in our hand luggage. The Holy Father has agreed to this. But the bones will have to stay here. They are well enough protected as it is," he said, his hand trembling as he waved the gun.

The shutter of Mr. Utz's camera clicked and stayed open for a full second. So did Mr. Utz's mouth. "Monsignor!" he gasped finally in his high-pitched voice, stunned at the sight of his friend holding the gun.

"Let's just close this up, go back up stairs, and agree on a plan to evacuate the manuscripts," Msg. Pacelli went on. "I cannot let you do this, Charbel."

He looked like he was about to squeeze the trigger. Mr. Utz saw it as well, and in the next instant lunged at him with an agility you would have thought impossible for a man of his stature. It must have been the Marine in him that surfaced. As he tackled Msg. Pacelli the revolver went off with a deafening report that echoed down the hallway and in the upper reaches of the Scribe's room. Dona's hands instinctively flew up to protect her ears. Msg. Pacelli was buried beneath Mr. Utz's large body and didn't seem to be moving. Father Charbel rushed over and kicked the revolver to the far side of the room, then leaned down to help Mr. Utz get back to his feet.

Mr. Utz brushed his clothes back into some kind of order and stood looking down at the figure of Msg. Pacelli, flat on his back on the floor. "Father Frances," he said finally. "You almost got yourself

killed. You just can't do things like that.
Understand?"

Msg. Pacelli sat up, unhurt, and started to say
something then stopped, too embarrassed and too
ashamed for words.

Just then, an alarm sounded at the entry to the
corridor. At the sound of it, Father Charbel quickly
replaced the glass cylinder in the brass holder and
returned it to the recess inside the cabinet, then
closed the cabinet doors on the chest containing St.
Peter's bones. Then he rushed to the wall near the
entrance, where I had noticed a tiny yellow light
when we came in. Now the light had turned to orange
and it was flashing.

"Matthew, Mark, Luke, John," he said,
pointing to the four tiny lights. "Those are our alert
codes." He opened a grey metal panel to reveal a set
of monitors. One camera panned his office from above
the vault door, and the second showed the room
above us with the cipher lock. The third revealed
Ishoo in the surveillance center. He was wide awake
now, peering into the bank of monitors with alarm.

"What is it, Ishoo?" Father Charbel said into
the microphone.

"Car bomb, father. Down at the checkpoint at
the entry of town. Apparently, it took out the whole
position, gates, barriers and all."

"I'll be with you in a few minutes. Confirm
Alert Code Luke to the brothers."

Turning to us, he said, "We'll have to
continue this visit later on. That's a promise. But now
we have to hurry."

We received an update once we reached Father Charbel's office. The car bomb was exceptionally powerful, and left a giant crater where the barrier across the road into town had once been. The Suburbans belonging to the Assyrian units of the Iraqi police had been tossed into the air like bowling pins. Because of the crater, there was no way for vehicles to enter the town and reach the road leading up to the Monastery except by crossing the rolling fields of spring wheat—an easy task for off-road trucks, as long as no one was shooting at them.

It was already 5 o'clock and starting to get dark. All thoughts of the lunch Father Charbel had planned for us were gone. If this was the beginning of the attack by the Emir of Jihad, then Saddoun had lied. He said it wasn't planned for several more days. I sent a brief text message to LTC Wilkens to inform him of the car bomb attack, and received a reply almost immediately: "Heard same from PTT at Marez. We are saddling up."

The PTT were U.S. advisors embedded with the Iraqi police. They would have learned about the car bomb attack and transmitted the information to command elements at Camp Marez outside Mosul air base, where a Stryker brigade from the 25h Infantry Division was now stationed. With the U.S. preparing to pull out of Iraqi cities and towns in another two months, they had already abandoned most of the forward command posts inside Iraqi neighborhoods in favor of the large fire bases on the outskirts of the cities. While this made the U.S. presence less visible to ordinary Iraqis, it also made it more cumbersome to mount rapid response operations. Even with guns blazing to get through Mosul traffic, it would take them a good hour and a half if not more to reach al Qosh from Camp Marez. I shared this information with Mr. Utz, who had a much clearer picture of the military situation than the others, but of course I couldn't tell him about the meeting in the desert with Saddoun.

"What kind of defenses do you have, father?" he asked. "Security's fine, but it won't do you much good if they just blow your guys away."

"You're right. Please, come with me."

As we went out into the cloister, we saw brothers emerging from their cells and walking rapidly toward a door at the far end, while others were coming back out and heading for the main courtyard, carrying M4 carbines with the large-mouthed 40mm grenade tube mounted beneath the barrel.

"That is our armory," Father Charbel said. "We keep the swords mainly for ceremony these days."

We entered the armory, and the room with its steel lockers was familiar from the surveillance monitor we had seen earlier in Father Charbel's office. At the far end, supervising the distribution of weapons, was a huge red-bearded monk with large meaty hands.

"This is Father Brian, an Abouna whose family emigrated to Ireland three generations ago," Father Charbel said. He clapped him on the back as he introduced him, and laughed.

"How many men do you have?" Mr. Utz asked.

"Twenty-six, sir," Father Brian answered.

"Are they trained on these weapons?"

Mr. Utz eyed the young monks skeptically, shaking his head.

231

"Before I took my vows, I served with the Special Air Service in Hereford. Did one tour in Afghanistan, another one in Basra. *I've* trained them. And yourself?"

"I'll be damned," Mr. Utz said, grinning. He liked what he had heard. "I'm a Marine."

Father Brian took an M4 from the locker behind him and held it out in two hands. "So here's the 30 second drill. The M4 is basically a re-engineered M16, like you blokes used in Vietnam. Slightly smaller, shorter barrel, more modern, better sights. It can still jam, but most of the time it's just a magazine misfeed you can clear by pulling back the bolt and letting it slam home a new round. Switch from single shot to three-round burst with this lever on the left-hand side. You won't hit anything over 300 meters, max, so hold your fire. Best bet when the bad guys are further off is to use the M203 grenade launcher. Sight flips up like this," he demonstrated. "Remarkably accurate out to 500 meters."

"How much practice do you give your men?"

"They have to requalify every six months. We've got an indoor range so not bother the neighbors," he grinned.

Mr. Utz took the weapon and turned to Governor Aiken. "Governor, you think you can handle one of these?"

"Last time I did reserve duty was fifteen years ago. But Hell, yes."

Brother Brian fitted us out with Kevlar vests, helmets and web gear holding six spare magazines, grenades, and a walkie-talkie. He gave Dona a Beretta M9 handgun just in case. By common agreement, Msg. Pacelli was to remain a spectator should a fight break out. He had stopped grumbling by now and meekly followed Father Charbel's instructions.

We headed out through the archway beyond the cloister to the main courtyard, where our own guards had taken up position. The distant explosion, the alarm and the sight of all the monks scurrying around with their weapons and gear clearly made them nervous. Bassam came up to Msg. Pacelli and asked him what was going on.

"I think you'd better ask Father Charbel," he said.

The main gates into the courtyard had been closed, and I saw that they were backstopped by a two-foot high crash barrier similar to those used at U.S. embassies that popped up from a recessed area and were designed to stop a ten ton truck ramming it at 60 kilometers per hour.

Just then, my U.S. cellphone vibrated with another message. "Clear the courtyard," it said. "Arriving by helo. ETA ten minutes."

Father Charbel gave the orders in rapid fire. It was a drill they had practiced often since told they would host the president of the United States a few years earlier. He had Bassam move our cars to a covered area at the far end of the courtyard, then had eight monks exchange their weapons for large brooms and sweep the area of any debris that could get kicked up in the downwash from the rotors and foul the turbines. As the monks reached the far end of the courtyard, we heard the air cavalry helicopters approach. A minute later we could see them, approaching directly from the greening fields of spring wheat to the south. The lead OH-58D Kiowa Warrior was unarmed, and had external seats attached to the hard points normally used for weapons stores. You could tell because men with helmets and weapons looked as if they were riding the skids, with the telltale mast-mounted site scouring the surroundings below. Suddenly, we saw a white plume streak up toward the unarmed helicopter, apparently a missile or a rocket fired from somewhere below the monastery. The pilot veered off to the left, and the rocket exploded a few hundred meters beyond his previous position. Then the pilot put the helicopter's nose down hard and headed straight for us, while the second Kiowa Warrior made a large sweeping turn, taking it back around to the area where the rocket had been fired. As the rotors from the first chopper whooped the air all around us, we heard a loud explosion. Colonel Wilkens unstrapped himself and jumped to the ground and ran toward us, head down, followed quickly by Mojo, Deron, and two soldiers from the Third Brigade Combat Team, all in full combat kit, who were riding on the other side. Deron was carrying an M82, a Barrett Light Fifty, similar to the one the Kurds had used out in the desert. The rotors slowed but continued to turn.

Father Charbel went out to greet him.

"Lieutenant Colonel Danny Wilkens, father. From SIGIR. I understand there's been a car bomb attack. We spotted fifteen pick-ups full of jihadis and three trucks in the area."

Father Charbel took the hand Wilkens extended, his other hand holding the M4 by the rail-mounted carrying handle. "I'm guessing there's one less by now."

Col. Wilkens indicated the helicopter pilot, who sat impassively behind the glass cockpit, his face obscured by black helmet, sunglasses, and microphone. "His partner's got another three Hellfire's on his Kiowa. But with the new rules of engagement, he can only use them if we are fired upon."

"And what's SIGIR?"

"Special Inspector General for Iraq Reconstruction. We're a government accounting unit, actually."

"Accounting unit?" He glanced toward the helicopter and at the four soldiers who had accompanied Col. Wilkens, and gave one of his great belly laughs. "Remind me to pay my taxes on time if I go to America."

The co-pilot signaled Wilkens and pointed up to the sky. He nodded.

"They'll make another pass on the bad guys and radio recon to the Stryker team before heading down to Diamondback to refuel and rearm," he said. "I reckon the Calvary ought to be here in under an hour."

The sun had gone down over the town just before the helicopters arrived, and now night was falling rapidly, as it did up in the mountains, with a sliver of moon rising over our attackers. We were now at Code John, full battle alert. Father Brian was giving orders to his monks to man different positions on the forward ramparts when the first mortar rounds landed at the rear of the courtyard.

Deron was chewing gum and didn't flinch as his thumb toyed with the optical sighting mechanism on his sniper rifle. "We'd like something high up, concealed, with good visibility," Mojo was saying.

Father Brian pointed to two monks who were disappearing into a stairwell to the left of the main gates. "Follow them."

Father Charbel patted his walkie-talkie. "Channel three," he called to Mojo. "I've got a sixty tucked away on a little courtyard out back that's been waiting for a moment like this. Call coordinates to me. We played this game with the Palestinians all the time."

He ran off into the cloister, while Col. Wilkens and the other two soldiers followed Deron and Mojo to the turrets in the outer ramparts to the south and east. I went with Gov. Aiken, Mr. Utz and Dona to the lower end of the ramparts in search of a good firing position. I had a pair of laser range-finding binoculars Father Brian had given me and showed Dona how they worked. With our bare eyes, we couldn't see anything below: just rocks falling off into hidden ravines. The switchbacks in the road climbing up to the monastery from the valley provided plenty of cover to our attackers.

Another mortar round crashed into the courtyard, and I thought I saw a wisp of smoke down below. "Let me have a look at those," Mr. Utz said, holding out his hand to take the binoculars from Dona.

He scanned the valley for a minute, then shook his head. "Hell, they've got their mortar halfway down into the valley by the electric poles. It's about two and a half klicks. We don't have anything that can hit them from here."

Just then, we heard the whistle of a mortar round after it passed overhead in the other direction. We could see it explode just beyond the electric pole down below a full three seconds before we heard the blast. A second round soon followed, ten meters or so to the left.

"I've got 'em," Mr. Utz said excitedly. "Charbel smoked 'em out. They're on the move."

There was still enough light to see the pick-ups down below now as they rounded one of the switchbacks and moved up the hill closer to us.

"Look! There's another group much higher up," Mr. Utz said, pointing over to the eastern approach to the Monastery. "They ought to be in range of your buddy's Light Fifty."

They played hopscotch with Father Charbel and his 60 mm mortar for another fifteen minutes or so, trading rounds, moving, setting up again from a new position and firing until Mojo spotted them and called up the coordinates. From time to time we heard the sharp *craaack* of Deron's Barrett M82 and then a distant explosion echoing into the mountains. We saw red flames shoot up a good kilometer beneath us where one of his incendiary rounds connected with the engine of a pick-up. The lower walls of the monastery were lit by yellow floodlights set in the rock cliffs, and more lights outlined the road for the final 500 meters or so. But the cliffs themselves were now in darkness. Suddenly, something slammed into the stone rampart just below our position and we saw two robed bodies leap into the air and fall crashing onto the rocks below.

"What in God's name was that?" Gov. Aiken said.

"Probably a 120—a big mortar," I said. "Further out."

"I can hear them. Now where are those snakes?" Mr. Utz said, passing the binoculars back to Dona and scanning the rock face just below us with the Trijicon optical sight on his M4 carbine. It wasn't a true night vision scope, but the crosshairs were lit and the magnification allowed you to pick out objects with minimal light.

Mojo started swearing over the walkie-talkie and then I heard Col. Wilkens shouting, "Truck bomb—fall back! Fall back! We don't have a shot from here."

Mr. Utz was scanning the road closer to the monastery. "Wait a second. I can see them. I've got the shot."

"Sir, we've got to go."

"Go ahead. I've got the shot."

He fired off three rounds from the M4 and we could hear shattering glass, screeching tires, and the motor of the truck revving wildly.

"Come on! Let's go!" I said, grabbing Dona and Gov. Aiken and dragging them to the stairs.

We leapt two steps at a time down the winding stone staircase, and when we reached the courtyard I saw monks streaming from the ramparts and Col. Wilkens and his team running full speed toward the far end of the courtyard. Over the walkie talkie I heard Mr. Utz panting. "My bolt is jammed. I'm going to try a grenade." Then we heard the explosion but we kept on running and a second later we heard cackling laughter over the walkie-talkie. "It's a fizzle," Mr. Utz said. Then in a voice filled with awe: "Well I'll be..."

An instant later, an explosion more powerful than anything I have ever witnessed ripped a hole into the front end of the monastery, including the heavily-armored gates and part of the stone ramparts and the outer walls that were well over a meter thick. Everything just collapsed and seemed to be sucked into a gigantic hole by a powerful vacuum, and then in the next instant it all exploded outwards scattering stone and metal and bodies in every direction. Dona was shrieking and running but I managed to throw her down onto the ground at the far end of the courtyard as the heat from the blast hit us and my heart pounded with utter terror. I glanced behind me, half-expecting to see the twisted grimace of some gigantic demon in a whirlwind, but through the smoke and the flames all I could see was blackness: a huge black hole, perhaps fifty meters across, starting from where the truck exploded well beyond the ramparts.

Col. Wilkens was standing up, waving his arms in the archway that led into the inner cloister. "Come on! Before they find their way in!"

One of the soldiers who had come with him in the Kiowa detached a square microphone from his web belt and handed it to him. "Sir, it's the 6-17th."

He depressed the button. "A little air support would be welcome right about now," Wilkens said into the device. "We just had a VBIED[6] packed with fuel-air explosives. Our perimeter is down. I think that qualifies under the new ROE."

The radio crackled from the small speaker located in the handset.

"Confirm: VBIED with FAE?"

"Roger."

The radio went silent for a long moment. Then the voice said, "Copy that. We're on our way."

Father Charbel was waving his arms from the far end of the cloister. Father Brian activated the steel blast doors, sealing off the archway and the cloister from the main courtyard. He started giving orders to the remaining monks to man positions in the refectory and the chapel overlooking the courtyard.

"If they've got another one of those, we're chopped meat," he said.

"What in the world *was* that?" Gov. Aiken said. "Gary, everything else. Just vaporized."

---

[6] Vehicle-borne improvised explosive device

"Probably fuel-air explosive," Col. Wilkens explained. "Foo gas. We used it in Vietnam to clear landing strips in the jungle. Saddam got the technology from a Pentagon supplier in the 1980s thanks to a German intermediary and juiced it up."

He depressed the button on the black microphone again. "Dark Angel 4, what's your ETA?"

"Five minutes. Maybe ten."

"That means ten," Wilkens said, off-mike to us. "What about the Stryker team?"

"About the same. They should be reaching the al Qosh checkpoint by now."

"We're hot."

"Roger that, Colonel. We're pushing it."

He handed the microphone back to the soldier. "You heard the horseman. That means we've got ten minutes of living Hell."

We took up new positions upstairs overlooking the wreckage of the main courtyard. A few monks remained along the eastern portion of the outer wall, defending our flank, although the sheer cliff would be difficult to breach, especially at night. As Father Charbel explained to us, there was basically one way in. And now it stood wide open to our attackers. The only advantage we had was the wreckage below. The truck bomb not only destroyed a good portion of the outer wall of the monastery; it also had transformed the road into a deep pit. It would be difficult for our attackers to bring up a second bomb, at least by truck.

If Col. Wilkens was grim, I was amazed by Father Charbel's sang-froid. He almost seemed to be enjoying himself. We were protected from the courtyard by the thick stone walls of the chapel, and peered down at the intruders through long narrow slots, built in the days when the monastery was defended by archers and pots of boiling oil. He put a finger to his lips, pointed, and then inserted the barrel of his M4 carbine into the slot and fired. I watched through the sight of my rifle as a young bearded man below clutched his throat and staggered backwards onto the ground.

"There, Yohannes," he said. "That one's for you."

Did Father Charbel know that I was still an innocent? That I had never killed a man, or fired a gun in anger? For an instant, the words of the commandment, "Thou Shalt Not Kill," swirled through my brain, and then I saw the bearded man below pull a long-stemmed grenade out of his backpack and hand it to a gunner with an RPG tube aimed directly at us: and I fired. A quick three-round burst threw the man to the ground, writhing. At the same time, Father Charbel took out the one with the RPG tube.

"*Khaya gyanukh!* —Well done!" he said.

Dona sat in one of the hard pews just behind us, her head bowed, hands over her ears, sobbing quietly.

We did indeed come from two different worlds. Was hers any better than mine?

12

Wednesday evening

The jihadis kept on coming. At one point there must have been thirty of them swarming over the wreckage along the outskirts of the giant crater where the entry to the monastery had been. Father Charbel and I picked them off one by one, but other popped up out of the darkness, screaming *"Allah O Akbar!"* scrambling over their fallen comrades, their AK-47s blazing.

A group of them was trying to maneuver a pick-up truck over the blocks of stone, backing and charging, backing and charging, with six men pushing from behind. They finally managed to get it inside the courtyard, and they raced up to the barricaded archway below us. I could see a long fat object in the bed of the truck. At just that instant, I heard Col. Wilkens' voice over the walkie-talkie. "They've got another bomb. Just below. All guns to the archway."

I had two magazines left, each with 30 rounds. Father Charbel had three, since he was firing single shots. Because of the angle, we could only hit the men at the rear of the pick-up. "We've got to go back downstairs," Father Charbel said, "if we want to have any chance of stopping them."

Father Brian met us downstairs by the blast doors, along with Col. Wilkens.

"We need some kind of opening," Wilkens said. "We can't reach them from up above."

Father Charbel stood side by side with Father Brian, and pointed to the seam between the two blast doors. "There's your opening, Colonel." He crossed himself, slammed a fresh magazine into the M4 and gripped it tightly at waist level, then he nodded to Father Brian to activate the doors. "Stand back and cover us," he said. "And close the gates after we drive them back."

The next ten seconds were the longest in my life. I was standing above Father Charbel in a staircase, at a forty-five degree angle behind him, and so I couldn't see what he and Father Brian started to shoot at when the doors separated. They were both firing three-round bursts, methodically going from one target to the next as the doors separated and slid back. Even if I had wanted to shoot into the pie-slice that was open to me, I couldn't see anything because of the smoke. I saw Father Charbel stagger once, then twice, then seem to recover and open fire again. "Close'em up," Father Brian shouted.

From up above, on the other side of the archway, I heard more firing, single shots. And then I heard Mojo's voice over the walkie-talkie. "They're pulling back. We'll concentrate fire on the stragglers so somebody can go out and take care of that bomb."

They opened the gates again, and LTC Wilkens rushed out and pulled the dead driver out of the pick-up truck. Before getting in, he pulled off the man's belt, straightened the wheels of the pick-up, and tied the steering wheel so it wouldn't turn. Then he reached down a grabbed a piece of debris. He gunned the motor of the pick-up, jammed the debris over the accelerator to hold it in place, then threw it in reverse and popped the clutch. It was all he could do to throw himself out of the pick-up and roll onto the tiles before the truck up-ended into the crater caused by the first bomb.

243

They were firing all around him as he ran back toward the archway in a crouch. He threw himself forward onto the ground as the gates closed. We could hear the bullets ricochet off the armor plate of the doors, like raindrops on a tin roof.

Father Charbel had been hit twice in the chest, but the Kevlar vest held and with his tremendous strength he had remained on his feet during his daring sortie. He was less lucky with the bullet he took to his left thigh. We now could see the blood seeping through his brown robe. He grimaced, and put his foot up on a stone step and pulled up his robe to expose the bottom of his briefs. He said to Dona, "Young lady, would you get somebody's belt and tie it on here, please?"

Although the jihadis had retreated momentarily, they hadn't given up the attack. We had just a few minutes of respite before we heard Mojo's voice over the walkie-talkie again. "They're coming back," he said. "Onesies and twosies. RPGs. Rampant."

Father Brian ordered the half dozen monks who remained with us at the archway to return to the upper levels. Father Charbel had collapsed onto the stairs and was leaning back against the wall, exhausted from the pain and the loss of blood.

The soldier with the radio handed the microphone to LTC Wilkens. "It's the AIRCAV, sir."

"Always good of you to show up," Wilkens said.

"We know you'd return the favor, sir," the voice said. "We've got eight pickups and two trucks out here. Any of them yours?"

For the first time since the battle began, Wilkens smiled. "Nope," he said. "They're all yours, Dark Angel."

In the distance, we could hear bursts of .50 caliber machine-gun fire and the dull thud of rockets from the OH-58D Kiowa Warrior helicopters echoing off the mountains, and then a few seconds later the explosions as they hit their targets below. We counted ten large explosions in the next minute or two, and then all we heard was the whooping of helicopter rotors as the Kiowas circled around for a recon run and then faded away. The other soldier who had come with Col. Wilkens got out a plastic package from his web kit and went over to Father Charbel by the staircase. "Let's have a look, father," he said.

Father Charbel rolled over onto his side and hiked up his robe so the soldier could inspect his wound.

"Dark blood is good. Looks like the bullet ripped through the muscle and not an artery. We've got a medic with the Stryker team. But let's wrap you up in the meantime."

He withdrew a paper envelope from the plastic first aid pouch and took out a large compress packed with a gooey mess of anti-septics, coagulants, antibiotics and pain-killers, which he applied over Father Charbel's wound. "The Army medical corps developed this after Vietnam. It's absolute magic. In another minute, you won't feel anything."

He released the belt tourniquet slowly, making sure the wound didn't start bleeding again, then secured the compress with a stretch bandage and tape around Father Charbel's thigh. He checked the pressure point beneath the knee to make sure it wasn't too tight.

Governor Aiken was staring out at the crater where the ramparts of the monastery had been, holding his M4 carbine by the carrying handle, his helmet askew. "I can't believe that Gary is gone. Just like that," he said. "I've got to tell his wife and kids," he added.

"He died like a Marine," Col. Wilkens said. "That's what you tell her. He died with his boots on and his rifle blazing."

"But there aren't even any remains." Then, turning around to face Wilkens: "Can you explain to me how that stuff works?"

Col. Wilkens shook his head. "I'm not an expert. But FAE bombs are said to be the most powerful conventional explosive in existence. They give the impression of a small nuke. Ordinary explosives contain nearly 40% oxygen to make them ignite. FAE bombs get their oxygen by sucking it out of the air, creating a vacuum effect. The bomb case is packed with a compressed liquid fuel mixture, which is dispersed by a small pyrotechnic charge to form an aerosol cloud. I think that's the last thing that Mr. Utz saw before he died."

"You mean, after he laughed because he thought it was a fizzle."

"That's correct. A fraction of a second later, when the cloud reaches the right density, a pyrotechnic charge ignites it, setting off the fuel-air explosive effect. The Israelis used one of these on a PLO headquarters in Beirut in 1982."

"Ha!" said Father Charbel, his cheerfulness returning as the Army medicine kicked in. "I remember that. Missed Arafat by an hour and a half. We called it *une bombe à implosion*—a vacuum bomb. An American journalist was in the basement, held hostage. The Israelis waited until he was moved and so they missed Arafat. Too bad!"

Suddenly I realized I hadn't seen Bassam or our guards since we crossed each other in the courtyard shortly before the battle began.

"Where's Bassam?" I said. "Did anybody see our guards up on the ramparts?"

Father Charbel's small eyes widened and the bristles of his hair seemed to stand straight up. "Pacelli!" he bellowed. "Where is that overweight son of a priest?"

He started to get up, then the pain returned to his leg and he grasped the rail of the staircase with a grimace. He beckoned for me to come help him and grasped onto my shoulder with a bear-paw grip. "Come on!" he said.

"Sir, keep pressure on the wound if you insist on moving," said the soldier who had dressed his leg.

Col. Wilkens came with us as Father Charbel hobbled quickly along the arcade of the cloister to his office, where we found Bassam and most of the guards. Behind him, the vault door to the crypt stood open.

"*Mayye tamele*—He's down there?" Father Charbel shouted at Bassam. It was more a cry of indignation than a question.

"He said it would be more secure during the attack," Bassam said.

"And so, what? You were going to lock yourselves in there if the jihadis came?"

Bassam was taken aback at the question. "Actually, yes. Didn't you know?"

"Why didn't I see this?" he said, more to himself than to us.

"How did he know the combination?" Gov. Aiken asked.

"He bought the vault door and sent technicians from the Vatican to install it."

As Father Charbel spoke, I suddenly recalled Msg. Pacelli standing behind him down below as he punched in the combination of the cipher lock giving access to the Scribe's room, where we had left the chest containing St. Peter's bones, unopened. Had he seen the combination? Was that why he had been standing so close behind Father Charbel?

"Let's see how far he got," Father Charbel said. "Come on!"

He hobbled down the steep staircase until we reached the round chamber with the painted cupboard containing the Ledger of the Order of St. Hormizd. The rest of our guards were waiting there, guns drawn, tense. They lowered their weapons when they saw it was Father Charbel.

"Is he inside?" he asked Samir, one of our drivers, pointing to the door with the cipher lock, which stood half open.

"*Eh, Abouna*. Yes, Father."

"How long?"

Samir shrugged. "Since we came down here."

"He truly is a *lascar*—a rascal," he said. "Colonel, if you would do us the honor? It's like a guest book."

He opened the Ledger of the Order to the last page, which we had all signed earlier in the day before the attack. LTC Wilkens added his name below ours.

"And now we will complete the visit that got interrupted earlier on. I'm sorry Mr. Utz didn't get the chance to see the Sacred Relics, but soon enough he'll be seeing St. Peter in the resurrected flesh."

"Sacred relics?" Col. Wilkens said.

"You missed that part, Colonel."

"I've heard about a book. But not relics."

"I'm about to show you St. Peter's bones," Father Charbel said with a mischievous grin. "That is, if they're still here."

We found Msg. Pacelli seated at the copyist's table inside the cavernous Scribe's Room, head buried in his hands, weeping quietly. He was expecting us and lifted his head to reveal bloodshot eyes.

"Where is it, Charbel? You've hidden it!"

"You couldn't get at the Sacred Relics."

"I gave up on that almost immediately. You never opened the cipher lock."

"So what is it you are looking for, Frances," he said quietly. "If you are seeking to harm anything under my protection, I assure you I will not hesitate to kill you."

Col. Wilkens gave me a querulous look, but said nothing.

"The *Secret Book*, Charbel. The Book of the Order. Where is it?"

He waved his hand to indicate the vast shelves of manuscripts and books on the four walls around us, most of which had no lettering on the spine to identify their contents. "Where do you keep it? This is what the Pope is seeking."

"And why should I surrender the Diaries of the Founders of our Order to the Holy Father?"

"Because, Charbel, the final battle has begun," Msg. Pacelli said. "'After me, many false prophets will appear and deceive many people.'[7] The

---

[7] Matthew 24:11.

time has come to do battle with them and their evil offspring. With your help, we can defeat them."

Father Charbel went to the tall cabinet with the swords, which Msg. Pacelli had already opened, and pressed two fingers into the painted eyes of the gilt icon of St. Peter. A small panel opened near the bottom, exposing a cipher lock. He tried to bend down to key in the combination, but the wound in his leg prevented him.

"*Yohannes, m'ayenni*—Help me," he said.

I came forward and he leaned on my shoulder with one hand as he bent his other knee to the ground so he could punch in the combination. I made sure Msg. Pacelli couldn't see his fingers.

The gilt panel moved aside into a recess cut out of the stone with a decidedly modern, electronic sound. Inside the chest was a shelf set near the top containing several volumes with dark covers set on their sides. Beneath them was a golden urn held in place by dark purple velvet. Father Charbel stood up painfully, and carefully took out the first two volumes and brought them over to the copying table by Msg. Pacelli. He opened the first one, and the handwriting was immediately familiar. Here finally were the complete originals of the various fragments I had seen, all gathered and bound into two volumes! Like me, Dona couldn't take her eyes off the open page, wondering what other secrets the diaries contained."We were planning to reveal these at the same time we brought out the Sacred Relics," he said. "After all, why should anyone accept the authenticity of the bones of St. Peter unless they can see the chain of custody."

"Keep the bones," Msg. Pacelli begged in a whisper. "Let us use the Diaries in Rome."

Father Charbel didn't respond. "Yohannes, bring the urn," he ordered.

250

I was stunned. I couldn't believe he was actually asking me to put my hands on the golden urn containing St. Peter's bones. Was it an honor, or a curse? There was no time to ask the question; it just flashed across my consciousness like a dark cloud scudding before a thunderstorm. I grasped the handles of the urn, one in each hand, and gently pulled it from the velvet cushions holding it in place and brought it over to the copying table. It had a wide opening the size of my hand, sealed with a flat cork. Father Charbel pulled out the cork and reached inside. He withdrew what looked like a gun bag made of thick linen and laid it on the table. It was tied with a simple leather thong, like a belt, which he undid, unrolling the linen before us to reveal the bones.

"Two complete femurs. Remains of nine fingers. Thirteen ribs, even a few teeth. Fragments of what might have been the skull, and part of the pelvis. But no sheep bones, no pigs, no mice," he said. "Just the remains of a man, powerfully built, between sixty-five and seventy years old, who died a violent death over nineteen hundred years ago. We change the linen at least twice a century."

We said nothing as we crowded close to Father Charbel to gaze at the Sacred Relics. I suppose if you just looked at the bones themselves, without knowing the story of how they got to al Qosh, it would be easy to dismiss them as a hoax. But the Pope's letter, and the diaries of the founders of the Order of St. Hormizd, provided powerful testimony that authenticated the Sacred Relics.

"I have to agree with Msg. Pacelli," Col. Wilkens said. "I don't want to get in the middle of Church matters, but the reason I am here is because a very good friend of mine told me something about this secret book. He said it must not be released here in Iraq, because it would inflame the Muslims."

For the first time since we made our initial pilgrimage down into the crypt, Msg. Pacelli gave a look suggesting hope. "I see the outlines of a compromise, Charbel."

"Really?"

"You take your meeting with the Prime Minister and tell him about the Sacred Relics. You keep the letter from the Pope, and the sections of the Diary that describe the Sack of Rome and the evacuation of the St. Peter's bones to al Qosh. No one can argue with that. Even a Muslim Prime Minister will agree to World Heritage Site status and the appropriate level of protection."

"And?" Father Charbel said, suspicious.

"You give us the early volumes of the Diary, those written by Bahira and his son. We get to use them in Rome."

When we got back upstairs to Father Charbel's office, his walkie-talkie crackled with Father Brian's Irish twang.

"The Stryker team has arrived. Time for a meet and greet."

Msg. Pacelli was clutching the two volumes of the *Secret Book* of the Order, but Father Charbel pried them from his hands and placed them carefully in a locked drawer in his desk. He wanted to package them properly in airtight plastic before surrendering them. The Order had copies, of course, and would continue to train new generations of monks to commit the early texts to memory. "I'm only doing this because we'd be making them public anyway," he said.

Beneath the archway leading into the wreckage of the courtyard, Father Brian was talking with the commander of the Stryker team from the 25th Infantry's Third Brigade Combat Team. His men were establishing a secure perimeter beneath the remains of the Monastery ramparts and would go out on patrol awhile later to make sure all the jihadis were gone. He saluted when LTC Wilkens came up.

"Sergeant Jonathan Jordan, sir. 2-27th Infantry, Wolfhounds. Looks like we missed the party."

He surveyed the wreckage of the Monastery ramparts and the giant crater where the entryway had been. What remained of the courtyard was littered with weapons, blood-caked rubble, bodies and tattered bits of clothing blowing in the wind. His men were already hauling away the dead and checking for survivors. He was hoping they'd get at least one prisoner in good enough shape to question. "What were your casualties?"

"Four of my monks, and one Marine," said Father Brian.

"We've got no Marines up here."

"Former, I guess. Civilian. Working for a humanitarian aid group."

"Humanitarian aid? I like that," the Sergeant said, nodding toward the dead jihadis.

Sgt. Jordan sent his medics to treat Father Charbel and a half-dozen brothers who had suffered non-critical injuries during the battle. Because of the advancing hour, we decided to spend the night in the Monastery.

"See if you can manage helo-transport for us in the morning back to Erbil," Col. Wilkens said. "We've got some urgent business to attend to."

13

Thursday

Because of the wreckage at the Monastery, we drove down to the entrance of town the next morning to await the helicopters. It was the first we had seen of the damage done by the car bomb that took out the Assyrian police checkpoint the day before. A pair of 19-ton Stryker wheeled combat vehicles with their distinctive anti-armor cages had replaced the police Suburbans. U.S. soldiers from the 3rd BCT were manning a new checkpoint, as cars slowly maneuvered around the large crater and chunks of roadway and jagged sheets of corrugated grey metal from the shutters of the blown-out store fronts. Bassam and his team planned to drive Msg. Pacelli, Governor Aiken and Dona back to Erbil, while the rest of us hitched a ride from the 6-17th Calvary.

"I found his watch," Gov. Aiken said. "I went out early this morning and looked all over the place for something, anything. I wanted to take something to his wife. This is all I could find."

He held up Mr. Utz's heavy gold wristwatch and shook his head. "I can't believe that Gary is really dead."

"I can't either," Dona said. "*Yohannes, dre balukh*—Be careful."

She took both my hands in hers and looked into my eyes, but I turned away to hide my annoyance. I had gone out on plenty of missions before when I worked for Triple Shield without having someone to spook me, and frankly it was better that way.

"Saddle up," Col. Wilkens said, pointing to the horizon where an armed Kiowa and a larger, UH-60 Blackhawk were now visible over the rolling green fields. "We've got a couple of visits to make. I've arranged with Richie and Capt. Stewart to meet us at the airfield with ground transport."

✝

Cory Reed was not expecting us when we showed up at his office in the U.S. consulate complex in Ainkawa. When we burst in, he had boxes of documents on his desk, which he was feeding in quarter-inch stacks into the oversize shredder behind him.

"Whoa, Bucko!" he said. "You're not supposed to be here."

"What does that mean, Cory?" Col. Wilkens said.

"I mean, you were supposed to be up at that pile of rocks in al Qosh. Warning them. Or whatever it was you were going to do."

"So you expected us to be dead. Is that it?"

The sags of flesh beneath his jaw drooped ridiculously as he realized he had fallen right into the trap.

"Let's see what Mother has brought us," Richie said, plucking a file folder at random from the box of documents on Reed's desk.

"Hey, you can't—that's classified," Reed blubbered.

"I can," Richie said, deftly pulling the folder out of Reed's grasp. He took a few steps backwards, and started leafing through the papers it contained. "Ooh, and guess what? There are no stamps. It's as classified as my monkey."

"Hey. Guys. Sit down," Reed said. "It's Thursday noontime. Everybody's clearing out for the weekend. Why don't we have a nip of something and talk this out."

He started to open a deep file drawer in his desk, but Wilkens kicked it shut with his foot.

"I don't know what you've got in there, Cory. But we don't want any. You're under arrest on charges of wire fraud, money laundering, false official statements, conspiracy, and violations of the Procurement Integrity Act."

"Gee, is that it?"

He was eyeing something under his desk. Wilkens saw it and kicked his chair so he rolled backwards and slammed into the filing cabinet against the wall. He went over to the desk, and pulled out a Heckler & Koch MP5 machine-pistol loaded with a thin 32-round magazine, its skeleton stock folded over the right side, the snub-nosed barrel scarcely protruding beyond the front site. He turned it to one side and looked at the selector switch by the trigger.

"Fully automatic. That's real cute. Let's add 'intent to commit murder' to those charges."

"Wait a second," he sputtered. "This is Iraq. A man's got to have some protection."

"He's also got to know when to use it," Wilkens said. "Cuff him, Jed."

Watching Capt. Stewart place hand-cuffs on Mr. Reed gave me almost as much satisfaction as slugging him out in the desert the other night. Except that this time, I was just a spectator.

"You can't do this," Reed whined. Then: "How much do you want?"

"Like maybe you'll give me a cut, say half of your share?"

"Something like that."

"Is that what you're giving Jasper C. Ganz?"

"I'll give you Ganz."

"First, I want you." Turning to Capt. Stewart, he said: "Add 'attempting to bribe a government official' to the charging documents."

Reed ground his feet against the concrete floor, as if he could physically prevent Capt. Stewart from marching him out the door.

"Don't think you're safe, soldier boy," he growled. "Not even at the Sheraton. If you really do this, my guys will get you anywhere."

Late that afternoon, once we had finished processing Cory Reed with the American Military Police at the small base by the airport that was run by the South Korean contingent of Multinational Force-Iraq, LTC Wilkens ordered his driver to take us to the headquarters of the Kurdish Islamist Party in New City.

"I want you to meet a friend of mine," he said. "Someone you would never suspect. Burhan Salahuddin."

I knew this man—not personally, of course, but by reputation. He was indeed an Islamist, someone who wanted the KRG to declare itself an Islamic Republic, ruled by the Koran as constitution. What type of friendship could he possibly offer us Christians except to live in his Islamic state as *dhimmis*—second-class citizens—who must pay the *jizya* to purchase tolerance from our Muslim masters?

"Burhan is for real," Col. Wilkens said. "He has been a *very* good source for us."

The Party headquarters lay just beyond the New City emporium, a sprawling neon-and-glass attempt by the KRG to imitate an American shopping mall—without the customers and the extravagant choice of goods. It was chock-full of clothing stores where you could buy cheap Turkish suits and Vietnamese jogging shoes and Gucci knock-offs made in Iran, where the cashiers sat drinking tea for want of anything else to do.

Although Erbil had so far escaped the jihadi car-bombs, jersey barriers and a guardhouse decorated with the green and yellow flag of the Kurdish Islamist Party blocked entry to the small street. When the guard on duty saw LTC Wilkens, he waved us through. A clean-shaven man about my age was waiting on the broad cement steps of the drab Party building.

"Mr. Salahuddin is expecting you, Colonel," he said. He was dressed in a Western-style suit with a loosened tie and his English was perfect, but I had never seen him around Triple Shield.

He ushered us into a stuffy conference room with a polished wooden table and 24 swivel chairs, and then knocked before pulling open the sliding doors at the far end. Beyond the partition was a sitting room, with large comfortable armchairs, two sofas and a low coffee table, all covered with a dull grayish-green Damascene fabric. The only decoration in the room was a large golden frame set on the far wall with elegant black calligraphy of the Muslim profession of faith, the words of the Koran said to be written in gold letters around the throne of Allah.

The interpreter, whose name was Sami, offered us coffee and soft drinks. A few minutes later, Mr. Salahuddin joined us. He was instantly familiar. I had seen his picture in the newspapers, but he was much smaller than I had imagined him. He stood a full head shorter than Wilkens and me, but his large forehead and trimmed black beard with its streak of white right down the middle made him look bigger than he was. He wore a blue and grey Turkish suit and a bright blue tie. From the very start, a puckish affability emanated from his eyes that was infectious. It was hard not to like him.

"So today, do you have time, Colonel?" he asked, as he made sure we were served more tea and Turkish sweets. "The last time you were here you had so many questions, and so little time."

"Today I have time, Mr. Salahuddin. And I've brought my own interpreter—not because Sami doesn't do his job, but because I want him to hear what you have to say."

Our host turned to me and said in Arabic, "You are a Christian, correct? Who are your parents?"

It was a familiar question in Iraq. People think we are a big country, but in fact, we are an agglomerate of small communities. We like to say that if you put two people who've never met each other before in the same room and they start talking about their families, soon enough they'll find out that they are related in some way. When I told him my name and the name of my father, it brought an instant smile of recognition.

"See, he is from the clan of Tariq Aziz. Am I not right?"

I felt I was turning red. "My father's grandfather and his grandfather were brothers. That was a long time ago. It's not something we are particularly proud of."

"And on your mother's side?"

"Originally from Iran. My great-grandfather, Boutros Marcos Koriakos, was murdered in Tabriz during the genocide. My great-grandmother fled with their only child, my grandfather Issa, and settled in al Qosh in 1922."

His eyes lit up again. "Issa Koriakos?"

I nodded. The identity of my grandfather had apparently made his point. Turning to Col. Wilkens, he explained:

"It's because of his grandfather—or at least, his famous fight with Tariq Aziz—that I had to flee Iraq in 1980. And it was in exile that I learned the inner beauties of the Holy Koran."

"In Turkey, right?"

"Yes. All the other Dawa party members fled to Iran, but because I am a Sunni, I went to Turkey. I am not a Saudi stooge, Colonel. We are an Islamist party. We would like to see Islamic rule in Kurdistan. But we don't want to see a dictatorship—not a religious dictatorship, or a secular dictatorship. And that's what we have today with the KRG. Tell me how they are any better than Saddam Hussein?"

They had a long discussion about Islam, and moderation in Islam. For the most part, I let Sami translate, because clearly he understood the thinking of Mr. Salahuddin better than I did. Perhaps Col. Wilkens was trying to suggest that Mr. Salahuddin was a potential ally to the Christians, but I couldn't see the point of it.

"You mention Jihad," he was saying. "I am a Muslim, so of course I do not reject the concept of Jihad. After all, it is in the Holy Koran. But I note that today the circumstances are not appropriate to wage Jihad. For starters, where is the Islamic Caliphate? Who is the Caliph? Osama Bin Laden? As much as he would like to be the ruler of the Islamic world, no one of any authority recognizes him. Ayatollah Khamenei in Iran? Try telling that to the Sunni Jihadis. Even though they work with Iran, and take money and weapons and even orders from Iran, they despise the Shias. Besides, Iran is not calling for Jihad anyway.

"Perhaps one day we will have such a caliphate," he went on. "Perhaps one day, such a recognized Caliph will call for Jihad, and I will obey that call. In that case, it is possible that we will become enemies, Colonel. But that day has not come; indeed, the conception of such a day has not yet been born in the mind of God, so that makes it a long, long ways away. Don't you agree?"

"Yes, I do. And that's why I'm here," Wilkens said. "First, I want to thank you for your help. Without the information you provided us, I never would have been able to nail Cory Reed."

Mr. Salahuddin just smiled, but said nothing.

"I can't go after the Kurdish minister. That's going to be your job. But at least I can make it clear to American contractors that they will pay a heavy price for embezzling the U.S. taxpayers and cheating the people of Kurdistan."

Mr. Salahuddin half-listened as Sami translated this, clearly already thinking of something else.

"Was I right about the north?"

"How did you know?"

Mr. Salahuddin gave a quiet laugh, and his eyes lit up. "This is Iraq, Colonel. People talk. Everyone knew that Abouna Charbel was going to be meeting with the Prime Minister on Sunday."

Wilkens cut him off. "But you knew pretty specifically when the Emir of Jihad was going to attack. That's why I went up there earlier than I had planned."

"Let's just say that the same people who helped me with the documents were also aware of that."

They played cat and mouse awhile longer, with Col. Wilkens trying to find out how he had learned the day of the jihadi attack on the monastery, and Mr. Salahuddin politely putting him off. My guess is that his first answer was as close to the truth as he could get: people talk in Iraq. The Kurdish Islamist Party has lots of members. Some of them work in government ministries. Others probably work under cover for the jihadis. Who knows? Perhaps some of the Kurds working for Cory Reed were not the reliable KRG puppets he always took them to be?

"What about the thing I asked you, Col. Wilkens. Were you able to help *me*?"

Wilkens gave him one of those looks he reserved for people he knew well who had retained the ability to surprise him, full of complicity and respect. "How did *you* know about the Secret book?"

"There are no secrets in Iraq, my dear Colonel. There are only stories that don't get told. When I saw this so-called Emir of Jihad meeting with religious authorities in Iran a few months ago, I started making inquiries. What could they possibly have in common—besides murder, of course. That was when I learned about this so-called Secret Book. And so I consulted some of *our* learned authorities, and understood how explosive this knowledge would prove if it ever it became public here in Iraq.

"I personally have no problem with the truth, whatever it might be. Surely if the Prophet Mohammed were receiving instruction from a Christian monk, that could only enhance his understanding of God—don't you agree? After all, before he began taking dictation from the angel, he was just an *al-Ajami*—an illiterate camel driver. He makes a big point of this in the Koran itself.

"I do not *worship* the Prophet, Colonel. I respect him. But I do not worship him. I worship God.

These silly people who riot in the streets over some Danish cartoons poking fun at the Prophet Mohammed are really showing how little faith they have in their own religion. If their faith in God were strong, they would know that God's ways are not the ways of man. You cannot insult God. But if God sees that you do not respect and honor him, then he will mete out his justice on you in his own time."

When we finally parted company several hours later, Col. Wilkens held his hands for a long time, as is the Arabic tradition among good friends.

"You are a dangerous man, Mr. Salahuddin. Because you are not afraid to speak the truth. I just hope you are well-protected."

The Kurd's eyes were laughing. "Colonel, you have understood nothing at all of our talk this afternoon! If God wants to protect me—he will. I also have a few bodyguards. But really, what can they do if it's against His will?"

We gathered for a farewell dinner that night at the Sheraton, hosted again by the owner, Mr. Hiram. He began with a long, solemn toast to the innocent who had perished. "It seems this is our lot as Asyro-Chaldean Christians," he said. "It is not an easy fate to bear."

I put down my glass without drinking and just sat there, shaking my head in disgust. But he had already had several *araks* before we arrived, and was so absorbed with his own self-importance that I don't think he noticed.

"We don't need your crocodile tears," I said finally. "We need your money—since you don't have any courage to spare."

He started passing platters of food down the table as if he hadn't heard. We ate mostly in silence. Msg. Pacelli tried to tell a few jokes, comparing the accent in English of the Holy Father with his predecessor, Jean-Paul II. "I keep on telling His Holiness he has to get rid of the Hollywood Gestapo lisp, but he just can't help it. Every time he tries to say 'we,' it comes out 'vee.'"

Mr. Hiram found this hilarious but no one else laughed, and I thought Msg. Pacelli was sweating more than normal. I knew the secret he was carrying in his bags, and he knew it and refused to look my way.

Dona excused herself before the dessert to go upstairs to prepare her luggage. A few minutes later, as Mr. Hiram was instructing the waiters where to place the gigantic platters of fruit, I left as well. Dona was waiting by the bank of elevators, her finger pressed on the "Up" button. We went in together, and our fingers touched as we both hurried to press the button for the 10th floor before the doors closed.

I tried to joke, as I had the other night before we went up to al Qosh. "We shouldn't meet like this —in elevators."

But I could see the tears forming in the corners of her eyes, and before I could finish my sentence she grasped my face in both hands and was kissing me wildly on the mouth. I could taste the salt of her tears with my tongue.

When we reached the 10th floor, she led me by the hand to her room without a word. And that night we cried together—in joy, in sorrow, in magnificence, in anguish, in the fullness of our union and the emptiness of our imminent separation.

264

I met a priest once who said that God's love was present in the love between a man and a woman, and that was what made sex so powerful and so precious. Sex was like a lamp, he said: completely useless until you turned on the electricity. God's love was the electricity.

How could a priest possibly know that?

LTC Wilkens and his team escorted us to the airport in the morning, where the Kurds had the courtesy to host our small group in the overheated VIP lounge for orange juice, coffee and sweets. The Governor of Erbil came to pay his respects in person.

Once the ceremonies were over, Col. Wilkens came over to the sofa where Dona and I were sitting quietly, trying to soak up the last drops of each other's presence.

"How would you like to come to America?" he asked. "Today. Right now. On the first military aircraft we can get down to BIAP[8]."

"What do you mean?" I said. Both of us sat straight up.

"I can bring you in under a visa waiver program as a SIGIR asset. Commander's authority."

"Oh, Yohannes!" Dona exclaimed. She was thrilled, and her deep blue eyes filled with joy. She put a hand behind my neck and gave me a kiss, right there on the sofa, in public.

---

[8] Baghdad International Airport, part of which was still under U.S. military control.

"What about Rita? My mother? And Yousrah?"

"You can apply for them once you're in the United States."

"He's right," Dona said. "I can help you with the applications. At that point, it's family reunification."

I thought for a moment. A year ago, this was precisely the outcome I had been hoping for, and Yousrah and Marcos were eager to come with me to America to start a new life. Now, with Marcos dead, and Rita fully engaged in the Movement despite her kidnapping, I could hardly walk out on them.

"I can't leave this," I said gently, stroking Dona's hand. "Not now. There comes a time when you have to stand up for something. I must stay here. I must fight."

Col. Wilkens nodded, but didn't insist. "Somehow I knew you were going to say that, little brother."

Tears were welling in Dona's eyes. "So did I," she said quietly.

I took both of her hands and shook her gently. I wanted to look her in the eyes. "My battles are here. My family is here. My country is here," I said. "You know that, Dona."

I was thinking of Father Charbel up in the chapel next to me, firing at our attackers through the archer's slits. The Americans got rid of the dictator. But God gave us our freedom; it's up to us to defend it and to use it wisely.

"Come back, Dona," I whispered. "Come back and join me here. Come back and fight for your people. We can make the future together."

Narrated Anas:

There was a Christian who embraced Islam and read Surat-al-Baqara and Al-Imran, and he used to write (the revelations) for the Prophet. Later on he returned to Christianity again and he used to say: "Muhammad knows nothing but what I have written for him." Then Allah caused him to die, and the people buried him, but in the morning they saw that the earth had thrown his body out. They said, "This is the act of Muhammad and his companions. They dug the grave of our companion and took his body out of it because he had run away from them." They again dug the grave deeply for him, but in the morning they again saw that the earth had thrown his body out. They said, "This is an act of Muhammad and his companions. They dug the grave of our companion and threw his body outside it, for he had run away from them." They dug the grave for him as deep as they could, but in the morning they again saw that the earth had thrown his body out. So they believed that what had befallen him was not done by human beings and had to leave him thrown (on the ground).

Virtues and Merits of the Prophet (pbuh) and his Companions (Hadith of Sahih Bukhari, Book 56, Number 814.

Research Note

This is a work of the imagination. But like many novels, *St. Peter's Bones* derives its inspiration from real events and real places, both historical and contemporary.

The germ of my plot grew out of a conversation with Christian activist Aaron Cohen over dinner in Amman, Jordan, where we had traveled on a mission trip to help Iraqi Christian refugees. We had been discussing the way Muslim scholars have interpreted Biblical prophecies, in particular those contained in the Book of Daniel and Revelations 17. (Aaron was completing a PhD on Biblical prophecy at the time, but he is better known for freeing slaves in Sudan and Burma with the Abolish Slavery Coalition and Christian Solidarity International, a remarkable group that truly is doing God's work here on earth). In passing, he mentioned the controversy over the authenticity of the relics of St. Peter that has raged ever since Pope Pius XII announced in 1950 that they had been discovered by Vatican archeologists in a sub-basement of St. Peter's basilica. "If St. Peter's bones are in the Vatican, than the Whore of Babylon mentioned in Revelation 17 is clearly Rome," he said. "But if St. Peter died while taking the Gospel to Babylon and his bones are in Iraq, then we have to take this passage literally."

Aaron himself favored a literal interpretation of scripture, arguing that if God meant Babylon, he would say Babylon; if he meant Rome, he would say

Rome. Obviously, scholars continue to debate this subject. But when I returned to Washington, DC from that trip to Jordan and northern Iraq, I began researching the controversy that Pope Pius XII had fueled, and found it to be full of unanswered questions.

Several books have been written about the discovery of human relics beneath the Vatican in secret excavations during World War II. The first, and most controversial, was published by Vatican insider Margherita Guarducci in 1960, a full decade after the Pope's revelation. (*The Tomb of St. Peter*, available online from www.saintpetersbasilica.org). A more balanced account, which refutes in part Guarducci's claims that the human remains where those of St. Peter, was published in 1982 by Reader's Digest reporter John Evangelist Walsh (*The Bones of St. Peter: The First Full Account of the Search for the Apostle's Body*, also available from www.saintpetersbasilica.org). I have quoted from both, as well as from the original New York Times story revealing the archeological find, at various points in my fictional work.

St. Peter himself, of course, adds to the controversy in his Epistle when he writes, "The chosen church which is at Babylon, and Mark, my son, salute you...." 1 Peter 5:13-14. The ancient Church flourished in the Tigris and Euphrates valleys until the advent of Islam in the 7th century AD, and the Church of the East long has contended that St. Peter himself proselytized Babylon.

For my purposes, however, I chose to sidestep this Biblical controversy and adopt the more widely accepted theory that St. Peter did, in fact, die in Rome, where Christian tradition has him crucified upside down in AD 66. As both the Guarducci and Walsh books pointed out, the bones of St. Peter would have been objects of veneration from the start, and so were likely to have been preserved in Rome and guarded by devotees. Indeed, there is a Church of St. Peter and St. Paul outside the Vatican to commemorate the spot where Christian lore says the Romans executed the two disciples; this is the most likely place the relics were preserved until they were ultimately moved to the Vatican).

So how did they get to northern Iraq? And why?

My search for an answer to this question led me to an examination of Muslim conquest, and the repeated Muslim invasions of the Italy. Rome was sacked several times by Muslim hordes. "On the second occasion, when Saracens broke into the city in 846, pontifical records tell us that they carried out 'unspeakable acts' of desecration at the site," writes Queens University scholar John Curran. "As a barbaric act of destruction, they may have opened the grave [of St. Peter] and destroyed the remains."[1]

The Saracen attack of 846 AD was so dramatic that Pope Leo IV was forced to flee the city, appealing for help from neighboring kingdoms. [2]

These events gave me the broad outlines of my plot. Onto this structure, I grafted the story of the monks of the Order of St. Hormizd, whose existence was suggested to me from apocryphal tales of the

---

[1] John Curran, "The Bones of St. Peter?" Available at http://theshepherdsvoice.org/catholic/the_bones_of_p eter.html

[2] Another useful source on the spread of Islam is Andrew Bostom's *Legacy of Jihad: Islamic Holy War and the Fate of Non-Muslims* (Prometheus Books, Amherst, NY): 2005, as well as the excellent review that focuses on the events of 846 AD that can be found here: http://chiesa.espresso.repubblica.it/articolo/44479?eng=y

Christian influences on Mohammad that I had heard during my nearly thirty years of travel throughout the Middle East as a war correspondent and reporter.

Not content, however, to just invent a story as grave as that of the founding of Islam, I spent a great deal of time with authentic Muslim sources, starting with the most famous of them all, Ibn Ishaq's *Life of Mohammad*. Ibn Ishaq recounts the influence on Mohammad of a Coptic monk named Bahira, as well as the influence of his wife's cousin, a convert from Christianity who was known to have translated the Gospels into Arabic[3]. I adapted his account of Mohammad's early success as a caravan leader working in his wife's employ as part of the "Secret Book" of the Guardians of St. Hormizd.

Muslims themselves have debated for centuries the influence of Jewish and Christian sources on Mohammad. A Muslim website aimed at explaining Islam to Western believers states the case that forms the basis for the Secret Book, the fictional text allegedly written by Bahira that intertwines with my contemporary plot:

> *Orientalists allege that Prophet Muhammad was subject to the Judeo-Christian influence of his time and that the Quran reflects this influence. It was suggested that Prophet Muhammad had faced two big problems if he were to embrace Judaism or Christianity. If he became a Christian, he would be bringing in the Christian Byzantine regime to Makkah, which would not be tolerated by the people of*

---

[3] See "Khadijah, Waraqa, and Ubydallah et. al,"available at http://www.mukto-mona.com/Articles/kasem/quran_origin4.htm,

iv

Makkah. The second problem was that he could not pretend that he knew more than the older members and priests of those two religions— Judaism and Christianity. Thus, in both instances, he could not acquire leadership. Hence, Orientalists suggest that the Prophet decided to reproduce the role of Moosaa (Moses) or 'Eesaa (Jesus), may Allaah exalt their mention, because he saw that "they were men, and he could do what they had done."

Orientalists allege that the monotheistic influence on Islam was due to the presence of Christians and Jews in Makkah. They also suggested that there was a monotheist informant from one of those religions. [4]

Citing Ibn Ishaq, this website also notes that Mohammad was just twelve years old when he first met the Christian monk Bahira while en route to Syria with his uncle. (This episode becomes part of the Secret Book.) The website goes on to refute allegations that Mohammad "received instructions from Waraqah bin Nawfal on Christianity."

British author William Muir, whose 1857 *Life of Mohammad* first aired these allegations to a Western audience, writes extensively about the Christian influences on Mohammad and represents the "Orientalist" view refuted by today's Islamists. [5] The most accessible modern day summary of these authentic

---

[4]http://www.islamweb.net/ver2/archive/article.php?lang=E&id=134204

[5] Muir's entire book is available online at http://www.answering-islam.org/Books/Muir/Life1/pref.htm

v

historical texts is Robert Spencer's best-selling account, *The Truth About Mohammad.* (Regnery: 2006).

The passage in the Secret Book about the three "goddesses" of Meccah—known to Muslims as the Satanic verses, because only Satan could have dictated such heresy—of course became famous to a Western audience because of Salman Rushdie's novel of the same title.[6] My particular twist to this story—comparing them to the Christian triune Godhead—is, I believe, unique.

Hamza's drunken slaughter of the she-camels being prepared for the wedding feast, and Mohammad's subsequent banning of alcohol, is taken from the authoritative Salih Bukhari (Volume 4, Book 53, Number 324). "Did the companions of the apostle of Allah drink wine? What an outrageous question is this!—you may say. Here is the answer—though most Muslims will simply deny the truth. You see, most of Muhammad's companions (except perhaps Umar and Abu Bakr) were habitual drinkers."[7]

The monastery of St. Hormizd does, indeed, exist in the mountains above al Qosh, much as I describe it in the book. The Assyrian Education Network provides a most useful history of al Qosh itself, which outlines the schism between the Eastern and Western churches.[8] With the advance of

---

[6] For some historical background on the moon god Hubul and the three "daughters" of Allah, see
http://www.bible.ca/islam/islam-allahs-daughters.htm

[7] The Salih Bukhari hadith, and several more like it, are cited in an interesting exchange among Muslim believers that can be found here:
http://groups.yahoo.com/group/mukto-mona/message/23760

[8] http://www.atour.com/education/20040922a.html

computer technology into ancient communities, the monastery itself now has its own website.[9]

Well after I had completed the first draft of *St. Peter's Bones*, I had the opportunity through Bill Murray, chairman of the Religious Freedom Coalition—another group that has done wonderful work to support the embattled Christians of the East––to meet Australian scholar of Islam, Mark Durie. His most recent book on dhimmitude, *The Third Choice*, is illuminating.

Mark sent me a link to a remarkable website, written by Muslim scholars, that told the story of the Nestorian monk Bahira and his alleged influence over Mohammad in great detail.[10] He also steered me toward the hadith from Sahih Bukhari, considered the most trusted of all the early Muslim chroniclers, quoted at the end of my book.

As for the rest of the plot, and the characters, they are the result of my three decades of roaming the wilds of the Middle East. While I have certainly used character traits and even snippets of conversation from real persons, the characters themselves are unique. However, the harrowing taxi ride in Amman described by the narrator in chapter 3 is a pretty faithful rendition of a real event that Aaron Cohen and I experienced in 2008.

One final note on the use of a fuel-air explosive in the battle scene at the end of the book. In 1982, I was taken hostage in Beirut by Fatah guerrillas loyal to Yaser Arafat. The day I was released (to French diplomats), I witnessed my first Israeli air

---

[9]http://www.kaldaya.net/2007/4_DailyNews_April2007/Apr 19_07_E1_FrNoel_memorel_rabbanhormizd.html

[10] http://www.mukto-mona.com/Articles/kasem/quran_origin4.htm

raid from above ground, after having been pummeled in the underground darkness for 24 days. From the next morning's newspapers, I learned that the raid had destroyed the building where I had been held just hours before, leaving a crater more than 50 feet deep where the building had once been. The Lebanese papers claimed the Israelis had used a new kind of weapon, which they called a "vacuum bomb." Later, I learned that it was an FAE weapon—the first time that a FAE had been used by a non-U.S. air force in combat. I have tried to faithfully describe the extraordinary destructive power of this weapon in the book. Without the power and intervention of my Lord and Saviour, Jesus Messiah, I would have been a victim of that attack. Out of those ashes, I was quite literally born again. Praise be to You, Lord Christ.

—Kenneth R. Timmerman

Acknowledgements

This book never would have come into being without the insistence and encouragement of Father Keith Roderick and Gen. Michel Kasdano. Both despaired at how little attention the American public was paying to the plight of Iraqi Christians, and urged me to create a fiction to illuminate the sufferings of the persecuted church. I thank Michel and Bishop Michel Kassarji of Beirut, Lebanon for their time, insights, and hospitality.

John Eibner, of Christian Solidarity International, deserves the recognition of all believers for his tireless work on behalf of Christian slaves in Sudan and the persecuted church in Iraq. I owe him a personal debt of gratitude for inviting me to join him and Gunnar Wiebalck on an aid mission to the Nineveh plain, a journey that provided much grist for my fictional mill.

Father Sabri al Maqdissi, of St. Joseph's Cathedral and the Chaldean Seminary in Ankawa, is an extraordinary human being who left a safe life and career in California to return to his native Iraq just after the liberation in 2003. He has risked his livelihood and position to denounce the gradual dispossession of the Christians of the north by the Kurds and believes that unless this tendency is reversed, in ten years no Christians will remain in the area.

William and Pascale Warda are true heroes to Iraq's minority and indigenous populations. Pascale was the Minister of Migration and Displaced Persons during the first post-war government, and has raised her significant voice ceaselessly to defend the powerless. I will never forget mourning with her in Tel Keif at the gravesite of three of her bodyguards who were blown up in a chase car the insurgents thought was carrying Pascale. William's Hammurabi Human Rights organization has rightly become the premier human rights group in Iraq, and he deserves support for his effort to bring food, shelter, and legal aid to displaced Christians living in the north of the country. A special thanks to Bishop Louis Sako of Kirkuk for his friendship and for speaking the truth. May the lion of the church you are seeking protect you.

In Amman, Jordan, I must thank Father Raymond Moussali of the Chaldean Eparchy, the women and girls at the Grace Church school, Wadah George Dallo, and countless others for sharing their stories with me. I praise the Lord for sending us pastors such as Rev. Ghassan Haddad, who introduced me to a number of Christian interpreters who had worked for U.S. forces in Iraq and were forced to flee after jihadi terrorists posted their pictures on local mosques. I fear that Father Clarence Burby, a Jesuit priest who is working with the Chaldean Federation of America to distribute aid to Iraqi Christian refugees, has many more difficult years ahead of him climbing the steep cobbled streets of Ashrafiyeh in Amman. I thank him for opening many doors that otherwise would have remained closed to me. A special thanks to Hanna Chamoun, Issam Ghattas, and Issa Matalky for their help on the ground, and to Nineb Lamassu for his help with the Aramaic language. And to all those men, women, children, political activists, and church leaders in the Nineveh plain who shared their personal tragedies with me, this book is for you.

What you can do to help

"The Christians of Iraq are facing extinction."
- *John Eibner, Christian Solidarity International*

This book is my testimony. Visit my website (www.kentimmerman.com) to find out more about what you can do to help our brothers and sisters who are suffering for their faith in the Lord.

Groups distributing aid:

• Christian Solidarity International (www.HelpIraqiChristians.com)
• Hammurabi Human Rights Organization (http://www.hhro.org)
• Iraqi Christian Relief Council (iraqichristianrelief.org)
• Chaldean Federation of America: Adopt-a-Christian-Refugee-Family (http://www.chaldeanfederation.org)
• Assyrian Aid Society (http://assyrianaid.org)
• Religious Freedom Coalition (http://www.religiousfreedomcoalition.org)
• Open Doors (http://www.opendoorsusa.org)

Learn more

http://www.aina.org
http://www.persecution.org
http://www.ankawa.com
http://assyrianchristians.com
http://www.chaldeanjordan.org
http://www.kaldaya.net

ALSO BY KENNETH R. TIMMERMAN

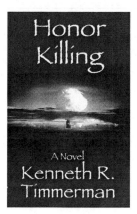

"Required reading. A great story... very timely in terms of the threat from Iranian nuclear weapons and the encroaching sharia program here in the United States."
Frank Gaffney, President and CEO, Center for Security Policy

Some have called it the CIA's greatest covert operation of all time.

"A must read... Fabulous... Incredible because it's scary—our own institutions undermining our own efforts against a genuine enemy... [Timmerman] names names... We're going to have to get this book in the hands of a lot of people... It's going to shock a lot of people.
- Rush Limbaugh

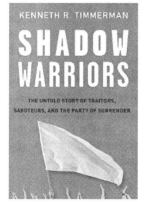

"An alarming but necessary book that reads like a thriller...."
- Michael Medved, nationally syndicated talk radio host

www.kentimmerman.com

FROM THE NOMINATION FOR THE
NOBEL PEACE PRIZE 2006:

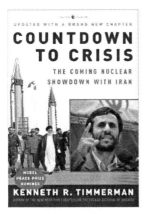

"The most urgent and disastrous threat to world peace today is the looming danger that Iran will produce nuclear weapons. . . . Kenneth R. Timmerman, a U.S. expert on Iran, has for more than twenty years exposed Iran's nuclear activities and intentions. . . . Despite the illusions of many in positions of power, he has been right, again and again. His latest book, *Countdown to Crisis: The Coming Nuclear Showdown with Iran,* lays out this ongoing scandal in chilling detail."
—**Per Ahlmark,** former Deputy Prime Minister of Sweden, nominating Timmerman for the Nobel Peace Prize

"With so many amateur intelligence experts clouding the public dialogue, it is a pleasure to read the work of an author of real professionalism. Timmerman adds texture and clarity to the gross failures of our intelligence establishment, and new visibility to the role of Iran in the Islamist war against America. "
—**John F. Lehman,** 9/11 Commission member and former Secretary of the Navy

www.kentimmerman.com

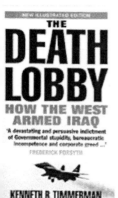

"A devastating and persuasive indictment of Governmental stupidity, bureaucratic incompetence and corporate greed..."
—**Frederick Forsyth**

"Filled with carefully reearched information about how greed for profits leads companies to support an unscrupulous dictator..."
—**Simon Wiesenthal**

"Many of the facts Ken first reported wre later confirmed to me and my colleagues in classified briefings..."—**Rep. Chris Cox**

"Your prose has the right sort of tension to make its way."
—Lawrence Durrell, author of *The Alexandria Quartet*

www.kentimmerman.com

Breinigsville, PA USA
06 January 2011
252723BV00001B/1/P